BOOKS BY DAVID GRIFFITH

THE BORDER SERIES

Blackwater Crossing
The Death Dealers
Without Redemption

BLACKWATER CROSSING

BOOK ONE IN THE BORDER SERIES

DAVID GRIFFITH

BLACKWATER CROSSING

CHAPTER 1
LONNIE

LOSING MY LEFT STIRRUP was the first sign of trouble. Two jumps later, the feather-footed roan bucked his way to the end of the arena while I skidded into the Montana gumbo like a bumbling rookie. I pushed to my feet, flicked the biggest watery lumps off the front of my shirt and slogged back to the mud-splattered bucking chutes. The drone of the rodeo announcer punctuated each long step.

"Folks, that's five-time national finalist Lonnie Bowers. It's a rare occasion when we see Lonnie hit the dirt. Stock contractor Ray Kalin has brought some outstanding bucking horses here today. Let's give Lonnie a big hand."

I stood next to the chutes and unbuckled my fringed black and tan chaps while the sold-out grandstand on the far side of the Dillon arena made a polite noise. These ranch folks knew and loved rodeo. They deserved a better performance than I'd given them.

I threw my chaps in the general direction of my riggin' bag and walked over to the unsaddling area to retrieve my saddle and bronc rein. I had just wasted the best horse I'd drawn in a month of grueling days and long nights on the road. My battered ego didn't need another wallop. Neither did my scrawny bank account.

Only a few broncs in a stock contractor's string will take you to the pay window. The rest are just filler material. Sometimes one of those second-rate horses will outdo themselves and you'll win a few dollars, but it's a rare event. That's just the way it is, and all of us in the game know whether we have a shot at the money before the chute-gate ever opens. Air Wolf would have taken me to the pay window, but I'd blown it. Another opportunity might be weeks away.

Over at the unsaddling chute, I picked up my well-worn bronc saddle and flopped it down beside my riggin' bag. That bag held my life: chaps, spurs, and bronc rein, as well as other sundry items of my trade. I dug to the bottom, looking for a spare shirt. Today, when I needed it most, I didn't have so much as a dirty sock to wipe the mud off my clothes; a perfect finish to the rest of my loser week.

My best friend and traveling partner, Brian Besser, had his bull rope clove-hitched to a rail in the area restricted for competitors behind the chutes. He was rubbing rosin into the handhold while I put away my gear. The rosin is a timeworn ritual, for the most part practical, because it keeps your gloved hand from slipping through the bull rope, but it's also the rider's time to focus his mind on the job in front of him.

Brian raised an eyebrow and gave me a sidelong glance as I stomped by him. "That cost you the big tamale, Lonnie." His voice was quiet. Brian understood.

Tight-lipped, I just nodded. He was a horse I should have ridden.

For a moment, Brian stopped working rosin into his rope.

"I've never seen Air Wolf drop that left shoulder the way he did with you. He jerked those swells away and left you hanging out in right field."

I looked out to the black arena mud, my despair turning to anger. Why hadn't I played it safe, instead of going for broke? At least that way I might have won something. Brian punched at my arm with the back of his gloved hand. "Let it go, Lonnie. There's always another day."

"Yeah, but I needed this one." The defeat lay rancid in my throat, and I tried to swallow the bitterness.

"I know you did." Brian turned back to his rope. "We'll get 'em next week!" Both of us knew what the paycheck would have been if I'd lasted two more seconds.

My jaw set hard. I turned away, wrapped the latigos on my saddle, and tucked in the stirrups. My failure was due to more than too many miles and not enough sleep. My reactions hadn't been quick enough, and I'd left the best part of two thousand dollars in the arena mud. That was a pile of money to me, and it was hard to handle the loss of it.

Contrary to my usual tidy habit, I stuffed my gear into my riggin' bag, shoved my saddle against the fence with my foot, and stalked out from behind the chutes. A hot dog stand on the roping chute side of the arena produced a bitter cup of black coffee. I leaned against the cold steel of the fence, pre-occupied with my failure while I watched the superbly trained roping horses barrel down the arena.

Out of the corner of my eye, I watched a couple of tourists in sunglasses and stenciled T-shirts sidle up beside me. Mesmer-ized by the events around them, they carried on a running com-mentary that revealed their ignorance. Obviously, it was their first rodeo. I continued to listen to their inane comments.

The heavyset dude kept glancing at me. I turned toward him and nodded a cool greeting. His piercing blue eyes were disturbing, and I turned away, intent on ignoring him. Right now, being nice to fans was low on my priority list.

"Are you one of the riders?" Those searching eyes were still fastened on me.

"Yes, I ride broncs." I attempted a smile—which was a mistake. The questions came, one after another.

"Did you ride today?"

Somehow, I knew that he'd seen me ride, that he knew who I was, and though I wondered why he asked, I didn't reckon I could ignore him. "Yes, I rode today."

"Did you win?"

"No." I wasn't going to elaborate on that.

"Aren't you scared when you get on a bull or bucking horse?"

"Sometimes."

"Why do they wear those leather things to cover their legs?" He pointed to a chapped-up rider standing by the chutes. Again, the question he'd voiced didn't fit with the eyes that studied my face, but I answered anyway.

"They're called chaps, and they help protect your legs from the saddle swells." Again, I glanced sideways at his face. It was vaguely familiar. Somewhere, I'd seen it before.

"What rodeos are you going to next?"

"I'll be at Moses Lake, Caldwell, Ogden, and Inglewood next week."

"Wow! You must spend a lot of time driving?"

"I used to, but now I spend more time in the air. My traveling partner has a plane, and we fly to most rodeos."

"That sounds exciting." This was from the other tourist.

For the first time, I glanced at him. Younger. Biceps straining against the T-shirt material. Gym rat? Somehow he didn't fit with the older, fat guy.

"What was . . . oh, right. No, I hate flying. However, it beats driving, and the guy I travel with is a pretty good pilot." Answering the questions from these two bedazzled tourists helped me forget my failure—at least for a few minutes.

"May I take your picture?" The old guy had a clipped accent, but not British—hard to pin down.

"Sure." I tipped my hat back and turned toward the camera. The picture would show a crooked smile, with straight, even teeth. My trademark high Indian cheekbones, dark eyes, and complexion inherited from my mother set me apart from most of my fellow cowboys. Folks sometimes described my features as rugged. None would call them handsome.

He snapped the picture. "Please, let me send you a copy." He dug out a couple of business cards from his wallet, and offered them, along with a flabby handshake. I took one, scrawled my current address in Vancouver, and stuffed the other in my wallet. The bull riding was next, and today especially, Brian would be expecting my help. I nodded politely to the tourists and left, suddenly uneasy that I'd given my address to these strangers.

Brian had drawn a high-horned brindle called Pistol Pete. He was a bull you could win on, but also a notorious chute fighter. The biggest challenge with Pete was to get outside without him hurting you.

The bulls were loaded in the chutes and ready when I made my way back into the contestant area. Another friend of mine was in the second to last spot, just ahead of Brian. Todd was a good friend, and he'd drawn a tough and dangerous bull—a gray, crossbred Brahma called Satin Pillow—so I detoured by to wish him luck.

I slapped his taped-up riding arm. "Hey, Todd, ride tough."

He nodded. His eyes slid away, but not before I glimpsed the uneasiness. For a moment, my hand rested on his shoulder. Todd didn't usually worry about rank bulls. I glanced back as I hurried down the line, but he'd turned toward the fence, busy with his stretching routine, preparing for the job ahead.

Brian would be last. He was fumbling under Pistol Pete with a wire hook, trying to catch the bell end of his bull rope. I took the wire from him and snagged the bell loop. He crawled over the chute and sat on Pete while I passed the rope up to him. He threaded the tail through the bell loop, pulled it snug, then jumped to the ground to work his rosin-caked glove onto his riding hand.

I stepped up on the catwalk so I could pull Brian's rope tight when he was ready, but I also wanted to watch Todd. He was in the chute ahead of Brian, taking the final wrap on his hand. Twenty feet out in the arena, Donny Brice hunched forward in his baggy short pants, his face deadly serious behind the clown paint covering his features. His hands rested on his knees, tense, and ready to do whatever the situation required to protect the next cowboy from those lethal horns. Todd scooted up on his rope. I watched the back of his straw hat shiver up and down in a tight nod. The gate swung open.

Satin Pillow burst into the arena with Todd in complete control. I watched him with one eye while trying to pay attention to the job I was supposed to be doing for Brian. He passed me the tail of his rope to hold taut, while his gloved hand zipped up and down, warming the already worked-in rosin. I sneaked another glance at Todd. He was going to be tough to beat. The crowd was on their feet, cheering wildly. Satin Pillow stayed in his signature spin to the left, and Todd's feet were reaching for new holds with every jump. Satin Pillow was always good. Today, he was exceptional, but so was Todd. A fleeting exhilaration submerged the earlier apprehension. Todd had just had a case of nerves, all too common when you have a dangerous one to ride.

The horn blared over the screaming fans, signaling the eight-second mark and the end of the ride. It was none too soon. Todd was getting dangerously close to the well. That's the inside of a bull's spin. You don't want to get bucked off in the well with any bull, but you sure didn't with a headhunter like Satin Pillow. His horns would smash your face to a bloody, pulsating mass of jelly. And Satin Pillow didn't just hook at you because you were in his sights. He was hunting to kill you. He hated anything on his back—or anywhere near him.

Todd made a desperate grab for the tail of his rope, trying to free his hand. He strained, his face contorted, teeth clenched, trying to throw himself toward the outside of that spin. Every breath held, every cowboy silent, hoping Satin Pillow would jump out of that sucking left-hand spin.

Donny was instantly in front of Satin Pillow's head, slapping at his nose, trying to pull him out of the spin and draw his attention away from Todd. But as hard as he tried, there was no turning that bull. He'd bucked off a hundred cowboys. He knew when he had one in trouble.

Todd's hand came free, but Satin Pillow slammed him down into the well. He stumbled to his knees and pushed upward to get away from those menacing horns, but it was too late. Satin Pillow's left horn struck his face and neck with the force of a baseball bat. Blood spurted from Todd's neck as he dropped under the hooves and into the rain-soaked sludge. The bull ground him into the earth, oblivious to the bullfighter's slapping hands. A younger bull would have turned on Donny in a flash. Satin Pillow paid no attention. Seconds later, one horn came away red with blood. Todd lay silent in the mud, unmoving.

It was over before any of us could even crawl over the chutes. I gripped the tail of the rope in my hands, the breath strangled in my throat. Brian looked out through the bars, horror stamped on his face. The bull raised his head from the still form in front of him to glare and hook at the pesky bullfighter's frenzied slapping hands. Finally, a pickup man's rope snaked out and settled over those sixteen-inch horns, then drug him toward the catch-pen. Paramedics rushed in, but all of us behind those chutes at Dillon could see Todd's lifeblood from his severed jugular pumping into the Montana sand. We stood frozen while they placed his bloody form on the stretcher. Everybody knew—Todd wasn't coming back.

Somewhere in the background, the rodeo announcer was talking, doing his job. "Folks, as soon as there is any news—"

"Brian, get ready. You're next." Ray Kalin, the stock contractor, reached through the chute bars and touched Brian on his chap-covered leg. "When the paramedics get out of the arena, you be ready to roll."

For a second, I saw the fear of death transfix Brian's features. "Get your mind on the job, pard." I slapped him on the shoulder, trying to make up for my shaky voice. "Block it out. You have a tough one to ride. You can do it!"

Brian's hat brim bobbed downward while he adjusted his rope. When I saw his face again, his eyes were still, his jaw clenched, every move focused. We would mourn for our friend later. Now was not the time.

The rodeo announcer continued giving his canned "hurt cowboy spiel" to the crowd. "These things happen, and folks we will let you know as soon as there is any word on Todd Landon's condition." Nobody in the grandstands on the far side of the arena could see the blood. They didn't know Todd was dead before they ever put him in the ambulance, and Dallas Bonner wouldn't be telling them. Those people were there for a fun afternoon, to watch cowboys ride some of the toughest bucking bulls and horses in the business, and maybe see a little blood and gore—but not too much.

The paramedics loaded Todd into the waiting ambulance. His score was a big ninety-one points. He would no doubt win the bull riding at this rodeo, but he would never know. I reckoned they could send the money to his wife and little boy.

Brian finished warming up his rope, his gloved hand again sliding up and down the sticky, rosined sisal.

"You can do it, Brian!" I tried to force confidence into him. He placed his hand in the braided handhold, and my shoulders strained to tighten the rope to his required tension. A short nod signaled it was enough. He reached over and took the tail of the rope, made a quick twist and tucked it into his hand. I'd kept everybody away from the front of the chute and Pistol Pete's head. He hated anybody up near his head, and he'd go berserk trying to hook at everything around him. Maybe it was our lucky day because he stayed quiet.

Brian eased up onto his rope. Instantly, Pistol Pete jumped ahead into the front of the chute, slinging those deadly horns around, but Brian was ready for that. He just hung on and nodded his head for the gate to open before Pete got any crazier.

I watched as that brindle-colored Brahma exploded into the arena. He made three high, looping jumps to the right. Then, like a striking rattler, he threw himself into his lefty spin, and flattened out. The spin got faster with Pete sucking backward through every high-kicking jump. That move could dump you right onto his head and those dangerous tipped-up horns.

Brian was, as always, the accomplished professional. He made riding bulls look easy. The moment the horn sounded, he reached down to undo the wrap on his hand. Pistol Pete catapulted him to the outside of the spin, well away from danger. Pete made a few more halfhearted jumps and started looking for the catch pen. He was a professional as well. His work for the day was over.

As the bull trotted out of the arena, Dallas Bonner's voice again crackled over the loudspeaker.

"That was four-time national finalist Brian Besser. And now we have the score. Eighty-nine points! That's enough to move Brian into second place, right behind Todd Landon. What an afternoon! What do you think of rodeo in Dillon this afternoon, folks?"

The crowd was on their feet and roaring their approval. They'd seen two bull riders make exceptional rides, and these ranch people appreciated rodeo at that high level.

Still panting from the exertion, Brian strode behind the chutes and set his rope down. A dozen guys congratulated him, including me. When somebody is hurt bad before your turn in the arena, it takes extraordinary discipline to concentrate on the job in front of you. What Brian had done was a cut above the ordinary. He had just ridden one of the toughest bulls in the business in the worst possible situation. All of us had immense respect for that brand of courage.

We packed our gear, said our goodbyes, and caught a taxi to the little county airport. Even though Brian had won a good chunk of the prize money in the bull riding, Todd's death overshadowed any good feeling. At the plane, we stowed each item and prepared to trust ourselves to the fickle sky. However, a fear I'd not known before stirred within me. Todd's death was abrupt, final, and it spoke to my own mortality. My jaw clenched with building anger at the seeming unfairness.

The Cessna gained altitude, and my mind turned to Todd's wife, Donna, and his little boy back in Logan Springs, Kansas. Why was life so unfair? Brian would try to tell you there was a God up there who had a handle on this mess, and that everything happened for a reason. That logic was beyond me, and the anger and sadness welled to the surface. Todd was a good friend and a decent human being. His death made no sense.

"Tell that to Todd's wife."

"Tell her what?" Brian looked across the cockpit at me.

"That there's some great cosmic reason for her husband getting killed. Todd was a good guy." I poked my thumb at the blue sky above us. "If somebody up there had a hand on the levers, He would have given the horn to somebody like— I don't know—that foul-mouthed Craig Klein, or Rody Jackson. Yeah—Rody! He's always fiddling with somebody else's wife. If there was any justice, it would be Rody who bought it, not Todd."

Brian glanced across at me and raised an eyebrow. I knew what he was thinking. If there was justice, Clarissa, my soon-to-be ex-wife, could add my name to the list of the damned—for good reason.

The Cessna leveled off at thirty-five hundred feet. Brian

pointed the nose north to British Columbia, and the ranch on the Blackwater River. I tugged my hat over my eyes and tried to sleep, but it was a long time coming.

Chapter 2
LONNIE

A JARRING AIRPOCKET woke me just over the Canadian border. I'd slept right through the too often rough Bitterroot Mountain Range, and didn't wake up until Brian dropped the nose toward Cranbrook to clear customs.

The under-worked agent shuffled out to look at our paperwork. He didn't find anything wrong with Brian or the plane, and my documentation was better than my looks, so he gave us the nod. We climbed back in and took off, angling toward the middle of the province.

An airplane was a necessity for Brian because of where he lived. We spent a good part of our time in his Cessna 180 Skywagon, one of those short-field bush planes that you can fly most anywhere and land in a cow pasture. We were still alive, so I guess it was a decent enough plane, but I hated flying. However, if I had to get my feet off the ground, it was comforting to have Brian in the left-hand seat. Year after year, he flew us through countless miles of bad weather to make "have-to-be-there" deadlines.

"Brian, are you sleepy?" I threw my hat into the back seat,

hoping he wasn't, so I could go to sleep again.

"No, I'm okay. We'll have to dogleg it up through the middle of the province. A thunderstorm is moving in from the Pacific, but if we can stay east of it until we get to Kamloops, we'll have 'er made."

That sounded good to me. Sometimes Brian made me steer that bucket of tin when he was too tired to stay awake, but it always made me queasy. Once he'd let me fly right into a cloud just to see my hysterical response. He got a great belly laugh out of my instant panic. Brian had an instrument flight rating, which I suppose meant he could play in the clouds whenever he wanted. Not me. I wanted to see what was coming toward us—like maybe a stray mountain.

We'd land at the Besser ranch sometime late this evening. Spending time there was always a rare pleasure. Mind you, anywhere would trump my bleak, memory-strewn condo in Vancouver. When my soon to be ex-wife Clarissa landed her first job in the insurance field, we'd plunked down the needed cash for our own digs and committed to five years in the big city. However, we both looked forward to the day we could ditch it and move to a smaller community. We needn't have worried. Our marriage didn't last five years. Clarissa had pulled the pin in March after I had returned from the big winter rodeos in the South, so it was just memories and me in the condo, and I avoided the place whenever I could. The ranch carried old memories as well, but it would still be better than where we had lived together.

Brian's folks ran a wilderness cow outfit snuggled next to the remote Blackwater River. Dozens of verdant meadows teemed with waving redtop, native bluegrass, and the tall sedges of the interior plateau. This time of the year, they welcomed extra help to drive cattle down out of the higher mountain meadows. The work was always hard, but a few days at the ranch would give both of us a much-needed break. We'd been in that plane for the last three weeks, mostly in the Midwest, with a few scattered hops down into Texas and Oklahoma. Four days from now we'd be flying south again, on another hectic run.

All the way to the Blackwater, I inspected the wing rivets and of course that whirly-gig propeller which was likely only glued on by luck and a ten cent cotter-key. Underneath us, the sun-cured Chilcotin grasslands gave way to the Lodgepole pine forests of the Cariboo. It was a time to worry—which is what I did best in airplanes.

My life was crumbling faster than I could put it back together, and I don't mind saying I was scared. Sure, I wasn't winning, but it wasn't just my anemic bank account. My six-year marriage to Clarissa was over except for the paperwork, and much as I wish it wasn't true; I had to take the blame for most of that. Too many grueling road trips chasing a World Champion buckle were difficult enough. Then she'd found out about the one-night stand in Fort Worth.

My face burned as I relived the scene . . . opening the door . . . her standing there, knowing everything . . . the bitter hurt and anger in her face.

I had no excuse. Stand around in a beer garden long enough and it won't matter if your face isn't movie star quality. You're a recognizable cowboy with a big gold buckle in a party-time town. She just happened to be there . . . an old friend . . . one too many drinks. Even if Clarissa hadn't found out all the sleazy details, deep inside, I couldn't make the guilt go away.

The purple, eastern twilight had just chased the orange sun down the far side of the Ilgachuz Range when the narrow strip to the east of the horse barn appeared under us. The small Cessna side windows revealed the emerald ranch meadows, flung haphazardly into the darker hue of the endless trees. Brian did a low-level pass to chase three black-baldy yearling heifers off the runway. I concentrated on the ranch buildings, which kept my mind off landing, my least favorite part of the business of flying.

A compact, weathered log house with a full-length front veranda nestled at the southwestern edge of the runway. A bunkhouse to the west of the house served hired help or overflow company. The corrals and barn to the southeast of the house ran down to touch the sprawling meadow that ran for a couple of miles west toward the mountains. The steel-ribbed roofing on the barn was a recent addition, and it reflected the last light of the northern sun as it disappeared behind the Itcha Mountains, seconds before our wheels touched the autumn-browned, grass strip.

Brian and I trudged the short distance to the house, both of us weary and of course hoping his mom had something to eat. This was my first trip to the ranch since Clarissa had left, and I wondered about my welcome. Brian's mom and dad had always made Clarissa and I feel like part of the family. Now that she was gone, did that still hold? I didn't know.

Divorce was anathema to Bob and Anna. They knew our marriage had crashed—and worse, what had caused it. Nevertheless, when they met us on the veranda, Bob shook my hand, albeit with some reserve. Anna hugged me with the usual warmth. A slight shadow crossed her face, but that was the only judgment of my actions Anna would ever show.

That dear woman had seen all the frequent trials and back-breaking labor of a backcountry rancher's wife. Her caring blue eyes always carried a warm welcome for those who were fortunate enough to come to the ranch on the Blackwater. They were the predominant feature in her work-lined face. Her calloused, red hands could deliver a newborn calf or bake a batch of mouth-watering cinnamon rolls with an equal amount of fluid grace and skill.

Bob had the coffeepot on, and he poured us both a cup while he quizzed us about the Dillon rodeo. He was an avid rodeo fan and had done his share of traveling the amateur circuit in B.C. and Alberta in his younger days. He always took great pleasure in hearing Brian's account of each rodeo, what bulls and broncs we'd drawn, and our coming itinerary. However, when Brian told of Todd's death at Dillon, Bob didn't seem to want to hear anymore, and when he walked by Brian to get the coffeepot from the kitchen, he squeezed his shoulder lightly.

"Good to have you home for a few days, son."

I walked over to the window and looked out into the now dark yard, broken by a sliver of pale moon rising out of the southeastern sky. Sometimes I envied Brian. Maybe that was why Bob's displeasure hurt more than I was willing to admit. My sire disappeared before I was even born.

Anna fried a couple of platter-sized rib steaks and added boiled potatoes, swiss chard, and the ranch standby, saskatoon pie with homemade ice cream. Neither Brian nor I had eaten anything since breakfast except a shared bag of peanuts in the plane, so we didn't disappoint her with a poor appetite. Later, we strolled into the living room to find a comfortable spot on one of the cowhide couches. Bob pumped up one of the gas lanterns and then sat back in his easy chair next to a side table that spilled over with magazines and books. His tattered old Bible balanced on top of the stack. He read it every morning, though I never understood why a hardscrabble, mountain-lion-tough man like Bob Besser ever had need of that book.

He picked up a damaged hames strap and continued hand stitching the torn pieces. "It would be a help if you two were to ride up to the Kushya Creek cabin this week and start pushing cattle down." He pulled the waxed thread through for another stitch.

"Yeah, that's kind of what we figured on doing." Brian stretched, and jacked his boots off. "What's in the barn pasture for horses?"

"Your dun horse is in there, and Lonnie can ride Snip. You can pack Chuchi. That will do him good. He's still a bit of a bronky knot-head." Brian and I both smiled. Three days on the trail would take a lot of the vinegar out of the rambunctious Chuchi.

Searching through the mountain meadows and draws for cattle, then moving them down country was hard work, but Brian and I always had fun. This time would be no different, and I'd looked forward to it for weeks. Brian had been doing this same ranch work since he was a kid, but for Clarissa and me, it had always been like a paid holiday. The talk was short, and I knew Brian would want to spend some time with his dad, so I excused myself and walked down the hall to the same guest bedroom where Clarissa and I slept when we were here. I turned back the sheet and crawled in, but the deep sense of loss for what I'd squandered kept sleep at bay.

***

SEPTEMBER MORNINGS can be frigid in the Blackwater country. Brian and I left the home corrals before eight, shoulders hunched against the morning cold. The horses' breath swirled like blown smoke in front of us as we rode single-file down the narrow trail toward the Messue Crossing. Brian led Chuchi, the chunky black packhorse carrying the three-day supply of grub and our bedrolls. He had mounted a spirited protest at his new calling, but with some firm persuasion, we got him lined. Brian had a hard dally on the horn with Chuchi's lead rope, and I brought up the rear. The little black packhorse dug all four feet into the dirt and fought to escape. I gave him a sharp pop with the end of my lariat-rope and he jumped ahead, jostling Brian's horse. That big dun gelding didn't even waver. He just heaved a sigh and plodded up the trail, dragging the still fractious packhorse behind him. Chuchi wasn't the first young horse he'd taught to mind their trail manners.

We followed the wagon track north and up to the long meadow until it intersected the ancient, westbound Indian Trail which ended at the far-off Pacific Ocean. We turned east, then skirted a few small, native grass meadows and dropped off the ridge, down to the Blackwater River. We rode without any talk, waiting for the weak warmth of the early morning sun. The brilliant, multicolored fall leaves of the poplar drooped with a heavy morning dew, while the starlings and sparrows chattered a noisy discourse. A beady-eyed Canada jay flitted from tree to tree, following our passage to the river, hoping for a handout. Overhead, a flock of Canada geese ka-ronked their way south, intent on reaching whatever sunny locale they searched for during the cold Canadian winters.

Cattle on the ranch spent the summer grazing the high plateau country, up against the Itcha Range. The pesky, blood-sucking black flies weren't as bad up there, but some of the younger cows always figured they didn't have to head for the lower pastures until too late in the fall. By November, the snow was so deep they couldn't get out, so they either starved or the wolves got them. Our job was to move them down out of the high country before the weather got bad.

Brian rode ahead of me on the narrow trail, with Chuchi holding to the middle. "You know, Lonnie; you can't improve much on what God created." Chuchi must have decided his neck had been stretched enough—at least for the moment.

"Yeah, it's a great mornin', except I have to put a question mark on your God part." When it came to religion, there was never any doubt where Brian stood, and I loved to needle him. Brian had this simplistic belief that some cosmic giant had created the world and everything in it. I liked and respected him, maybe more than anybody I'd ever run across, but you could pitch a horseshoe through the holes in his science. Many times, I'd had this same discussion with Clarissa. Neither she nor Brian would ever convince me that some wing-nut Jewish legends about some sky-guy power ranger had the slightest validity. Christianity was to me the epitome of intellectual dishonesty.

That issue had been the beginning wedge in our marriage. One evening, Clarissa had announced the astonishing fact that she had "given her life to Jesus." I had never felt so betrayed, and our arguments had been protracted and bitter. Clarissa was intelligent. She flew all over the country solving big insurance claims. She sat in high-level board meetings with hot-shot insurance executives. How could she have bought into that religious hocus-pocus? This person wasn't whom I'd married, and at the time, I considered it a deal-breaker. Just thinking about the subject brought all the old anger back.

I glared at the back of Brian's fleece-lined jacket.

"Your religion is based on total absurdities." The whole subject made me rabid.

Brian was quiet for several minutes while we both concentrated on Chuchi. He'd decided to throw another fit, again protesting the injustice of being a packhorse.

After we got Chuchi settled down and lined out on the trail, Brian scooted around in his saddle and grinned. "Why do you say that?"

"It just is."

"What you're doing isn't really working that well either. You think nobody sees the guilt and pain you're going through? How would you rate your life right now?"

I didn't care to answer that one. Chuchi laid his ears back and started another protest, which gave me enough reason to ignore Brian's questions. I rode closer and popped my chap-covered leg with my coiled rope. Chuchi's ears stayed flat against his neck, but he jumped ahead next to Brian's gelding.

Brian grinned at the now docile Chuchi. He reached over and rubbed his neck, and I hoped he'd forgotten the whole morbid religion subject. He hadn't. "All that stuff; Christianity and creation, evolution, the Big Bang theory and anything else that you believe or don't believe, just put it all in an oversized pair of saddlebags and ask God to sort it out. And you know something? He will."

I grimaced and shook my head. Brian was a great friend, but sometimes his fundamentalist, zealot theology got to me. I stared up at the cotton clouds and silently swore I was going to find a new traveling partner, but I knew I wouldn't.

We turned north off the Indian Trail and rode on down the deep-rutted wagon road. I halfheartedly sifted through Brian's words. Sometimes, what he said made sense, but mostly his religion speech gave me a big headache. I didn't want to deal with any of it—ever.

The fresh wood smell of the wind-stirred pine mingled with the tart odor of wild cranberries as we descended into the swaying poplar and cottonwood along the river. Today, I wanted to forget the tension, the failure to win—at anything, and just savor the feel of this cat-footed little bay gelding under me.

The trail leveled and opened to the shallow, tinkling waters of the Messue Crossing. We rode into the river and stopped in the middle of the stirrup-high stream to let our horses sip a few mouthfuls of glacier-cold water. When they'd finished, we splashed across the pebbled bottom to the gentle rise of the riverbank on the north side. The hillside, rich with native grass, opened up in front of us. For me, the Messue was a holy place—if there is such a thing, and we rode quiet, the telltale western breeze delivering the first biting chill of the coming winter. That early September morning, the gurgle of the water over the rocks, and the slight creak of saddle leather were the only sounds to break the silence, and even Chuchi showed some reverence.

Upstream on the other side, I spotted the smoke of a campfire. Three men, a woman, and two kids, native folks hunkered around it, their hands cupped around mugs of hot morning coffee. A tripod held a blackened pot over the coals. We rode up and dismounted. Anything less would have been rude in that country. In the bush, you always stop and trade news. A tall, angular-faced man in his sixties strolled forward to meet us.

"Hello, old friend. Good to see you." Brian shook hands with Jimmy John, the current chief of the Anaheim band. "You remember Lonnie?"

"Sure, I know heem." Jimmy turned to me with a big, snaggletooth grin and warm handshake. We'd met at the ranch two or three years ago.

"Where ya' headed?" Brian asked

"We're on our way home from Vanderhoof. Are you looking for cows?" Jimmy motioned us to the fire.

"Yeah, we're going up to the Kushya Creek cabin. We rode down to see if there was any cow sign."

"There are five cows and calves about three miles back on the trail," one of the others volunteered.

Brian nodded his thanks. We'd get those later if need be. The important thing now was to start pushing any cattle off the upper mountain plateaus to the west before any early snowstorms. Once we moved them down toward Kushya Creek, their cow brains would kick in, and they'd remember the right direction for winter hay and home.

We visited some more, and shook hands all around. The Bessers had always been on good terms with these folks, but in the last few years, it had been more difficult. They had a barrel full of grievances, some of them valid. The big one now was land claims, which all overlapped and likely would never be solved. I hoped the Indian side of my heritage helped to smooth things over for Brian's family.

With no more sign of wandering cattle, we rode back across the river, and angled southwest toward the already snow-dusted mountains and the headwaters of Kushya Creek.

At the top of the ridge, the Indian route, ancient as man, led us toward the Pacific tidewater at Bella Coola.

By mid-morning, the sun had taken the worst of the chill. Chuchi seemed to resign himself to the life of a packhorse. We shed our coats and made steady progress over the worn trail, occasionally skirting dead fall or swampy meadows. In the late afternoon, we cut south toward the mountains.

A canary moon peered out of the eastern sky as we broke into the cabin meadow. To the south and west, the inky purple Ilgachuz rose faint in the gathering darkness, mountains that had seen bitter battles over the rusty ocher and black obsidian that jutted from their slopes. In the distant past, the local tribes had used the red ocher clay to paint themselves pretty. The obsidian had a more lethal purpose. It was the preferred source for knife blades and spear points. When the white guys showed up with steel knives, the obsidian lost its allure.

We hung our gear from ropes on the covered west-facing veranda of the log cabin to keep them dry and out of reach of pack rats, but mostly porcupines. They can reduce a good saddle to chewed-up ribbons.

The moon lit the trail in front of us as we led our three horses down to the redtop grass meadow on the east side of the cabin. We hobbled our saddle horses, and picketed Chuchi as well. He'd get less to eat, but he could make up for it all day tomorrow while we searched for cattle.

Back at the cabin, Brian unlatched the door and kicked it open in time to see a furry intruder vanish through the ripped plastic covering the window. Bush rats stink almost as bad as skunks, and are more difficult to evict. We spent the next half hour shoveling together the pinecones, chewed up foam mattress, and other assorted cabin materials from the big nest under one of the two pine pole bunks.

Ready kindling had been stacked on the veranda from the last trip. I built a fire in the airtight stove, then started supper while Brian replaced the tattered window plastic and chopped more wood for the morning fire. I hoped the smell of steak and fried potatoes would overpower the rat smell. It didn't, but it helped enough so we could get to sleep, even with a wolf pack singing their melancholy mantra.

***

THE AROMA of frying bacon wafted through the cabin, which was enough to trump the frigid air outside my sleeping bag. It gave me the push I needed to swing my skinny, shivering legs out and stick my feet onto the icy floor. That fire hadn't warmed up more than two feet around the stove, and I'd forgotten to stuff my pants in the bottom of my bedroll. Consequently, they were the same temperature as the frozen floor boards.

Brian snickered at my discomfort. He'd bailed out and got the fire going, which meant tomorrow would be my turn. I shivered into my shirt and pants, stomped into my boots, then grabbed the water bucket and a towel before heading for the creek. After breaking the shore ice, I splashed two handfuls of water on my face, filled the bucket, and hurried back to the crackling stove.

We devoured Brian's bacon and eggs, and then caught up our hobbled saddle horses. They'd been tired enough to stay content in the meadow, which was fortunate. I had no desire to test-ride the half-broke Chuchi. By eight, we were picking our way southwest, following a chain of tiny meadows hugging Kushya Creek. Midmorning, we split up, so we could cover more of the plateau country. I rode to the east and immediately stumbled onto three cows with their calves. The cows were older, so they would likely have remembered the way home, but one could never be sure. I pushed them down from their summer Valhalla, and headed them north and east toward the home ranch. Throughout the day, I dug a few more cows out of the little pothole meadows and trailed them a few miles down the valley in the general direction of the Messue.

The sun was slanting into the Ilgachuz when the last two cows I followed, hooked up with four that Brian had brought through the end of a shallow draw. Between us, we'd found at least thirty head, most with calves. Tomorrow, we'd move west to the other side of the creek and repeat the exercise.

We spent the evening taking care of our tired ponies, chopping wood, and planning our coming itinerary. I blackened hamburger steak on the airtight stove. Brian usually took over all the cooking after a meal or two of my hair-frizzling charcoal. I was relegated to dishes.

As I sliced some potatoes into a pan, my mind turned to the coming week. Moses Lake would be our first stop for an afternoon performance. We would then fly to Caldwell, Idaho for the rodeo that evening. Two rodeos in one day were always difficult. There could be no hitches in planning, or inclement weather. However, it was a September run we'd done other years, so if the weather was decent, I knew we could make it happen. The day after Caldwell, I would have to catch a ride to Ogden, Utah. Brian would fly to Puyallup, Washington. The following morning, I would catch a commercial flight out of Salt Lake City to the Inglewood, California rodeo. Brian would fly the Cessna down, and we would meet there. The following day we would head north for a couple of Alberta rodeos. It was a tough run, but that was our life, and I enjoyed every minute, or at least I had until lately.

I glanced sideways at Brian, who perched precariously on one of the rickety plywood and pine stump chairs. "What bull did you draw at Puyallup?" He filtered another sip of the leftover morning coffee through his teeth before he answered.

"Wildfire."

"Is he any good?" I was well acquainted with most of the bulls in Roscoe Roger's string, but I didn't recognize that name.

"Oh, he's one of those mediocre types," Brian answered. "You might win something on him if all the tough guys get bucked off. What did you draw at Caldwell?"

"I have . . ." I turned the hamburgers over to fricassee the other side black. ". . . I have the notorious Sitting Bull."

"Oh, right. Now I remember. Lonnie, you be careful with him. He pancaked that rookie kid from Nevada on the back of the chute last year at Kennewick. Remember? That horse crippled him. He never rode again."

I remembered well. Sitting Bull could hurt you, and though I wouldn't admit it, he worried me. Both of us were quiet, immersed in our own thoughts as we listened to the silence of the northern night. Occasionally, the quiet was broken by a pop from the dry pitch-pine wood in the little airtight stove. My mind turned to Todd Landon. The danger of our sport seldom bothered me, but Todd's death at Dillon and the coming encounter with the unpredictable Sitting Bull moved mortality to the front of my consciousness. How could it not, with both Brian and Clarissa giving me constant reminders that if the worst happened—my soul was in mortal peril?

***

At six thirty, I scrambled into my icy clothes, then fumbled in the dark cabin for kindling to start a fire. Eventually, the stove threw off enough heat to mitigate the biting September air. The breaking dawn crept into the room while I shivered and stabbed at a half-dozen pieces of frozen ham in the skillet.

Brian lay wrapped in his bedroll, waiting for the fire to take the chill off. Of course it never did, and it was my turn to smile as he threw off the covers and danced around in his bare feet while he scrambled to cover his shivering body. By the time we'd taken on breakfast and a quart of caffeine, it was time to catch our horses and get on with the day.

When I saddled my bay Snip horse, he stood splay-legged, his ears at half-mast and his back humped like he had a frozen chunk of ice under the blanket. I swung a leg over him, and he bucked around the clearing, showing his displeasure with the cold. I don't guess I would have felt any different if somebody had thrown a frosty saddle blanket on me. Fortunately, his protest was only halfhearted. Most days I could ride a rank bucking horse, but this well-muscled bay gelding might have tested my skills if he'd put his mind to it. Brian chuckled. His dun, of course, was a perfect gentleman.

Halfway through the first meadow, we stirred up a mama grizzly with two cubs. She stood on her hind legs, then dropped down and took a short run at us. A hundred feet away, she stopped, her head weaving back and forth, snuffling at our strange man-smell. Brian pointed out the remains of a fresh-killed calf moose up on the hillside. Apparently, she didn't intend to share it. We had no inclination to argue the issue and made a wide swing around her, then moved on up into the sparse-timbered hillsides toward the foothills of the Il-gachuz Mountains.

At the top, we split and went different directions. I spent the morning working the seven cows I had found down to the Kushya cabin meadow. One more day would see this part of the high plateau swept clean of cattle. Tomorrow, we could pack up and work our way farther down toward the Messue, moving all the cattle we'd found closer to ranch headquarters.

By the middle of the afternoon, I'd cleaned out every meadow on the west side of the creek. On a grassy hillside, I reined in my horse, stepped off and loosened the cinch. For several minutes, I stood and drew in deep breaths of the crisp, pine-scented air. I wanted to save each one, so I could breathe it again in the cities where we were forever confined by our chosen vocation. The sighing wind in the poplars and the nearby trickling creek provided a tranquil backdrop to the flittering robins and blackbirds, all of them flocking together for their long journey somewhere to the south. Nowhere was there any man-made sound.

***

THE NEXT DAY when we dropped off the ridge and into the long meadow at the ranch, we didn't have to kick those tired ponies up to keep them moving. They were as happy to see the barn as we were. Chuchi tagged wearily behind, permanently resigned to his fate.

After we'd unsaddled and rubbed the horses down, we trudged into the house, well content with what we'd accomplished. While we annihilated more than our share of a hindquarter of beef with baked potatoes and all the proper homegrown trimmings, we gave Bob our report. He seemed more than pleased, and I was glad we'd been able to take that chore off his shoulders.

Tomorrow, we'd be back in the Cessna, headed for Moses Lake. It was the first time I could remember not being thrilled at the prospect of another rodeo. Maybe after fifteen years I really was wearing down, and I wondered. Was I depressed because of my slipping career, or was it the soon-to-happen divorce from Clarissa?

We turned in early. Moses Lake was only four hours away, if everything went well. However, if we had to skirt a thunderstorm or had trouble at customs, it was good to have a cushion. At the ranch, one never knew what storms lay over the horizon. Weather reports there consisted of gazing at the sky and using your best judgment.

Early the next morning, we took off into the rising sun, then turned south into a solid wall of east-marching cloud, heavy with rain and turbulence from the Pacific. For a couple of hours, we bounced on the edge of dark, angry thunderclouds that threatened to chase us from the sky. They drove us far to the east of our flight path. Lightning streaked in the distance. Occasional rain squalls slashed across the windshield. My stomach churned, threatening a full-fledged revolt, and even Brian looked worried.

CHAPTER 3
CLARISSA

HUNGER DROVE the male cougar to the top of the ridge. His patchy, dull coat no longer kept the cold from his emaciated frame. Three days earlier, he had killed a spotted fawn, but the fresh meat hadn't stopped the steady wasting away. The cancerous rifle bullet lodged deep in his vitals was a fire in his gut, constant, vying for supremacy with the gnawing hunger. He crouched on the pinnacle of overhanging rock, searching the prevailing wind for prey.

Arthritic, and angered by the pain, he growled through his broken teeth. The whipping wind blew hard against his flared nostrils, and his once keen ears, now dulled with age, twitched in concert with the writhing, blunt-tipped tail.

The wind brought no sound or scent of prey. Stiffly, the cat rose and padded away from the rock, his dun fur melding with the autumn-yellowed grass. Each stray breath of air was filtered for the scent of game as he quartered down to the lightning-scarred bull pine. He clawed his way up to the massive forked branch. A snarl escaped at the familiar shooting eruption of pain in his belly. He flattened against the bare wood. His ropey tail twitched with the hunger lust in his body. Suddenly, his nostrils distended, searching the telltale breeze. The enticing aroma of horse drifted to him, mixed with the stench of human. Saliva coated his tongue. His emaciated body hugged the limb, his gristly neck thrust forward. The once powerful hind legs coiled further under his body, waiting for the right moment while he searched for the origin of the strengthening scent.

Below on the trail, the horse moved closer, unaware of the danger.

The cat trembled. The human smell screamed a warning, but now only the hunger mattered, and like a giant spring, he launched into the air.

***

THE BITTERNESS with Lonnie, and my soon-to-happen divorce, was a potent drug in my woman's soul. As so often happened in the early dawn, the long-held anger and wrenching hurt of that distant afternoon became my first coherent thought of the day.

Still tired, I untangled myself from the wadded sheet, threw off the jumbled covers and slipped into a long-sleeved blouse and a pair of blue jeans. Barefoot, I padded into the bathroom and sponged the sleep out of my eyes, then brushed my streaky blond hair back into a ponytail. Fumbling through the bottles and jars, I found the moisturizer that soothed my often wind-burned cheeks, then applied the eye cream that did a passable job of hiding the bags under my eyes. The world didn't need to know about my lack of sleep—or the reason for it.

The picture window on the east wall of the two-bedroom

rancher I called home framed the major portion of my world. The pasture where my horse grazed led down to the road that ran past our house. On the far side, a steep bank dropped off to the meandering river nearly a thousand feet below. Nine years ago, I'd left this forgotten old British Columbia mining town. Now I was back again, settled in the place where I'd grown up, where both of my parents were buried.

My dad never felt he missed anything growing up in our backwater mountain town. Neither did I. Lillooet was a beautiful sanctuary, tucked into my special mountains, peaks that soared to the sky, solid, immovable, always comforting.

I shrugged a faded jean jacket over my brown knit sweater to ward off the autumn chill, grabbed an apple to munch on, then pulled on my riding boots. Outside, the autumn dew lay heavy on the sun-burnt fall grass. Swishing through its wetness to the rust-stained log barn, I called toward the pasture. Monte, my much-loved gray gelding whickered softly, then trotted to meet me. He nuzzled my pockets, knowing there was always something special for him. Sure, he was just a horse, but Monte had been a real friend in a time when those had seemed in short supply. I spoiled him with apples and carrots, and entrusted him with all my hurts and dreams. As far as I knew, he never told anyone. At the barn, I poured a handful of oats in his bucket, and turned my face to the weak sun that had started to burn off the river mist with its miserly September warmth. After he'd finished eating, I haltered him and smoothed his dappled coat with the soft-bristled brush.

Monte stood as always with one hind foot cocked into a resting position while I saddled him. He seemed to understand my need for a regular morning ride. Honestly, he probably didn't know that or care. For both of us, it was a time to see new country, and it helped to ease the loneliness of a shattered marriage. Sometimes, riding even banked the smoldering fire of resentment in my heart against Lonnie. But now I was at a crossroads, and I needed to decide. Where should I go from here? My marriage was over. What had happened was more painful than anything I'd ever known, but now it was time to put that part of my life behind me and focus on whatever might lie ahead.

After I'd saddled up, I leaned over the log fence and gazed down to the distant river. The phone call I'd made last Monday still made my face flush with remorse. At the time, I'd tried to quiet the fluttering inside my chest. With shaking hands, I'd dialed the number of one of our company lawyers. I knew Robert Bentall well. We'd worked together on a number of different insurance claims, but that day I'd not sounded anything like the capable and decisive insurance adjuster he'd worked with in the past. My whole body trembled. Doubts cascaded over me in a snow slide of worry. Did I want this? Was a divorce from Lonnie the answer, and if it was, where did I go from here?

The secretary put me through. The conversation played through my mind as though it had happened minutes ago. The receiver trembled in my hands as I'd waited for a response.

"Rob here.

"Rob, it's Clarissa Bowers."

"Clarissa—how are you?"

"Fine." I'd made a conscious effort to steady my voice, if not my hands.

"Hey, what's the weather like in Lillooet today?"

"Great." I'd tried to match his jocularity. "Just another of our famous sunny fall mornings."

"Sure, rub it in. You know what it's like here in the city. Rain—as usual."

I tried to laugh, but it escaped as a nervous titter, which elicited a moment of silence from Rob.

"Hey," he started uneasily, trying to cover the awkward moment. "I need some direction on that Tremblay file. How about a meeting this week? Or is that something Andrew will deal with?"

I sat up straight. This was territory I could handle. "No. That claim is mine. I probably need to walk it through the process." The fluttering queasiness inside me had eased, but my hand still trembled when I reached across the desk for my day planner. "Does one o'clock Wednesday work?"

"Uh—sure, let's try for that. If anything changes . . ."

"Rob," I interrupted. "I called for another reason."

"Sure. Wha—"

"I know you don't do them, but I don't know who else to call, and I don't want to pick just anybody out of the phone book. Rob—I need a lawyer."

"You've got the best." A brief silence as the urgency of my call blasted through. "Oh—you mean . . . as in not a corporate lawyer."

"I need a divorce lawyer." When I said those words, the dam broke inside me, and hot tears rolled down my cheeks.

"Clarissa, I'm sorry." This time, there was a long pause. "That's a difficult road, but sometimes it's for the best. I will personally make sure you're well represented. Leave it with me."

"Sure—and thanks." I fumbled for a tissue to wipe away the cascading tears.

"Say, how about lunch Wednesday rather than the one

o'clock meeting. We can discuss both issues." The invitation was warm, appealing, and after all, it was a business lunch. But there was much more than lunch in the warm tone of Rob's invitation. And though a hundred voices inside me shouted a warning, I'd accepted.

When I'd walked into Mesalas, Rob was waiting at the bar. He took my jacket, his hands lingering on my shoulders as he escorted me to a chair. From there it progressed to reaching across the table to cover my hand with his, and . . .well, I should have listened to the inner warning. I now had the phone number of a very good divorce lawyer—and a clear indication that a corporate lawyer and friend intended to become much more, which vastly complicated my life.

I turned away from the fence and swung into the saddle. After a lap around the pasture, I pointed Monte up the Farwell Canyon trail while I mulled through my past. Was I finished— washed up? Could I find new direction and a future? Doubts taunted me as I rode. Yeah, you're a real success, Clarissa Bowers! The big-city insurance executive, one month away from thirty, with a cracked-up marriage, a well-used Volkswagen Jetta parked in front of a rented house, and right back in the same hick-town you left nine years ago. It wasn't much to show, unless you counted my shaky new faith. A tear slipped down my face, and I mopped at it with the sleeve of my jacket. What good had that brought? The God of that new faith had let me down rather badly.

Monte broke into his effortless running walk, and I pushed the reminder of my broken marriage away. The morning was too nice to dwell on those dismal thoughts. I scanned the trail ahead for deer. Maybe today I would see one of the spooky mountain sheep. They often ghosted up the ridge on this seldom-used trail.

The seasonal stream of snow water that trickled down the canyon seldom stayed later than July. However, this September, it was still murmuring through the rocks. We followed the trail up the boulder-strewn slope and into the wind-stunted pine. No game appeared, which was unusual, and I lifted the reins to stop Monte in the trail while I scanned a belt of fir at the top of the ridge. This morning I decided I would ride to the top of the mountain. Few knew of it, but at the very top, a hidden grotto was carved into the west side of the mountain. It was my own private hideaway, a place to cope with the bitterness that threatened to overwhelm me. As I rode up the trail, I tried not to dwell on all the hurt. It wouldn't go away, and I gritted my teeth in anger. Lonnie Bowers would soon be my ex-husband. We were finished. And God? Maybe he had been a mistake as well, just a crutch when I was emotionally strung out and needy.

Lonnie and I met during our first year in college. I had fallen hard for the smiling, confident rodeo cowboy with his black curly hair and flashing brown eyes, and we were married the following summer under the towering oaks in my parent's backyard in Lillooet. After college, we returned to Canada. I landed a job at a large insurance company with offices in Vancouver, and Lonnie continued to rodeo. Riding bucking horses was what he did best, and it was a childhood dream that he was living. The years passed, and the separations became more difficult. We either didn't know what to do about the growing rift or were too stubborn to change. One of us had to give up something to make our marriage work. Neither of us would, and increasingly, the man I loved wasn't there. And then, my life spiraled out of control. At least, that's the way it seemed.

I found out from another rodeo wife that Lonnie was having an affair. Three days later, he came home from the rodeo in Fort Worth. When he walked into our apartment, I stood at the end of the kitchen counter, my arms crossed to keep my hands from trembling. The door closed behind him, and when he looked at me, I think he knew what was coming. His saddle and riggin' bag slid to the floor.

"Is it true?" My voice cracked across the room, charged with every bit of the venom and hurt that had boiled through me for three days.

"Is wha—?"

"Don't lie to me!"

"Clarissa, what are you talking about?"

"Did you sleep with that woman?" His face turned a pasty gray, and no matter what he said—I knew it *was* true.

"I didn't . . . Clarissa; there was a birthday party for . . . things got out of hand. . . ." He was pleading, which just made me angrier. His guilt-ridden eyes slid from my face to the carpet.

Suddenly, the volcano of anger drained away, replaced by deep sadness and a spreading pool of disgust for this man I'd loved so passionately.

"Get out! Leave!" He stood stock-still for perhaps ten seconds. The pallor in his face turned to a dark crimson. He fumbled at the floor for his saddle and gear, his stricken eyes riveted to mine. Then he turned, and like a sleepwalker, blundered through the door. Somehow I made it into the bedroom, fell across the bed, and wept until there were no tears left. Our "forever" marriage had lasted four years, two hundred thirty-one days.

In the early dawn, I packed everything I wanted from what

had been our home, loaded my Volkswagen Jetta and drove away. The only remaining sign of my presence in our Vancouver condo was the angry, tear-stained note on the counter. He'd come back for his stuff and find it soon enough. I'd changed my mind. He could have the condo. Our marriage was over.

The wind was stronger now, blowing our scent straight up the trail. Probably that's why we're not seeing any game this morning, I thought. I watched Monte's ears swiveling forward, then back, seeking sounds that only he could hear. He snorted his uneasiness, and there was an unfamiliar tenseness in his gait. I had to urge him every step up the rocky trail. I saw nothing, and I wondered what he smelled.

Suddenly, his ears lay flat and he whirled. A dark shadow dropped from an overhanging tree limb above us. The tawny form landed, clawing and tearing at my horse's neck, the hind feet in my chest. A cougar! I grabbed for the saddle horn, trying desperately to stay in the saddle. Monte bolted in terror, and I felt my face scrape through the dirt as my body slammed into the ground. The cat landed on top of me. Fear-laced adrenaline gave desperate strength to my arms. I screamed and punched at the tawny hide. His teeth tore through my jacket and into my arm. I tried to roll over to protect my torso from his flesh-shredding claws. Blood spurted from my now bare shoulder. "God—help me!" I screamed as he let go of my shoulder and reached for my throat. I rolled, kicking wildly, trying to keep the cat away from my head and face. His fur was now bloodstained—my blood. For the moment, he seemed to give up on my throat, and sunk his teeth deeper into my shoulder. Again, I screamed, then tried to twist away but my strength was rapidly soaking into the red soil under me. Black spots danced over the cougar's fur. I couldn't fight anymore. A calm acceptance took hold of me, and my body went limp.

God—thank you. I quit struggling and tried to lift my arms to protect my head. The cat again let go of my shoulder, then bit through my right forearm and into my face. The blood ran wet inside my shirt and jean jacket. Woozy and distant, the reeking, sour odor of the cat's emaciated body was now overpowering. Would losing consciousness be easier than the ripping, tearing pain? But I didn't want to die! Anger again gave me strength, and I kicked at the cat's protruding ribs as a crushing sadness welled up inside me.

Lonnie, I wish you were here. I should have told you how much I loved . . . I hoped you'd find ... . . I had no strength left. What was I going to say? Something about God, but I couldn't remember. Besides, God hadn't solved anything for me. Everything in my life had gone wrong, and now I was going to die.

A dusky shroud covered my eyes. The cougar's lips pulled back in a snarl, but somehow there was no sound. He was heavy, standing on my chest. I waited for the teeth in my throat, the final gush of my blood running down my neck to soak into the thin mountain soil. My arms would no longer work to protect my face and head, but an unexplainable contentment wiped every bit of my fear away. I was at peace with my God. Some way, Lonnie would find his own peace.

I didn't understand why, but the cougar suddenly slumped across my bleeding body. The vicious anger faded from his glazed eyes, which seemed now a mirror image of my own. Before everything dissolved into a black void, a bushy, bearded face blocked the sky. I tried to shrug. He wasn't at all how I'd pictured angels.

CHAPTER 4

LONNIE

BRIAN BOUNCED THROUGH the turbulence as we inched our way steadily south to the American border. The storm had pushed us far enough east, we had to cross the border to the north of Spokane. We cleared customs, then scooted down to Moses Lake, barely in time for the two o'clock performance.

The taxi from the airport dumped us at the Moses Lake rodeo grounds just as the Grand Entry was leaving the arena. That was close enough to a photo finish for me. I preferred a few minutes to unwind, swill a cup of coffee, and circulate a bit before having to think about a three-quarter ton adversary. It wasn't to matter here. I was teamed with a nondescript brown horse called Nighthawk. We crow-hopped around the arena for a whopping sixty-two points. Brian's bull must have eaten from the same trough, because he was awarded a starve-to-death sixty-five points. With those scores, there would be no prize money.

The minute Brian was finished, we rustled up a taxi to get us back to the airport. Barring anything unforeseen, we'd make it in time for the eight o'clock performance, but it was going to be tight.

I shoved our gear into the appropriate storage bins while Brian checked with the weather people. They must have given him some degree of confidence. He checked my storage plan, nodded, and we barreled down the runway. An hour and fifteen minutes of flying time should get us to Caldwell, but after we landed, we had to get from the airport to the rodeo grounds, which would take another half-hour. The problem was that the same Pacific front we'd fought all day was moving down from Canada, and we had to duck further south to avoid it. We made it, but the broncs were already in the chutes when we pulled into the rodeo grounds.

"Go!" Brian yelled. "I'll take care of the cab." I jerked my saddle and riggin' bag from the trunk, and bolted for the chutes. Brian had lots of time before the bull riding, and though I dreaded this horse, he was one I couldn't afford to miss. The big paint stud horse they called Sitting Bull was always dangerous. He had to be tied in, because he would often throw himself over backward and try to crush you against the back of the chute. But if you did get into the arena without him crippling you, you could win—if you could ride him.

Sitting Bull stood in the third chute, his thick pinto hide already gleaming with a sheen of sweat. His heavily muscled neck telegraphed the strength this hurricane would soon unleash. I hurried to get my saddle on him. He snorted, occasionally casting a wall-eyed glance in my direction. My good friend Bobby Williams tied him in and stood ready on the arena side of the chute. He took another wrap and a firm grip on the tie-rope while I gingerly placed a foot over the top of the chute and onto my saddle. As soon as Sitting Bull felt the weight, he threw himself violently backward. Bobby's tie-rope held. Immediately after he's settled back to earth, I slipped into the saddle and nodded for the gate. Bobby released the horse's head at exactly the right moment. Sitting Bull reared around the outside post at the back of the chute, but I avoided getting crunched, and he bucked well enough, I won third place. My bank balance needed that, and so did my confidence. After a long string of bad horses, my riding was getting sloppy. Brian won some money as well, so it was a profitable evening.

Brian and I caught a ride to the Sands Motel. It had been a long day and I was beat, but after we checked in, I forced myself to wander down to the honky-tonk that spilled music into the street. When I walked into the noisy lounge, I spotted Bobby Williams and Troy Spencer standing at the long counter in front of the bar. I snaked my way through the close-packed bodies on the dance floor.

"Heya, Lonnie." Troy turned toward me with his crooked-tooth grin and hollered over the wailing music. "Y'all want a beer?"

I held up my hand and shook my head. "Where you guys goin' tomorrow?" I shouted.

"Ogden," Troy yelled back.

"Got any room for a passenger?"

"Sure. It's just me and Bobby."

"What time are you leaving?"

Troy did a quick mental calculation of the mileage. "We'd better be hittin' the road by nine or so. You stayin' here?"

"Yeah . . . room two eleven. I'll be ready." I turned to Bobby and gave him a light punch in the arm. "Thanks for the help tonight, bud." He just nodded and smiled, and I left before the next cheatin' cowboy dirge. Helping a friend get out of the chute on a bad horse was what we did for each other. Bobby had done it well, and I appreciated it.

***

THE NEXT MORNING, I rustled around early and got my gear together. When I headed for the door, Brian was on the phone listening to the weather service. He had to be in Puyallup for a night performance, but it sounded like it was clouding up with a low ceiling on the Pacific Coast end. He'd be making good use of his instrument flying skills, and I was glad I didn't have to go with him. Sitting in that cockpit with nothing in front of you but murky cotton was about as comforting as driving a car with a blindfold over your eyes.

"Keep that tin bucket in the air. See ya' in Inglewood," I whispered. He winked, and gave me a thumbs up. I shouldered my bronc saddle and grabbed my gear, confident that tomorrow night we'd meet at the Inglewood rodeo in sunny, southern California.

Bobby and Troy were sitting in the front seat of Bobby's high-mileage black Buick, with Troy at the wheel, both itching to get on the road.

"Come on, Lonnie," Bobby hollered. "Get your butt in here. We gotta' be there tonight, not next week. Did you have to redo your makeup?"

"Stuff it." I stowed my gear in the trunk, and bailed into the backseat. Bobby and Troy were always fun to travel with on a short-term basis. We were all near the same vintage, so we had lots of common history. Many times over the years, we'd been thrown together in different travel circumstances, in every corner of the continent. I settled in, looking forward to catching up on the recent events in their lives.

Troy turned east onto the interstate and Bobby station-hopped through a half-dozen different country music options before sliding in an ancient George Strait CD. I leafed through my day planner to check my flight time for tomorrow morning out of Salt Lake.

Troy cocked his right arm over the seat. "What did Brian draw at Puyallup?"

I closed my calendar and stuffed it in my leather satchel. "A bull called Wildfire. He's not that great. I don't think he'll win diddly on him, but you know how it is. You gotta' try."

Bobby started chuckling. "Wildfire?" Troy and I looked at him and then at each other, wondering what was so funny about Wildfire.

"Remember that rodeo at Baton Rouge, Troy? Lonnie, you fell off the fence you were laughin' so hard."

I chuckled at the shared memory. It was the last bull of the night in an otherwise forgettable late February performance; all contained in a cold and clammy indoor arena. Bullfighter Wilbur Dobbs had fastened a rope from the catwalk high overhead. The rope was part of his clown act, and maybe an added safety feature if a bull caught him in the middle of the arena.

Bobby turned to Troy. "Didn't you win a bunch at that rodeo?"

"Yeah, but I wasn't there that night. I don't know where I was—maybe the Yuma rodeo. So what happened?"

"It was that pinto bull of Tommy Cripps. Same name as what Brian's got at Puyallup. Wildfire. He was always the last bull out at one of Tommy's rodeos. He wasn't much of a bucker, but he was a real headhunter. Bull riders hated him, but the crowds loved him. He'd clear the arena fast, mowing down everything or anybody that got in his way. So that night after Wildfire had made a couple of rounds, everybody was perched high on the fence, including us. The crowd is still oohing and aahing, but the show's over, so the boys opened the catch-pen gate and Wildfire snorted his way out of the arena. Right then, some mop-topped, hairy legged guy decided to jump into the arena and run across to the other side—bare-butt naked. Only the catch-pen gate didn't latch. And wouldn't you know it? Wildfire knocked the gate open, and out he came again, with lots of fight left in him. The first thing that came into sight was this weird guy with no clothes, right in the middle of the arena. The guy is loping for the other side, his fists high in the air. He doesn't even know Wildfire is back in the arena until the crowd's laughter goes up about two octaves. A stride later, that bull tossed him four feet in the air and then commenced to bellerin' and hooking at him. Now plumb terrified, Streaker picks up about three gears in mid-air, his arms and legs just a'pumping. He's still in the middle of the arena and Wildfire is lining up to really freight-train him when the guy sees that rope hanging from the catwalk."

Troy and I were both busting a gut hearing Bobby retell the long-ago event. Troy was having trouble keeping the Buick in the right lane he was laughing so hard.

"When that guy's peddling feet started contacting dirt again, he did a hard right and scampered for the nearest safety—the rope. I swear he hit it at forty miles an hour. Wildfire blew some more bull snot all over his exposed parts, and gave him a boost up the rope, far enough to be just out of range of those deadly horns. The guy hung there with a death grip, too weak with fear to climb any higher, but Wildfire wouldn't leave. He was right underneath the rope, pawing the ground, wanting to tear the guy to pieces. Those Baton Rouge folks were pretty strait-laced, but they were all on their feet, I think cheering for the bull. After circling and pawing the dirt a few times, Wildfire shook his head, now disgusted with the whole business and trotted out of the arena. A couple of security cops ran in, got the guy to come down the rope and took him into custody." Bobby laughed again. "After that episode, I doubt he even took his clothes off in the shower."

Twenty miles down the road, we were still guffawing over the streaker incident. Bobby was fiddling with the radio again when Troy looked back from the driver's seat.

"Hey, y'all sure 'nuff did a good job on old Sitting Bull last night. Good ride."

"Thanks to my man, Bobby." I chuckled. "He's the one that got me out on that chute-fighting devil."

Troy kept Bobby's used-up Buick in the passing lane as we continued to discuss familiar subjects: cowboys, broncs, bulls, and yes, women. That was a touchy subject for me, but of course, Bobby started it.

"Hey Lonnie, somebody said you and your wife are splittin' the sheets. How come? You're nuts, man."

"Private. Not up for discussion," I replied, and stared out the window. Both Bobby and Troy knew Clarissa. It wasn't the first time I realized I still really cared about her, and I had no intention of discussing her with Bobby Williams or anybody else.

It seemed Bobby couldn't take a hint, or more likely, being Bobby; he didn't care.

"Lonnie, if you dump that woman, there's going to be a hundred guys lined up to take your place. You ought to think about that before you cut her loose." Right then, I would have cheerfully throttled Bobby with the tie-rope we'd used on Sitting Bull last night. The whole subject of Clarissa always elicited a deep anger and regret. Even though I was disgusted with her newfound religious experience, and angry that she would do the Christian thing without . . . well, at least talking about it, I still missed her, and Bobby's comment didn't help. We were still married—sort of.

"Bobby, shut up, take a pill, and get on to something else. You'll be the first to know if we split the sheets, as you so tactfully put it."

Bobby glared from under the brim of his straw hat. "Hey, back off, Lonnie. We're on your side. I'm just telling you to think about life after rodeo. There is such a thing you know."

"As if you'd know. You're what . . . thirty-five? What are you going to do? Your riding arm is a medical mess, and you've never done anything but ride bucking horses from the day you got out of high school. So can the lecture."

Bobby shrugged his sudden disinterest in pursuing the subject further, and turned back to the radio. I glared at the back of his neck. All he had to show for the best twenty years of his life was a trophy case full of gold-plated buckles and a mortgaged trailer house on five acres out in the sagebrush near Rock Springs, Wyoming. Not that I was any different. However, I'd been lucky enough to get a college degree. I hoped that meant I could someday get a better job than sweeping out the local feed barn, which brought me back to what had started the whole argument.

I'd had no great desire to go to college, but my first week there, a long-legged Canadian girl with flowing sandy hair and a scattering of freckles across her cute, dimpled cheeks had captured my interest forever. And yes, I still loved that woman. Maybe it just took Bobby's crap to remind me of it.

CHAPTER 5

LONNIE

BOBBY'S COBBLED TOGETHER BUICK got us into Ogden in good enough time to grab a bite at a downtown café, avoid a fight with some pie-eyed local toughs, and make it to the rodeo grounds about five-thirty. Ogden has a big fair with a midway and nighttime entertainment, so I wandered around the grounds, peered disinterestedly at the exhibits and surreptitiously studied people's faces, wondering how many were like mine, cardboard cutouts, careful masks that concealed the mayhem inside. Behind the picture of the confident, self-assured cowboy with the tipped back hat and ready smile, was another portrait. Inside, where nobody could see, a little man taunted me and laughed at my clumsy bravado. You're not good enough, and you never were. You're at the end of your sorry career. You never made it, and your marriage is a wreck, and just what do you think you're going to do now?

I sure enough didn't know what I was going to do now, with my career or marriage. In my heart, there was no other woman and the nine-to-five routine made me shudder, but at thirty years old, the best of my rodeo days were behind me. I wandered farther through the crowd, and stopped to watch a middle-aged Carny taking ride tickets. His sleeveless, wrinkled T-shirt hung outside of a pair of army surplus jungle fatigues. The pants were at least two inches too long, held to his emaciated frame by a worn dress belt from a different era. The pants slopped over a pair of run-over black and white Converse tennis shoes with broken laces. His face spoke of defeat: eyes ravaged by drugs, the mouth puckered from years of cigarettes, his lips flat against his remaining yellowed teeth. I shuddered and turned away. No, I could never end up there—and yet . . . what if I didn't start winning?

I bought a cup of bitter coffee on the edge of the midway and sauntered back to the chutes, but the growing turmoil in my chest wouldn't leave. Could I ever just walk away from rodeo? Could I leave the deep friendships and seductive thrill of a thousand cheering fans? What would my life be like when I could no longer match my skill against an opponent that had the capability to injure or kill me? Not that any of us viewed the livestock as opponents. Most times, they're like old acquaintances, to be handled with respect and consideration.

I crushed the empty Styrofoam cup and jumped up on the catwalk behind the bucking chutes. The grand entry, which starts every rodeo, was just getting under way with all the pomp and nonsense of a Mike Perkins' show. Most of us rolled our eyes in disgust every time we came to one of Mike's circus spectacles, but the crowds loved him. He was a rodeo showman, and every year he devised another pageant to fill the folks with patriotic fervor. He worked the crowd like a carnival huckster until they became a part of the performance. And because filling those bleachers was what paid our prize money, we grudgingly became part of the act as well.

This year, Mike had the Liberty Bell routine. A team of fancy palomino horses pulled a low-slung wagon into the arena, the deck area completely obliterated by a huge fiberglass bell. While the national anthem played, the bell opened like the petals of a brilliant daisy. Standing proudly in the center was the current Miss Rodeo America, mounted on a flaxen-maned sorrel horse. She carried Old Glory high overhead for all to see. It put everybody in the right mood for the great American sport of rodeo.

After the national anthem finished, Troy pulled on his glove and tied it in place. I inched the latigo to just the right tension on his bareback riggin' while he held it in position. Troy was the fourth rider out, and he had a solid campaigner they called "Applejack." That big chestnut gelding always stood like he was on parade until they cracked the chute gate. Then he bailed into the arena and bucked his heart out. If you did your part, you were going to win some money. Troy nodded his red Texan head, then spurred his way to a whopping eighty-five points. He would win big at this rodeo.

I buckled my chaps and patted some rosin into the swells of my saddle. One stirrup leather seemed a little longer than it should be. Sometimes a tough horse like Sitting Bull or even a different level of humidity will cause the material in newer stirrup leathers to stretch. Rummaging in the bottom of my riggin' bag, I found a thin plug and stuffed it under the stirrup leather buckle to shorten it, but it still didn't feel right. In fact, nothing did and I wasn't able to shake my earlier malaise. It was Bobby's fault, badgering me about Clarissa. Or maybe I was just tired and fed up with my life. Tonight, the thrill wasn't there, and I couldn't pinpoint why.

The broncs trotted up the alley. Gates slammed shut,

locking each horse in their respective chute. Mine, a gangly black mare was in the last one, and she sure wasn't any budding princess. She had a roman nose and a parrot jaw. Her back was so wide you could have ridden her in a washtub, but her hipbones stuck out like she was a third world refugee. I saddled her, measured the right amount of rein, and waited my turn. When the chute gate opened, we scampered to the back end of the arena fast enough to be a derby contender, ricocheted off the fence, and started back again. It was a long eight seconds before the whistle blew, and even the pickup men had a hard time plucking me from the clutches of this frustrated racehorse.

I unbuckled my chaps and shuffled up the arena. A whopping sixty points wouldn't get me anything. Still, I did the good sport thing; high-fived a couple of kids, waved at a few others—and froze. That fat tourist guy, the one with the funny accent who had taken my picture in Dillon was sitting on the south side in the second row. Why would he be here? I ticked off possibilities in my mind. Maybe he was doing an out-west tour, taking in all the rodeos, and going to a dude ranch or. . . . Then why did he make me nervous? Those eyes; there was nothing soft and touristy about those hard, capable eyes, and once when I glanced back, they met mine. Somewhere in the past I'd seen them before, and it wasn't only at Dillon.

***

THE NEXT MORNING, I hitched a ride to the Salt Lake airport with a couple of young bull riders. My flight to Inglewood didn't leave for a couple of hours, so I wandered down through Terminal One to find a newspaper and something to eat.

After picking through some half-cooked eggs and sausage, I found a pay phone and tried to call Clarissa. It was something I still did at least once a week, which is tough to explain. We weren't friends, but we'd gotten past not speaking at all. I'd done wrong by her, but I still felt a responsibility toward her. I shoved the plate aside. That wasn't completely honest, and I knew it. I called her because she still meant a lot to me.

While the phone rang, my stomach turned into the usual mush and I tried to scrape the polish off the floor with the side of my boot. After the fourth ring, the answering machine kicked in. "Hello. You have reached Clarissa Bowers at Guardian Insurance. Your call is important to me. If you will leave your name and number, I will call you back just as quickly as I can . . . blah, blah, blah." I left a message that I would call tonight from Inglewood, then returned to my newspaper.

The front page had all the usual. Another hurricane in Louisiana, a couple of murders, a drug bust, and a new trade spat with China. The second page wasn't much better. A small plane disappeared somewhere in California. Nobody quite knew where. The pilot filed an Instrument Flight Plan from Puyallup, Washington, to Stockton, California. *No worries there. Brian was flying to Inglewood, not Stockton.* The single-engine plane with no passengers had taken off at eleven o'clock last night into high overcast. Enough doom and gloom. I glanced at the clock and moved on to the sports pages.

Chapter 6

CLARISSA

My eyes opened to hospital walls. Why was I still alive? For some miraculous reason I wasn't dead, and my eyes welled with tears of gratefulness.

I remembered the big cat ripping the flesh from my shoulder. Then there had been that bushy-bearded angel. Bushy-beard must not have been an angel, at least not a real one. I looked down at my right arm and tried to move it. Agonizing pain knifed through my shoulder, eliciting an instant tortured groan.

A capable-looking matronly nurse hustled through the door to my room, her face creased with years of service to hurting people like me. Caring, hazel eyes brightened her otherwise serious face when she saw I was awake.

"How're you doing, young lady?" She had a deep timbre in her voice, almost like a man's, but with a soft, comforting warmth.

"It could be worse." I tried to smile, but it turned into a grimace as pain shot through my lower face. "My face hurts the most."

She peered at the ragged, stitched-up lines in my face, arm, and shoulder, then adjusted the I.V. drip attached to my left hand. "You were about finished when they brought you into emergency. Dr. Jackson had to do some creative surgery on that arm to get everything reconnected. He'll be in later this morning to check on you."

"How long have I been here?"

"Oh, Clint showed up with you about nine o'clock yesterday morning. You were definitely critical."

"Aha—Clint," I thought. *"Whoever Clint is, I'll bet he has a big, bushy beard."*

"They would have airlifted you right to Vancouver General, but one of the top surgeons in the province happened to be here in the hospital doing other surgeries, so they wheeled you right into the operating room and went to work.

She explained the bed pan and buttons. "If you need anything, just push the call-button by your head."

She bustled out, and I was left to mull over why I had been spared. Few people live through a cougar attack. Why, and how had I escaped? Again, I tried to move my right arm with the same painful result, then turned my head and stared down at the forest of bloody stitches. My left arm seemed okay, and I brought my fingers up to my face to touch the whiskery feel of more sutures. Tears of despair trickled down the side of my face. What would I look like? Would my arm be crippled? Would I be like old Mrs. Fenton, forever destined to carry it next to my chest, the hand withering to nothing as the years passed? I lifted my left hand to my face, trying to trace the scars without touching them. *Why, God? What am I doing wrong? First my marriage, and now this.* More tears wet my pillow. The deep gashes in my arm and face didn't hurt any worse than the bloody wounds on the face of my soul.

When I'd embarked on this journey with God, it had seemed so right. Now—I wasn't so sure.

It started with Corrie Rice. She worked in the Personnel Department in our Vancouver office. We also belonged to the same women's gym over on Granville Street. Everybody knew Corrie. She was the most popular girl in the department, maybe the whole company. Corrie's intense, warm eyes and dimpled smile radiated genuine concern for whatever problem you might have, which was neat, until I found out that Corrie was one of those "Christians."

She wasn't my first experience with religion. My freshman year in college, I had roomed with a girl who was one of *them*. We had some great discussions about God, Jesus, and, the whole Christian thing, but I couldn't swallow the timeline of creation. Any scientific evidence I was aware of didn't leave that as an option. Lucinda and I ended the year distant and guarded.

Corrie hadn't been as easy to dismiss. More than anything else, she was my friend. She never preached, and she was always there when I needed her. We spent many evenings talking through those issues that I had argued over with my former roommate. But there wasn't the condemnation from Corrie, and for whatever reason, I didn't feel the desperation to defend what I believed. In the end, all my reservations and arguments crumbled. I decided I needed a Savior more than a guiltless theory; I needed peace in my heart more than control, and I needed Jesus more than my self-sufficient pride. The capitulation was complete.

A polite knock on the half-open door interrupted my reverie. Annoyed, I hastily wiped at the tears. I didn't want company. A big, tousle-headed man with a full beard and wire-rimmed glasses hesitated, then stepped around the door. "May I come in?"

I frowned, hoping he would go away. "Perhaps later." Either I wasn't forceful enough, or he didn't understand a polite "no," because he just walked into the room.

"I'm sorry for intruding," he said. He maneuvered his massive frame toward my bed. "I'm Clint Forsythe. I carried you down the mountain."

My face burned. "Oh, I'm sorry. I didn't know—forgive me for being so rude."

He smiled, and his eyes softened behind the wire-rimmed glasses. "I just wanted to pop in and see how you're doing. You had lost a lot of blood, and it didn't look like you were going to make it. God obviously had other plans."

Oh—so this guy is probably a Christian. Now it didn't matter what I looked like. It was more important to talk to this man—to hear about those terrifying moments on the mountain trail.

"Please—again—I am so sorry," I stammered. "What happened up there? And did anyone find my horse?"

"Actually we did, and he's alright. My wife and I went up yesterday afternoon to see if we could find him. He'd found his way down the mountain. I had a hunch you were living in the old Harkins place on the Texas Creek Road, so when I saw the horse grazing on the front lawn, I took the liberty of unsaddling him and putting him in your pasture behind the house. I hope that was all right?"

"Of course," I smiled. "He'll be fine there. Was he okay?"

"Yes, except for a small cut on one hock, and a few deep scratches on the left side of his neck," Clint replied. "I called

Doc Stone, and he stitched them up. Did a fine job. We'll keep an eye on him—that is, if you would like us to?"

"Thank you so much. That horse means a lot to me."

"You are most welcome."

"So how did you find me?"

"I went up Farwell Canyon early yesterday morning because I had an appointment with a massive muley buck, one I've tried to get for three years." A deep laugh rumbled from somewhere deep inside this big man. "He never showed, but I guess God had me up there for another reason. I was holed up in the rocks waiting for this monster buck when you and your horse showed up on the trail below me. The cougar attack happened right in front of me."

I shook my head, marveling at this . . . coincidence? *Did pure chance explain this man's being in that exact spot?* I wondered.

"It's hard to understand why your horse never smelled that big cat," Clint continued. "Horses can smell cougars a mile away, yet he walked right under that tree without ever knowing the cat was there. Just before the cougar made his leap, your horse finally sensed the danger. He shied at the critical moment, which may have saved you from a broken neck. The cougar probably wanted the horse, but there you were on the ground, already on his plate, so he just started chewing."

My laugh instantly turned to a groan, as pain shot through my upper body and face, but it had been comical, the way Clint told it. The nightmares would come later.

"When he knocked you off your horse, I froze for a moment wondering what exactly to do. I started running down the hill, but it was a hundred yards down a rocky slope. When I got to within thirty yards, that cougar let go of you and looked my way. His chest was two feet from your head, but there wasn't going to be another opportunity. I sent a bullet and a prayer his way. Thank God, they worked. He fell right on top of you. I dragged him off, certain you were dead. You were unconscious, and you'd lost a lot of blood from the torn artery at the top of your arm. I ripped up my shirt and used it for a tourniquet. My pickup was about a mile away, so I packed you down there and carted you off to town."

Clint's dark eyes twinkled behind the glasses. Lonnie's sparked the same way—or they used to.

"Anyhow, Clarissa. That is right, isn't it?"

I nodded, as gratitude welled up in me.

"I need to be on my way. I'm the pastor of Mountain Community Church here in Lillooet, and duty calls. If you would like though, I'll bring my wife Darlene up tomorrow morning. She would love to meet you, and I think you two would get along well."

"Please do. I would like that. And—and—thank you." I started to cry, but I think Clint understood. They were tears of gratefulness, all mixed up with trauma and the still biting pain in my arm and shoulder—plus the joy of just being alive. Why was I laying in this hospital bed—instead of the morgue? Coincidence? Luck? Or was it really a miracle? If it was a miracle, then why? My life wasn't important. Why would God care enough to keep me alive? My eyes closed in a restless sleep, filled with nightmares of big tawny cats with dripping fangs and bared claws.

***

I woke, ate, and slept again. My body was trying to heal, and maybe my mind was as well. The cougar attack played through my sleep. Daylight crept through the curtains and lightened my room. I dozed in and out of consciousness, exhausted from the recurring nightmares fighting to escape those enormous, reaching fangs.

Hunger finally brought me to full consciousness, which I suppose was a good sign. The nurse came in and told me I could get up, if I wanted. Any movement was excruciating, but the bathroom was infinitely more appealing than a bedpan, so with my I.V. pole, I forced my weak and rubbery legs toward the privy. The pole and I made it through the door and over to the sink. The mirror waited like a courtroom judge to pass sentence. I held onto the edge of the counter with my good arm, and forced my eyes upward to the glass. Ragged, bloody lines crisscrossed the right side of my face. They were festooned with black stitches, the same sprouting dead grass that covered my shoulder and arm. I slumped forward, horrified, but unable to look away. No matter how skillful the doctor had been who had stitched my face, the scars would always stand out as angry welts. Makeup could never cover the red slashes that ran down my neck to my bare shoulder. What would Lonnie think? Would he turn away in revulsion? I clenched my jaw. I didn't need to worry what Lonnie would think. He wouldn't see my bare shoulder—ever again.

Later in the morning, Clint walked into my room. A petite and attractive woman followed him. Clint introduced his wife, Darlene, and she stepped forward and squeezed my left hand with both of hers. We were immediate friends. Within minutes, I was telling her my life story, and she was listening as if I were the princess of Persia. She asked whether there was anyone who needed to be notified. I told her both my parents were gone. I had no brothers and sisters. In fact, I had no family other than an elderly aunt in Georgia whom I had only met twice in my life. Lonnie was somewhere on the road. He still called regularly, but I didn't want him to come. That would be too painful. He would find out soon enough—if he cared.

Darlene and Clint listened without comment when I told them briefly about my lack of family and why I had moved back to my hometown of Lillooet after my marriage disintegrated. After a half hour, they stood to leave. Clint asked if he could pray for me. That sounded embarrassing but I nodded. His prayer was short. He asked God to heal me, to reach down and let me feel his power in my life, and after that— Amen. Darlene squeezed my hand again with love and concern in her eyes. "Clarissa, do you have chores or things that need looking after at your house? We'd love to help if there's anything we can do."

"Well, I have two cats. They're barn cats and I'm not worried about them, but it would be good if somebody opened a new bag of Kitty Chow in the next couple of days. And, there's a standpipe in the yard, if you wouldn't mind filling the water trough for Monte."

"We'll be glad to do it," Clint said. "It would be a privilege to be able to help."

"You have done so much." My eyes filled with tears of gratefulness to these strangers. No words would come that were adequate. "Thank you for . . . for everything." I had never meant it more.

CHAPTER 7

LONNIE

THE LOUDSPEAKER announced my Los Angeles flight. I grabbed my clothes bag, then hurried through the concourse to gate thirty-six to join the last straggler walking down the ramp to the plane. Fumbling through my wallet for identification, I grabbed my driver's license and boarding pass and shoved them toward the attendant. Stuffed in the same slot as my driver's license was a plain white business card. I glanced at the name. The card belonged to the fat tourist looking guy who had been at the rodeo again last night. In small, bold print, the name stared back at me. Frederick Roseman. Underneath in larger block letters was the company name. Stirling Associates.

Vague memories from my distant college past cascaded through my mind as I sidestepped past the two Southwest flight attendants at the front of the plane. The intense recruiting activities in my senior year by the few elite companies like Stirling Associates, Blackwater, and a half-dozen others, not to mention the CIA and other government three letter agencies. That name was one of many from that time. But why would he show up now?

Few people outside the security business know the name Stirling Associates. Birthed after the embarrassment of the Iran-Contra affair, Stirling's appearance was a direct result of a congressional effort in Washington power corridors to shield politicians from the carnage that followed that public chapter of finger pointing and bloodletting. Now, when a counterintelligence operation went awry, a few civil servants were thrown to the wolves, but no politician had to stand before a Congressional Hearing and fumble for nonexistent answers. Stirling Associates took the rap. The neocons called them unprincipled scoundrels who had stepped way beyond their orders, bad actors who had breached acceptable protocol. The liberals screeched and pontificated, government security contracts were cut, and a few low-level bureaucrats were shuffled from Washington to the hinterlands of Nevada. But the clandestine, necessary, and often dark business of espionage and intelligence gathering never slowed.

I shuffled forward, waiting for the lineup to stow their overhead baggage. Was it just coincidence to have run into him twice in hardly more than a week? I wedged my bag into the overhead. Maybe the guy was a rodeo fan who spent his vacation time following the professional rodeo circuit, watching his favorite cowboys. Perfectly normal people did that sort of thing. It didn't necessarily have anything to do with Stirling Associates or their often clandestine activities. But my reasoning rang hollow.

My college major had been Counterterrorism and Foreign Intelligence at a small regional college buried in a five-stoplight Wyoming town. But the curriculum was cutting edge, and graduates were hotly pursued by every national intelligence agency as well as private security companies. I'd switched to the program after nearly flunking out of both Education and Business. The course was fascinating, and even though I missed classes because I was off at rodeos, my grades were more than acceptable. However, there was no desire in me to work for the government, or anybody else. I loved the free life of a rodeo cowboy. Punching a time clock and taking orders held little appeal, so I kept riding bucking horses. I'd worry about the future when it came.

After settling into my aisle seat, I pulled the business card out of my shirt pocket. The guy had written a short note on the back offering his best wishes and assistance. The address was somewhere in Albuquerque, New Mexico. Strange. Were they still trying to recruit me? They'd already kicked that can, and it hadn't worked. Assistance? I neither wanted nor needed any from this bird.

The stewardess started the seatbelt, oxygen mask routine. Most of my two hundred fellow hostages ignored her. I stared at the name on the card. As the flight attendant finished her spiel, I slipped it back in my shirt pocket. If I didn't start winning some money, I might need a real job. I scowled at that possibility. If I did, it wouldn't be with Stirling Associates. The rodeo arena provided enough adrenaline. I had no desire to play their cloak-and-dagger spy games.

***

THE WHEELS HIT the Los Angeles runway acceptably late, but it was only a short hop out to Inglewood and the Best Western where Brian and I had reservations. Maybe there would be time for a nap. My horse tonight was a good one, and I wanted to be ready. Cotton Ginny would take me to the pay window, presuming I did my part.

I picked my saddle and riggin' bag off the carousel. The airlines had lost them enough times that I was always relieved when they coughed up from the bowels of airport mayhem. Smoggy warmth mingled with the petroleum city smell and instant clamor of a thousand frantic cars as I trudged from the air-conditioned neutrality of the terminal to the waiting cab line. Brian should be at the room. It would be good to reconnect and hear the gossip from another far-off rodeo.

At the hotel, the desk girl and I bandied the usual questions and answers.

"No, Mr. Besser had not arrived."

"Yes, we would be checking out tomorrow morning, and no I would not need any help with my luggage." I offered a nearly used-up Visa card for a key and trudged up to the room.

After I'd dumped my gear in the closet, I recalculated Brian's flight time from Puyallup to Los Angeles. If he were in the air by eight . . . five and a half hour flight time . . . that should put him in L.A. by one thirty, say two at the latest. He should be here within the hour.

Flopping down on one of the beds, I toed off my brown ropers. My eyes closed, and I tried to concentrate on every detail of my coming ride, every little quirk that Cotton Ginny might have tonight. Frederick Roseman . . . something disturbing . . . Clarissa . . . should try to call her again.

Some noisy kids in the hallway jarred me awake, as they badgered their stressed-out parents to go to the swimming pool. The bedside clock said five. Time to head for the arena. Brian must have had to skirt some bad weather, or maybe he couldn't get off the ground in that fog-bound northwest rain-hole. This late in the day, he would go straight to the arena from the airport. I'd see him there.

I splashed some water on my face, caught a cab at the front door and arrived at the arena an hour before the seven o'clock performance. Finding my way to the chutes at the north end of the Coliseum, I said a few quick hellos, shook some hands, and scoured through the riggin' bags piled around the chute area. Brian's bag wasn't there. Why? The possibilities clicked through my mind one after the other.

"Hank," I hollered to the other side of the chutes. "Let me borrow your phone?" I'd left mine in the room. Brian might have his turned on, though we seldom used them. The Canadian phone company wanted a pint of blood every time you touched the thing outside of Canada. But I had to try something.

Hank Porter dug out his phone. "Sure. Need to call your girl?"

I scowled. "No. Brian hasn't shown up. He was flying in from Puyallup, and he should have been here by now." I dialed Brian's number.

"Brian here. Leave a message, and I'll get back . . ."

I snapped the phone shut and handed it back to Hank. A tiny ball bearing started to roll around in the pit of my stomach.

The biggest factor was always weather. If he hadn't been able to get out of the Seattle area until later this morning, it would mean he wouldn't be arriving until . . . no, that didn't work either. The flight down was an easy four hours, and he would have called the Best Western and left a message if anything went wrong. That was what worried me. Brian would have called to let me know if there was a problem, even if he had to use his Canadian phone. He knew that I would have to make other flight arrangements back to Puyallup, so we could then fly to the Alberta rodeos. At any rate, my worries would have to wait. It was time to go to work.

I unwrapped the latigos on my saddle, then pulled on my bronc-riding boots and short shanked, dull-roweled spurs. My mind played through the rodeo at Spanish Fork, Utah. Cotton Ginny was a hard bucker, and she followed the same pattern every time. Gib Stewart had won first place on her there. All I had to do was keep my mind on the job and not make any mistakes, like I had at Dillon.

My fringed chaps buckled snug around my upper leg, and I patted some of the sticky, powdered rosin onto the swells of my saddle before checking my saddle and stirrup length. There could be no equipment failure tonight.

The eight broncs trotted up the alley to the chutes. The slide gates clanged shut. I picked up my saddle, halter, and buck rein and prepared my mind to win.

The chunky brown mare they called Cotton Ginny was in chute number one, over close to the left wall of the arena. That would give the mare lots of room to make her big, high kicking circle to the right. I jumped up on the catwalk and talked to her while I slipped my bronc halter over her nose, buckled it, and looped the rein over her neck. I always missed Brian when I was saddling a bronc. He was ranch raised and had an uncanny skill to quiet a nervous, chute fighting horse. That wasn't necessary with this horse, but it was always good to have his calm, capable help.

Cotton Ginny had been taking cowboys to the pay window for at least ten years, and I had a fondness and respect for old campaigners like her. They weren't just adversaries in the arena; they were fellow athletes. I checked my saddle to make sure it was cinched tight enough. When the last roper left the far end of the arena, I was ready.

Cotton Ginny stood like a sentinel, now and then cocking an ear back to listen while I talked to her. I measured out the amount of rein to give her. Too short, and she could jerk me over her head. Too long, and I wouldn't have the steadying balance point that I needed to stay in the saddle. It's a procedure peculiar to our trade, and knowledge of how much rein a horse requires is always shared with other bronc riders. Climbing over the top of the chute, I put some weight on the saddle with my foot and eased down, always watching her ears. If a horse is going to rear over backward, it has to start at the head, and those ears will be the first sign of danger. There would not likely be trouble with this mare, but it was my habit to be cautious. More than one cowboy had been crippled in the chute because a solid, old horse like Cotton Ginny, for no apparent reason, had suddenly turned upside down. I slid my boots into the narrow wooden stirrups, continuing to talk softly to her. Scrunching my butt into the saddle, my mind blocked out everything but this bronc. I tucked my chin against the whiplash of that first big jump, and nodded my head. The chute gate swung open and Cotton Ginny bailed out into the arena sand. From that point, my body reacted to her every move, and we became one. With the precision earned from a thousand other broncs, I followed the curve of her powerful body with my spurring feet, my eyes fixed on the rippling mane behind her pointed brown ears. My rein hand extended out over her neck. We'd gotten "tapped off right." Ginny was having one of her spectacular days, and I was putting in a solid spurring performance on my end. She made her big looping turn to the far side of the arena before the horn blared, signaling the end of the ride.

Larry Kantor's big dun pickup horse crowded in on my left side. He took my bronc rein, and I slipped over the back of his saddle and hit the ground on my feet. It had been a good ride and by the sound of the applause, the fans had liked it well enough. However, it was the judges who would decide whether this was a payday.

Cotton Ginny tossed her head beside Larry's big gelding as they loped out of the arena. I grinned and tipped my hat to her. Both of us enjoyed our work.

"Ladies and gentlemen, we have a new leader in the bronc riding here tonight. The judges have given Lonnie Bowers . . . eighty—one—points!" Announcer, Pete Jarvis elicited his usual enthusiastic response from the crowd.

Yes! The old thrill was back. If that score stayed in first place through the final performance tomorrow night, I would be able to pay a few more of my screeching creditors.

I gathered up my gear and grinned my way behind the chutes. When things go well in the business of bronc riding, it's a huge rush. I was a hero, for the moment. However, I'd been around long enough to know that in this ego-charged atmosphere, star status was short-lived. At best—it would last until breakfast.

The bulls were clanging their way through the alley and into the chutes. Brian's bull was in the number three chute. I wrapped up my saddle, folded my chaps and tucked them into my riggin' bag, but he still hadn't arrived.

The bull he had drawn was a good one—if you could ride him. Brian could. He'd done it a year ago at Salinas. If there was any way to make it, he would have been here to get on this bull. The worry knot in my stomach picked up another layer. Had there been some mechanical failure? We'd flown through those northern California mountains a dozen times, and they were often miserable. You could run into snow, hail, or sleet about six months of the year. Brian explained to me that because of sudden changes in temperature, a plane can pick up airframe ice. That disrupted the airflow over the wings and of course, down you went, out of control. Carburetor ice robbed engine power, with the same devastating result. It was all a bit daunting to somebody like me who abhorred airplanes even in the sunniest of weather.

Marty Gray, the chute boss, called for Brian. Then he saw me standing on the back of the chute.

"Lonnie, where's Brian?" he bellowed.

I shrugged. "He was flying in from Puyallup today. I don't know what happened."

Marty swore. I didn't blame him for being angry. Popeye was one of their best bulls, and he was matched against Brian, one of the top bull riders on the circuit. His ride could have been one of the high points of the performance, and now he had failed to show up.

I turned away from the chutes, all the euphoria from my ride gone. A dozen guys fired questions. Why wasn't Brian here? Had he landed on some backwater strip to avoid a storm system he couldn't avoid? It was too early in the fall for real bad weather. But he wasn't here, and the ball bearing in the pit of my stomach turned into a roiling nest of snakes.

CHAPTER 8

CLARISSA

I GRIPPED THE WINDOW SILL and stared down at the lined parking lot. Yellow leaves skittered over the dappled pavement. The word from the nurse was that if there were no complications, the doctor might release me. I was more than ready.

A late-model silver Mercedes with tinted windows pulled off the street and parked in a corner stall. The door opened, and I caught a glimpse of black leather. Then an expensive pinstripe suit stood and glanced toward the hospital before reaching into the back seat. Roses—a basket full. He was tall, athletic and immaculate in his lawyer attire and my heart skipped a beat. There was no doubt where he was bound. I hurried to the bathroom mirror, grabbed a brush and peered at my reflection. I lowered my hand and dropped the brush on the counter. Five minutes wouldn't fix anything. I couldn't hide the hideous line of stitches along my jaw. My arm and shoulder were mangled and useless. I was a far cry from the crisp and confident businesswoman he had taken to lunch, and my stomach lurched with dread.

When Rob stepped through the door holding the roses in front of his brilliant smile, I stood with my back against the window—wishing I could jump out of it.

"Clarissa. It's great to see you." His voice was warm, and I relaxed a little.

"Hi, Rob."

He extended the roses. "Where would you like them?"

I motioned to the tray table by the bed. "They're beautiful. Thank you." His eyes slid from my wounded face to the stitches slashing across my once whole body, then fell away.

"What a horrible thing to go through." He set the flowers on the table.

"Please, Rob, sit down." I motioned to the plastic hospital chair and tried to give him an encouraging smile. "The flowers; they're so nice. Thank you for coming all the way up here to see me," I stuttered nervously.

His eyes once again flickered to my mutilated shoulder and arm, then moved back to my face to study the ragged stitches that skirted my jaw. "So how did it happen?" His voice was soothing, his words comforting to hear.

I tried to relate the events on the mountain as best I could. "It was a miracle," I finished up. "I guess God has something more for me to do, or He wouldn't have saved me."

Rob's face was impassive, but his eyes ridiculed me. "Yes, of course. You were very lucky."

"No." I turned and again stared out at the parking lot. "I don't think 'lucky' had anything to do with it." The temperature between us cooled, and he steered the conversation to business and client files we had worked on together. A half-hour later, he stood to leave.

"Get well soon. I miss working with you." He turned on

his thousand-watt smile. I thanked him again for coming, and for the beautiful flowers. Before he left, he bent over and brushed my forehead with a kiss, but it didn't feel right. In fact, it felt all wrong. However, I bulldozed my misgivings aside. Rob had driven four hours to deliver those flowers. It was a rare occasion when Lonnie brought anything but dirty laundry. And at the last, it had been an event if he even came home. But it didn't matter, and as much as I wanted it to be otherwise, my heart was dead. The toothpaste smile, the money, the flowers, all meant nothing. I'd given my heart to a man a long time ago. Getting it back wasn't going to be easy. My chin rose, and my teeth ground together. Nevertheless, I was going to try.

That afternoon, Clint and Darlene picked me up. We drove through the brilliant fall leaves to my little rented house. Everything appeared the same as I'd left it when I rode up the mountain five days ago. Clint opened the passenger door. I gingerly slid out and stood beside the car to survey my little domain. Monte stood with his head hanging over the fence. His ears pricked up and he whickered at me. I limped over and scratched his ears, then worked down his neck to his chest. My fingers traced around the deep scar on the left side of his neck. Like my own, it would always be a reminder of our traumatic morning on the mountain.

Clint carried my bag and flowers in while I petted Monte. I hurried inside. "Would you stay for a cup of tea?"

Clint grinned. "Thank you, but no. I have a sermon to prepare, but we'll stop by to check on you tomorrow."

After a week of having strangers poke and prod me, solitude sounded blissful. I think they understood my need. "Tomorrow then? Would you come for dinner?" I asked. "I have some lasagna in the freezer. Even one-armed, I can whip up a salad of some sort."

Darlene gave me an appraising glance. "Okay, we'd love that. What can I bring?"

"How about some French bread to compliment the lasagna?"

"Sure," Darlene smiled, her eyes twinkling. "How about I bring the salad too?"

"Sounds good." Our eyes met, understanding, building a friendship I was beginning to treasure.

"If you need anything, call us," Clint said. He jotted down their home phone number and the one at the church on my notepad by the phone. At the door, they both hugged me.

I waved goodbye, already looking forward to tomorrow evening. This small-town pastor likely had little time to call his own, but he and Darlene had embraced me as if I was one of their own congregation, and I was grateful.

A gnawing hunger moved me to the kitchen. The fridge was spotless. Bless Darlene again. She had thrown out everything that was rotting while I was confined to a hospital bed. I searched through the freezer, extracted a loaf of bread, and found a can of tuna in the little kitchen pantry. By one-handing a daub of mayonnaise into the tuna, with a little of it dribbled on the counter, I managed to make a sandwich. Later, I stretched out in the recliner and had a nap. It appeared I would need some time to get my strength back.

I longed to tackle the outside chores. Instead, I spent the rest of the afternoon moving between the recliner and the outside step letting the autumn sun warm my injured body. If it could only do the same for my battered heart, I thought. My eyes turned to Rob's fading roses on the dining room table, which oddly made me wonder about Lonnie. Why hadn't I remembered to check the phone messages? In my groggy state, it hadn't even occurred to me. I shuffled to the answering machine. Two were from my boss, Ben Thomas, with best wishes and a short update on some important insurance loss files. He had been supportive and understanding, though aghast at what had happened. I am sure in his downtown Vancouver office, he wondered why anyone would live in such a dangerous backwater. Two other messages were get-well wishes from colleagues in the company. The last two were from Lonnie. The second message Lonnie sounded irritated with a hint of worry in his voice at his inability to reach me. A dim spark, one I wanted to stamp into the ground ignited a fiendish delight. Lonnie . . . anxious about me? How curious.

CHAPTER 9
LONNIE

THEY HELD BRIAN'S BULL until last, but finally Marty threw the gate open and the big brindle Popeye trotted into the arena without him. I took a deep breath and flipped through the possibilities again. *Brian would be okay. He was an absolute whiz in that plane. All I had to do was track him down.* Then I thought about Clarissa. Brian might have left a message with her, knowing there was a possibility I would call her. I hurried down the arena concourse to find a pay phone.

Every time I dialed Clarissa's home number, my stomach started flip-flopping. I wondered where she was, whom she was with, and what she was doing. Twice this week I'd tried to reach her, with no answer either time. That always started the anger and suspicion, which in our estranged circumstances, didn't make a lot of sense. Hunched into the phone, I tried to block the still excited din from the exiting crowd. Her phone was ringing in faraway Lillooet. In Inglewood, a pair of well-shaped Wranglers filled my vision, but I forced my eyes upward. The flowing, sandy hair was startling, so like—like hers. My eyes followed the woman, wishing she'd turn around. Did she have the same prominent cheekbones with the freckles so faint but appealing across her straight nose, and . . . oh darn, she wasn't home—again.

"Hello?" The sound of her voice sent an instant high-voltage surge into my chest cavity. It was short-lived. She was a thousand miles awa—in more ways than one.

"H-hi—how are you?" My eyes snapped away from the Clarissa look-alike.

"Lonnie?" The usual chill in her voice was missing.

"Yeah, where have you been? I've been trying to get hold of you for a week."

There was a moment of silence before she spoke. "In the hospital. A cougar attacked me. Up Farwell Canyon." Her voice cracked.

I froze, and my fist tightened around the phone. "A cougar? Are you all right?" Dumb question. Of course she wasn't, if a cougar had attacked her. "What happened?"

"I was just riding up the trail—"

"You were riding? A cougar attacked you while you were riding Monte?"

"Yes, we walked under a tree, and he jumped right—"

"That ding-bat horse walked right under a cougar?"

"It wasn't his fault. The wind—"

"How bad are you hurt?"

"My right arm and shoulder are torn up pretty bad. There's some nerve damage, and I'll have some big scars on my face . . ." Again, her voice broke.

In the silence, my face flushed. Her horse wasn't the lame-brain. It was me. Clarissa was hurting more than she ever had in her life and so far, I hadn't been much help.

"When Clint carried me down the mountain—"

"Who's Clint? He was with you?"

"No. He's the pastor of Mountain—"

"You really know how to get hooked up with those Christians," I laughed.

Silence. "Why don't you give it a break, Lonnie? All you ever do—" Her voice was tight, anger choking back any more tears.

"Hey—I'm sorry. I didn't mean it *that* way." A canyon of hurt and history created more distance between us than the miles.

"Did Brian call?" Our conversations always ended this way. There was no use thinking it would ever be any different.

"No, he didn't. Why? Where is he? You told me you were doing this run together."

"We got drawn up wrong. Last night he had to be in Puyallup, and I was in Ogden, Utah. We were supposed to meet here in Inglewood, but he must have weathered in somewhere. So I thought he might have called and left a message with you."

"No." Her voice was now controlled, distant, with the usual icy chill.

"Okay, I just wanted to check. Uh . . . well—take care of yourself."

"Sure, Lonnie."

"I'll call in a couple of days."

"Good bye."

"Good night." I ground the receiver into the hook and slumped against the wall while I stared unseeing at the coin slots in front of me. Even if this woman hated me for what I'd done, and though I was bitter about her Christian thing, I still cared about her. But once again, I hadn't been there when she needed me most, and again, everything had gotten crossed up when we'd talked, just like it always did.

I caught a ride back to the Best Western with a couple of young cowboys from Missouri. In the lobby, I thanked them and wished them well before I rode the elevator up to my room. Stepping out on the third floor, I had to sidle by two coverall-clad repairmen. Apparently, they were working on the ice machine, or at least arguing about it, because they didn't have much for tools. Both appeared to have spent more time in the gym than fixing refrigeration problems.

In front of my door, I fumbled through my riggin' bag for the room key. That red message light on the phone should be flashing. Brian better have called. Kneeing the door open, I crabbed sideways into the room with my saddle and gear. The lights were on. Relief surged inside me. He was here. Then I looked to the far end of the room. Sprawled in the big recliner at the writing desk was the stranger who wasn't really a stranger anymore—Frederick Roseman. How had *he* gotten into my private hotel room? I'd had enough. My saddle and gear slid to the floor. I took four strides to the end of the room, ready to punch his fat face into next week, before I threw him out into the hallway.

Chapter 10

LONNIE

The fat guy just sat there. He never moved a muscle, but his watchful, hard blue eyes never left my face. My jaw set with anger, and I reached for the front of his shirt, determined to be rid of this joker.

"Lonnie." The voice was soft as a wolverine's pelt, and it stopped my hand cold. "You would like to know what happened to your friend, would you not? And I would like a few minutes of your time. Sit down." He waved at the only other chair in the room.

I backed up until my hand bumped into the straight-backed chair. The anger at his violation of my privacy was still strong, but if he knew something about Brian, I could wait to pass judgment.

"I apologize for invading your privacy, but a discreet meeting elsewhere would have been difficult to arrange." He leaned forward, those cool, intelligent eyes boring into mine.

Now wary, I pulled the chair out and straddled it, with the back in front of me. This was not the bumbling tourist I'd talked to at Dillon. I studied his square face with the high-blood-pressure cheeks. He still looked like a vacationing gad-about, though tonight he was better dressed, in slacks and a tweed sport jacket. Once more, I swallowed the rising anger and distrust. If he had information about Brian, I needed it. Throwing him out could come later.

The man in front of me spoke again. "Frederick Rose-man. Stirling Associates. You will remember that from my card, even if you don't remember it from years past. We do offshore security contracts and sometimes apprehensions for different government agencies. Occasionally, we also—"

"Can the speech. I remember who you are, and I most certainly know what you do. What about Brian?"

He sat back in the chair and his index finger tapped a slow beat on the desk. "Brian's plane is in Mexico."

"H—how did it get there?" Dread made my voice stick in my throat.

"We're reasonably sure a drug cartel grabbed him and the plane at Puyallup. He'd filed a flight plan to Stockton . . . when he never closed the flight plan . . ." My mind flashed back to the newspaper I'd read in the Salt Lake airport. *But why would Brian have filed a flight plan to Stockton, instead of Inglewood?* Suddenly, the answer hit me. If there had been an approaching storm-front, he would have skedaddled out of Puyallup right after the rodeo, before the weather closed in and made it impossible. Stockton to Inglewood was an easy flight with much less worry about the weather.

"They may have killed him, detoured out over Juan de Fuca Strait and dumped the body."

The man's voice jarred me back to the present. *Brian, dead? It wasn't possible.* I stared into his face while my mind searched desperately for answers that would discredit his seemingly half-baked theory.

For a moment, the finger stopped. "There is a chance they kept him alive."

"You mean they wanted him, as well as the plane?"

The man shrugged. "They always need good pilots to fly cocaine for them."

I snorted and stood. "Well Mister, let me tell you something. There aren't enough guns in Mexico to make Brian Besser fly drugs."

The cobalt eyes bored into mine, the index finger again tapping the slow beat on the rosewood table. His voice was suddenly gentle, as if he was explaining a teeter-totter to a child. "They are quite capable of using other more effective methods to ensure cooperation. He has elderly parents, other relatives they can reach if it becomes necessary. That's presuming he's alive." He shrugged. "He may be. No one has produced a body—yet."

I stretched my legs out and shoved my thumbs into my pockets, my mind again ricocheting through options. Brian couldn't be dead. But if he wasn't, was this man right? Could I trust his story? And why was he parked in my room like he had a first mortgage on it? So far, what he'd told me didn't warrant breaking into my room.

"So why are you here, and what do you want?"

"You."

"This is about Brian. I turned your job offers down a long time ago."

"Yes it is about Brian. Do you want him back, or not? If you do, working with us is your best—no, it's your only option for finding him."

I paced back and forth. This man knew way more than he

was telling. I knew Stirling Associates were a capable bunch. If anybody could get Brian out of whatever mess he was in, they could, even if some of their methods were a little less than Geneva Convention legal. I stood and paced, nervously flexing my fingers while I shuffled through options. *I didn't want to deal with this man, or his company. But if Brian had been kidnapped, could I get him out of Mexico on my own? If I threw Frederick Roseman out of my room, which no longer seemed like a wise choice, what then?*

Frederick's finger slowed its unrelenting beat on the desk, as if it was marking time for Brian.

"So where do these drug people operate?"

"They're headquartered somewhere in the Sierra Madre, on the Chihuahua-Sonora border." The big man sighed, and his shoulders slumped. "They're flying the stuff across the border, right under our noses."

"How are they doing that? You guys have the best technology in the world, and you're saying you can't catch one small airplane flying drugs over the border?"

"Oh, most of the time we know when they've crossed. The problem in remote or mountainous areas is getting agents to the site before the plane is unloaded and gone. They're very efficient."

"So how long have they been doing this?"

"About three months ago our intelligence people started picking up rumors of flights into the Big Hatchet Mountains in southern New Mexico. Usually, the cartels use the larger 210's, but for those, you need a decent strip. These guys are flying the smaller workhorse Cessna 180's, and unloading right in the desert. The landing strips are quick and crude. They fill a few holes, remove some rocks on a flat spot up next to the mountains and presto; they have a place to land. A few drug mules unload the plane and split, each in a different direction with their thirty-pound load of cocaine which they stash in some hole in the rocks. If the Border Patrol does get agents to the landing site in time, they only catch one or two guys. The cartel writes off the loss as part of the cost of doing business. When the time is right, the cartel mules move the contraband further north to Highway 9, or up to the Interstate where it's picked up and delivered to El Paso or Phoenix."

"And who runs this cartel?"

"A man by the name of Manuel Lourdes. On the other side of the border, he's known as *"El Lobo."*"

"And you're saying he has Brian?"

The man crossed one leg over another, peered out from underneath bushy blond eyebrows and nodded. "I do, and I don't think they killed him." Frederick's index finger never missed a beat while he talked. "Manuel's people steal the plane they need and are back in Mexico within hours. This is the second time they've grabbed a plane north of the border."

I leaned forward. "And the other pilot?"

His eyes slid away to somewhere beyond me. "Well, they did kill him." The finger stopped. "They dumped the body out over some wild country in southern Utah."

My stomach churned. *What if Brian . . . no, I wouldn't go there. Brian was okay.* "So why do you want me? I'm sure you have a whole train load of tough commando types."

The silence dragged. He sat watching me while he worried his lower lip with his thumb and index finger, the one that wasn't tapping like an obnoxious metronome on my desk. "You're right. We have sufficient of those types, all of them valuable men."

"Well good. So let's use a few to get Brian out of that snake pit." Once more, I pushed the chair away and tried to pace between the beds. I needed room to walk, to sort through this whole convoluted package. Who *really* engineered the kidnap? If Brian *was* alive and in Mexico, could I get him out without help from Stirling Associates? The questions piled one on another, but I had no answers.

"Why aren't you working with the Mexican authorities?"

"Because working with them has more often than not turned into a dismal failure. Security down there is sketchy. Too many times, we have set up an operation for them. Somebody is paid off, nobody of any consequence gets caught, and we lose months of intelligence work—and maybe an agent. This time we're going to go in, eliminate Manuel, rescue Brian, and come out. It will be quiet—and efficient."

I moved to the chair, turned it around and sat facing him, my arms crossed in front of me. He had my attention. If they were going in, I needed to listen. Brian's life might be at stake.

"Until a month ago, we had a contact close to Manuel's organization. He was caught. They found him hanging from a bridge with his index finger cut off and stuffed in his mouth."

The muscles in my legs tensed, and my hands gripped the wooden back of the chair.

Frederick grimaced. "Nobody gets strike two with Manuel *'El Lobo'*."

"So-o?" I leaned back. "You guys are really impressive. You can't catch a plane flying cocaine into your back yard, and you can't take care of your inside man either. Yet you want me to work with your dysfunctional organization? I don't think I'm interested. Somehow, I'll get Brian out—without you."

Minutes ticked by before Frederick spoke. "You can't get him out alone, Lonnie. No matter what you think, that is not possible. These guys are tough and smart, and they know how and when to kill."

I stood and again paced between the beds. For all my bluster about going it alone, deep in my gut, I knew he was right. My shoulders slumped in defeat. I didn't like any part of this, but did that matter? Was there a choice? The seconds passed, and at each one, I changed my mind. In the end, I knew what my choice had to be. "Okay, I'll do whatever it takes to get Brian out of Mexico. You happen to be the best of a few bad options to make that happen. After that?" I slapped the glass-covered desk top in front of Frederick. "Adiós. Brian and I are gone!"

He sat for a minute, chewing on his bottom lip, and then nodded in a precise, short, movement. "Okay—but you accept on our terms."

"What does that mean?"

"You're on our payroll, so you'll take orders. You do nothing on your own." He waited for a moment while I digested what he'd said. "If he's there, we will get Brian out. That is a priority. The pay check will be more than sufficient for your services. That should be welcome." The left side of his mouth twitched upward.

Ah, the subject of money. Somehow, I knew that he was well aware how little I'd won in the last three months, and I'd bet he also knew I had some credit cards that were fast reaching the maxed-out stage. I watched his passive face out of the corner of my eye, while I pretended to stare at the dark skyline.

Suddenly, he leaned forward, and for a moment the finger

stopped tapping on the desk. "Just remember, we're not here to play games with these jerks. We are hired to steamroll them. Regardless of what you might think of our efficiency, our people do that discreetly—and well."

"Which means . . .?"

"We will pinpoint their facility, do the reconnaissance, and . . ." he hesitated, "find out if Brian is there. That always requires local support. That's where you come in. I want you to be part of that process. You have the qualifications, if not the experience."

I met his eyes, trying to keep any expression from showing on my face. "I'm ready and willing to go in there for Brian. But doesn't it make more sense to send in your Special Forces dudes? That's what they're trained to do, aren't they?"

"Yes, they are, but I don't have guys available that can blend in and do the kind of advance work this will take." The man scowled. I wasn't sure whether he was aggravated with his people's lack of qualification, or my denseness, but I suspected it was the latter. "They stand out like . . . well, are you on the team, or not?"

My eyes traveled from his brown loafer shoes, past his charcoal corduroy dress slacks to the tiny triangular emblem on his jacket. Frederick Roseman had been straightforward, but I still wondered if he wanted me on his payroll more to watch me than for any of my supposed qualifications. If I were reporting to Roseman, I wouldn't be traipsing around the northern Sierra Madre looking for Brian, a loose cannon careening around his Mexican deck. I needed to trust him because he was the only reasonable option I had, but I was also pragmatic enough to know their first priority would be to stop a drug pipeline. Rescuing Brian would be at best, secondary, which sent a thousand volts of worry up my spine. I scrounged for other options—and there weren't any. His offer was the best shot I had for finding the man who was closer to me than a brother.

I shoved the hard-backed chair under the desk, and studied the poker-cold eyes in front of me.

"When and where do I start?"

He eased out of the recliner, stepped forward, and flipped a business card at me. "I'll call you in the morning."

I followed him to the door and looked out after he'd stepped into the hallway. Two familiar coverall clad repairmen appeared, and fell in behind him. The big blond man didn't smile or speak, but we understood each other.

I eased the door shut and looked at the business card in my hand. "Frederick G. Roseman." I'd forgotten the name. That wouldn't happen again.

CHAPTER 11

CLARISSA

THE PHONE WOKE ME and I hurriedly glanced at the clock. Eight. I should have been up and around long ago. I hated to be caught in bed, even if I was still recovering from the cougar attack.

"Hello?" I made an effort to sound businesslike, but my sleepy voice failed to cooperate.

"Hey, it's Rob. How are you?"

"Fine. And you?"

"Good. I know it's short notice, but I have business in Whistler today. How about dinner tonight? I'll drive up, and we'll go out to one of your local eateries. I don't suppose there's much to choose from, but we'll tough it out. What do you say?"

My mind whirled. Last night, Lonnie's phone call had brought all the familiar resentment rushing back. He'd acted like the cougar attack was my fault. It was time to move on with my life. Maybe this was the way to get started. "Alright. I think I can manage that." There, I'd done it, but arrows of doubt pierced my careful facade.

"I'll be in Lillooet by six."

I gave Rob directions to my house and replaced the receiver, ignoring the niggling doubts. This would be fun. Rob was a successful lawyer, motivated, and good looking. Then why did this feel so wrong? My stomach churned like a cement mixer, but I pushed the negative feelings away and planned what I would wear. My upper arm and shoulder looked like a scene from Dracula. A sleeveless gown wouldn't work. Only a sweater would cover that up and partially hide the stitched-up mess on my face.

That evening I struggled into one of my big-city skirts, topped it with a beige turtleneck sweater, then gobbed makeup on as thick as I dared. It did little to conceal the ugly stitched scars, but there was nothing more I could do.

At five minutes after six, headlights shone on my yard fence. I grabbed a jacket and met Rob at the door. I didn't want to invite him into my house, even for five minutes. Though Lonnie had never lived here, it just didn't feel right—not yet. My paranoia seemed silly when I looked up into his blue, patrician eyes. He squeezed my hand, then placed it in his arm as he escorted me to the car. The plush leather seat was a tall step from my Volkswagen Jetta or Lonnie's battered Chevy pickup. I determined to enjoy it. Tonight, I was going to move forward, have some fun.

"It's so good to see you." Rob idled the Mercedes out of my narrow, rough driveway and onto the pavement. His worried scowl told me it had never been off the pavement, and I smiled in the darkness.

"So, what does this muddy backwater offer for dining?" The sarcasm grated on me like a finger on a chalkboard, not a good start.

"Well, there's the Cookhouse, the Garden Patch, and Dina's, none of them what you're used to, but . . ."

"Uh, what would you recommend?"

"How about Dina's? It's Greek—and quite good." I decided I wasn't going to apologize for our little town. Dina's did serve good food.

"Sure. Just show me the way."

The waiter seated us in a back corner, and we ate excellent spanikopita stuffed with spinach. Throughout the meal, I relaxed, my self-consciousness draining away in the dim light as we talked about clients, files, and corporate strategy.

Both of us passed on dessert, but ordered coffee.

"So, uh, what do you do for entertainment out here? Oh, I forgot. I guess you ride a horse up in the mountains."

"Yes, I do ride a lot. I enjoy it."

"Can't say as I ever had the urge to gallop around the countryside. Are there other recreational pursuits?"

"It's pretty quiet if you don't like fishing and hiking, and other outdoor sports." I toyed with my coffee, avoiding his eyes, the meal suddenly spoiled.

"I like outdoor stuff. Golf."

"I don't think you'd like our golf course. A local sheep herd frequently wanders through the links. Players have to contend with, well—sheep fertilizer, and other country hazards."

Rob looked like he'd been kicked in the groin, but the waiter brought the bill which prevented him from commenting on our one-of-a-kind golf course. After the waiter had left with Rob's gold plastic, he twirled his cup, once again composed and in control. His eyes roved critically over my face. "I know a really good plastic surgeon. He could probably fix your face."

A plastic surgeon who could make my face smooth and beautiful, or at least presentable. How novel. I stared at his strong, sculptured jaw, the even white teeth under the chiseled aquiline nose. Curly blond hair contrasted perfectly with his blue Nordic eyes, and yet, it was a face missing something important. Suddenly, I understood. Rob Bentall was only interested in me if my face were fixed. He wanted a trophy. I would need a plastic surgeon to qualify.

I gazed out at the dark street. When I spoke, each word was measured, as expressionless as I could make them. "Thank you, Rob, for your very kind offer. I will let you know. Now, I'm quite tired. I still don't have my strength back, and you have a long drive ahead. Let's be going."

In the dark car, tears stung my eyes. I'd tried to move forward, past all the hurt of our broken marriage, but it was all wrong. Love didn't just go away.

Chapter 12

LONNIE

I DOUBLE-LOCKED THE DOOR behind Frederick Roseman. A trickle of icy certainty wormed its way into my chest. I'd made a bad bargain. Stirling Associates had the people and connections to capture or kill Manuel Lourdes, and find Brian. But how important was Brian to them? If Frederick had to sacrifice Brian to get Manuel Lourdes, would he do it? The question bothered me, because I wasn't sure of the answer.

After I'd tugged my boots off and undressed, I lay in bed dreading tomorrow, but eager for some kind of beginning. Where would we start? What would they expect me to do? I hoped my long-ago training in foreign intelligence operations had some relevance to this mess. Little else in my past had prepared me for these ruthless killers, not that it mattered. Brian needed help, and this guy was giving me the best opportunity to do that.

But what about Clarissa? The least I could do was show up and let her know I cared. I pictured her pretty face, scarred and disfigured with dozens of stitches. How would she face that trauma? And how would I react if I saw her? That thought only brought dejection, because it wouldn't matter to her what I thought. She'd made it more than plain she was done with me.

Too worn and weary to follow those thoughts further, I grabbed the remote and flipped through a dozen channels, but none of them took the lonely ache away.

When I finally slept, my dreams were of cougars and bandoleered Mexican banditos in tasseled sombreros who held me down and shoved cocaine through my clenched teeth. My hands were smeared with blood. Clarissa screamed. I desperately wanted to help her, but I couldn't find her. It wasn't a good night.

***

THE HOTEL DINING ROOM opened at six. Baggy-eyed from lack of sleep, I sipped coffee and tried to rationalize my decision. How could I let Clarissa know I cared? A get-well card would probably be a waste of a postage stamp. But what else could I do? I'd committed to go into Mexico to find Brian, and there was no backing out now.

Frederick showed up before I'd finished my first cup of coffee. His eyes swept the room, noting every exit before he eased his bulky frame into a chair, his back to the wall. When the waitress stopped to take his order, he ordered a cup of tea. I shuddered and leaned back when she brought it. Even the smell of tea first thing in the morning made me nauseous.

Frederick noticed, and slid the cup and saucer as far away from me as he could. "A rather un-American habit, I suppose?"

I growled my agreement.

He chuckled, or as close to that as he could likely muster.

I studied his still face and wondered. He seemed a man little accustomed to laughter.

"I acquired the tea habit in Wales. A number of years ago, we did a job for the Brits. They needed help with some . . . shall we say, Irish issues. Fascinating people, the Welsh, but they make horrible coffee."

I nodded warily, not ready for small talk with this man. I would have liked to have dug into his personality and past. Who was this man who cased a hotel dining room with one quick glance, sat with his back to the wall, his chair far enough from the table that he could easily reach the bulge under his left arm? Spy master? Conductor of assassins?

Frederick's eyes, like an airport beacon tower, traversed the room at regular intervals. Two minutes after he'd sat across from me, he pushed his cup away and leaned forward. "As of this morning, you are on our payroll. However, there are a few things you need to know about—"

I held up a hand. "Just so it's understood. We have no deal after getting Brian out. You guys—"

"You've already made yourself clear . . . a long time ago." His eyes bored into mine. "I understand, and accept the terms." Suddenly, he stiffened. Two dark-suited businessmen with swarthy Latino faces were waiting to be seated. One had an overcoat slung over his arm, his right hand concealed by the material. The waitress brought them our way, past several empty tables. Frederick's chair eased further back. His hand moved inside of his jacket as if he were fumbling for glasses, but his eyes never left the dark-skinned strangers. The waitress stopped two tables over. The man with the coat draped it over the back of a chair. The covered hand was empty. I exhaled noisily, and wiped my instantly sweaty palms against my pant legs.

Frederick spoke softly, his eyes still locked on the two businessmen. "Good eye. You immediately saw the possibilities in that covered hand. We have to train most agents to do that. Years ago, I thought you were an asset worth cultivating. I haven't changed my mind."

"And those are . . .?"

He shrugged away the sarcasm. "You have presence."

"What's that mean?"

Frederick placed his hands on the table; his fingers intertwined. "Do you watch basketball?"

"Sometimes."

"Have you ever noticed how some players have an innate sense of where the ball is going to be before anyone else?"

"I suppose—yes."

Frederick shrugged. "A long time ago, that's what I saw in you. A good intelligence agent has a sense of what's coming down, before it ever happens. That's what I mean by presence."

I laughed nervously. "Thanks, but—"

"Besides, you're fluent in Spanish, and a well-known rodeo cowboy. We don't have to give you a new resumé and hope you remember your lines. That's the best cover an agent can have. And you're a Native American—well, mostly."

"I'm pleased to know I'm the right color?"

He shrugged, unbothered by my remark. "Also, you're a Canadian. In many environments, an agent with a non-U.S. passport is more effective. Not everybody in the world loves us." He shrugged. "Of course, we can duplicate a passport, but that always make for a horrid diplomatic stink. Most countries take offense at us replicating their documents. So, we try to do it legitimately."

I scrutinized the dark wainscoting around the edges of the

room, and the high-back cane chairs that hugged the faded rose tablecloths while I mulled over what Frederick had said. As much as I wished it to be different, the time was long past to do anything about my relationship with Clarissa. My duty now was to get started on whatever this man wanted me to do, and ultimately to rescue Brian. I shoved my coffee aside and looked him in the eye. "Okay. I'm ready. Where do we start?"

Frederick toyed with his spoon. His eyes never left mine. "I understand your wife had a tragic accident."

"How did you know that?"

"We know because we take the time to dig up everything. I don't like surprises. I am aware of your tenuous relationship with your wife. That is your business. Our business is to give you the time and resources to take care of whatever domestic responsibilities you might have so you're mentally and emotionally ready when we need you. In the weeks ahead, your work will include some level of danger. We want to make sure your mind is focused on the mission." Roseman reached into his inside blazer pocket and handed me an envelope. Expense money—and a credit card. "I don't care where you go, just be ready to go when we call."

I nodded, grateful that he had made going to see Clarissa possible, but more worried than ever about what information this man and his organization might have dug up? I decided I probably didn't want to know.

Frederick leaned forward and continued with drill-sergeant precision. "I want a number where you can be reached at all times." He pointed at my shirt pocket. "The envelope contains open-ended tickets. If you're interested, there is a flight that leaves at two forty-five this afternoon. Direct to Vancouver. A car is reserved for you. Leave your old truck wherever it last died." He grimaced. "It may be necessary that you have a decent automobile so that you actually arrive when you're supposed to."

Expense money and a car weren't part of the rodeo business. That was a perk I'd never had, so I ignored the slur against my old pickup, which truthfully, did have some issues. Instantly, I made a decision. "Thank you. I will be on that flight."

He nodded, pushed his chair back and stood. Our interview was finished. One of those big, square hands reached toward mine and this time I noticed the strength. The left corner of his mouth turned upward, but there was no humor in his face as he released my mangled hand and turned to leave.

"Frederick?"

He turned, eyebrows questioning.

"I'll be ready—and thanks." I waved the envelope. Likely it was a flight home for nothing. She wouldn't care to see me, but I had to try. It was the least I could do.

Frederick nodded, and I watched him stride into the lobby like a great-maned cat. My face flushed. Why had I ever thought of him as overweight?

***

MY PLANE splashed onto the tarmac in a Vancouver deluge, and I made my way through Canadian customs with only the routine questions. At the Hertz counter I signed for Frederick's rental car, then drove through the restless traffic to my condo on Broadway.

Clarissa and I had bought a one-bedroom unit on the eighth floor of the chrome and cream modernist building because Clarissa worked downtown. Of course, that reason didn't live here anymore.

When I clomped through the ornate carpeted Kitsilano Towers lobby with my dusty bronc saddle slung over my shoulder, I passed a couple of stuffed suits. They avoided me, my saddle, and eye contact. As usual, I felt like an alligator trying to slither unobtrusively through a herd of penguins.

The elevator deposited me and my gear at the eighth floor. After pawing through a month's' worth of debris at the bottom of my clothes bag, I finally found a key. The heavy white door opened to the musty smell of emptiness, and I vowed again to never come back here. After I returned from seeing Clarissa, I would call a real estate agent and get it on the market. I resolved to talk to her about selling this last item we had in common. The Vancouver market was still roaring. We might even make a few bucks.

I jacked my boots off and sauntered through the unused, bone-white tile kitchen. It was just the same as when I'd left. A dirty coffee cup with a brown ring under it shared space with unopened bills on the counter, none of them paid. I sighed, and wandered over to the ornate glass doors that led out to the patio, where I seldom went. Looking over the edge always made me dizzy. My fondest dream was to have a house where I slept no more than three feet off the ground.

The patio door rumbled open, and I stepped outside into the gathering darkness. Far below, a thousand headlights rushed at each other like fireflies gone berserk. In the distance, the salt-water barrier of the Georgia Strait confined the hordes of clamoring cosmopolites from spilling into the bay where ships hovered in wait. My eyes wandered from one glassy tower to another. What were all those distant people doing behind their illuminated windows? Were they cooking supper? Snuggling in front of the TV? Or were they getting lonely divorces from people they'd once loved? I turned away, empty and depressed, and picked up the waiting phone. I couldn't put off the call any longer. Brian's folks had to know.

After three tries, I got a shaky connection to Brian's dad at the ranch on the Blackwater. Bob and Anna, like most people on remote ranches or trap lines in the north, had an archaic radio phone on a shelf in the kitchen, powered by a car battery. Most evenings they monitored it for a couple of hours. It not only brought calls for them, but because everyone within range could hear one side of the conversation, it supplied a constant stream of news from their distant neighbors. The two-way radio reception was full of static, but at least I could tell Bob what little I knew about Brian's apparent abduction, and that I would call him as soon as I had any other information. The connection faded out, and I didn't try to call him back. I had no other news, and neither of us were much for chitchat.

After talking to Bob, I shrugged into my oilskin rain jacket and headed out for something to eat. The Brite Spot was a block from our building. It wasn't the greatest restaurant, but it would work for tonight. My female neighbor from across the hall arrived at the elevator just as I punched the 'down' button. Sherri was like a lovable Labrador puppy—a very good-looking one. The moment she saw me, she ran up and threw her arms around my neck. "Lonnie, it's so good to see you."

"Likewise, Sherri." Alarm bells started going off in my head like fifty caliber machine gun rounds, while Sherri's manicured nails slid feather-light across my neck. The elevator door opened . . . and closed with us still on the seventh floor, and I stabbed behind my back at the button, while Sherri held me with her seductive blue eyes. The second time the elevator arrived, I made a concerted effort to disengage from her clingy hug and toothy smile, and dived for the now open door. She followed, and gushed on about how wonderful it was to see me and would I like to come by for a drink later and tell her about all the fun places I'd been, while she flirted with those huge, angel blue eyes that didn't seem at all innocent.

"Sherri, I just flew in from L.A. this afternoon, and I'm beat. And . . . I have to leave for Lillooet early in the morning. Clarissa was in a horrible accident. She was mauled by a cougar, and I need to go up there and be with her for a few days." That last wasn't all true, but it was close enough. Sherri and I were not going to happen. Even though my marriage was probably over, it didn't make this right.

The sky-blue eyes opened even wider. "Oh Lonnie, I'm so-o-o sorry." Her soft hand rested on my arm. "Please, do let me know if there is any way I can help."

Well, maybe I'd misjudged her. She sounded genuine enough. We rode the elevator down to the lobby, and she hailed a taxi at the door. "See ya, Lonnie. If you change your mind . . ." No, I hadn't misjudged her. She left the invitation, along with a little finger wave dangling seductively in front of me. I nodded without smiling, and turned up the street.

Hunched against the misty Vancouver rain, I strode toward the Brite Spot. How was Clarissa handling this tragedy? What did she look like? Was she badly disfigured? Tomorrow, I had to be prepared for anything—that is, if she even consented to let me come. Soft light spilled from the restaurant windows and splashed over my cold form as I reached the door. Tomorrow I would do whatever I could do to make up for the times I hadn't been there for her—with no expectations, and no strings.

I ordered the Brite Spot's version of chicken-fried steak, which bore no resemblance to the real version I'd had two weeks ago in Missouri. I shoveled down most of the gristly cardboard and left, wandering back through the still falling rain to my empty condo. When I stepped through the door, the red light on the answering machine flashed in the darkness. I'd checked it before, so it had to be a new call. I punched the button and growled as I listened to the recorded message from MasterCard about how I needed to call them right away. I hit the delete button. That call could wait. I had more important calls to make.

I sat down on one of the bar stools at the counter, took a deep breath to calm my fluttery insides and dialed her Lillooet number.

"Hello?"

"How are you doing?" My voice rasped with emotion at hearing her soft tone.

"I'm okay." As usual, her tone changed after the initial hello. An immediate barrier went up, which was painful, but I understood. I expected no more.

"How's the pain?"

"Better today. Some of the stitches are even starting to itch a bit."

"That's a good sign." After fifteen years of riding bulls and broncs, I had a veteran's handle on pain, broken bones, and stitches. Steeling myself for the rejection I expected, I approached the subject. "I'm home. I thought . . . well, I thought I might drive up tomorrow—that is if . . . if that would be okay?" My left hand was sweaty on the receiver, and my right trembled in spite of the grip I had on the pen. Nervous circles and arrows took up most of a page on a yellow legal pad, while her silence screamed accusations at me. It was hopeless. I shouldn't have expected anything different. There was too much bitterness. I shouldn't . . .

"Oh . . . I don't know. Clint—the pastor and his wife may be here tomorrow evening, but . . . sure . . . I'll be here." Her words were rushed, flippant, like maybe she couldn't give a rip whether I showed up or not. Whatever. At least I could see her. I finally exhaled, excited, but already scared.

"I . . . okay . . . I'll be there tomorrow. Does early afternoon work?"

"Sure."

That one-word answer made my day, enough I hardly heard the rest of her answer.

"I'll see you tomorrow then, Lonnie. And thanks, I know you're busy."

Ouch. There it was—as usual. The irony; barely masked, and well deserved. My face burned. If Frederick Roseman hadn't more or less sent me home; once again, I wouldn't be here.

"Goodnight then." There was nothing more to say, and I went to bed with mixed emotions, but mostly very afraid of tomorrow's meeting. In the dark, I replayed the conversation while I drifted into sleep. Had her familiar anger and scorn been replaced by a wary caution? Maybe; I wasn't sure. Perhaps she was just making an attempt to be polite—and distant. I wondered again what damage the cougar had done to that face I'd loved. Would it matter? I honestly didn't know. Now I only wanted to protect her, and try to make the hurt go away. I needed to look into her eyes and have her know that I still loved her and cared about her, even if we went ahead with the divorce.

CHAPTER 13

LONNIE

MY STOMACH FLOPPED around like a fly-hooked trout from the moment I awoke that Monday morning. If this went wrong . . . well, it couldn't.

After my morning shower, I stood in front of the mirror and primped like a sixteen-year-old kid on his first date, but the telltale gray hairs and deepening lines in my face gave the lie to that. I growled through my apprehensiveness while I shaved. Then I cut myself, which made me look even worse. I did the best I could with the blood, dug out a newer pair of creased-down-the-front Wranglers and topped them with a tan Pendleton shirt. That was pretty much my uniform seven days a week, the only difference being the color of the shirt. I buffed up my brown roper boots and gulped down a cup of coffee. On my way out the door I scowled at the mirror, then headed for the elevator. A Starbucks drive-through provided another cup for the road. That was the only breakfast my churning stomach could handle.

The miles fell away under the wheels of my rented Chevy Malibu while I tried to plan a suitable meeting. Though I'd made an effort to call regularly, we hadn't seen each other since Clarissa had cleaned her stuff out of our condo last April. The mountain of hurt between us hadn't gone away, but I knew; this was the right thing to do. It's just that I was a bit of a coward when it came to facing her. If she heaped more scorn on me, I'd wilt like a September daisy.

I kept to the speed limit, but the switchback hill down to Lillooet appeared before noon, long before I was ready. I pulled to the side of the road and nervously punched in her number. She answered on the first ring, which I hoped was a good sign.

"Hello?" Her voice was guarded, and distant.

"Hi, this is Lonnie." *Why had I said that? She knew who it was.*

"Hi."

"Hi. I, uh, I'm in town. I'll come out . . . that is . . . if it's still okay?"

"Yes, of course."

"I'll just grab a quick bite then, and be right over."

"You're welcome to come have a sandwich here—if you'd like?" Her voice had lost some of the defensiveness, but it was still cool.

I reckoned it was more her compassionate nature than any concern over my hunger. She'd feed any stray dog. "No, that's okay. I'll grab a bite downtown, but thanks anyway."

"Okay, after lunch then." She recited directions to get to her place which I wrote on the back of the rental-car contract.

"Alright, I'll be there about one-thirty."

Everything had been porcupine-polite, both of us with sheathed quills and staying well on the neutral side of nowhere. I snapped my phone shut, and the butterflies in my stomach immediately turned into a thousand screeching bats. I should have just sent a get-well card. This was a huge mistake.

At a deli on Main Street, I ordered a sandwich which tasted even worse than last night's cardboard chicken-fried steak, if that were possible. Maybe I should have taken her lunch invitation. The food would have been a lot better. I resolved to be less of a coward, and that lasted—until I turned into her driveway.

A weathered log barn stood at a crazy angle behind a yellow, bungalow-style house.

Weathered rail fencing circled the front half of the property. I knew it was the right place, because that gray horse Brian's dad had given her stood with his head hanging over the fence next to the barn.

Part of me wanted to just drive by and forget the whole business, but it was too late for that, so I parked in front of the house. I took as much time as I could to get to the door, hoping she would do something to make our meeting easier. I forced myself to rap four times. The sound was timid and weak. Why didn't she have a doorbell? Those sounded the same for everybody. Maybe she'd decided she didn't want to see me after all. I rapped on the door again, this time more resolute and manly, or at least, that's what I hoped.

The knob turned, and the door slowly creaked open like something out of a Hitchcock movie. She stood on the other side of the threshold, silent, and frozen. I gazed into those expressive gray-green eyes, the same as I always had. Only this time they were the unreachable eyes of a stranger.

I shuffled from one foot to the other. Everything I'd planned to say fled. What could I tell this woman I had sworn to love, protect, and be faithful to for life, this partner who had shared every intimate secret—and been betrayed? My eyes slid from hers, down to the angry, raw scars with the black catgut stitches. I forced my eyes away from them. Deep inside my soul, I knew my reaction to those scars would be important. It wasn't likely I'd passed.

"Hello, Clarissa." The stilted greeting probably sounded as bad to her as it did to me. I hadn't called her that name since our second date. I'd had my own special pet name, but I couldn't call her that, and 'honey' or 'dear' didn't work any better, and well, it was a bad start, and she wasn't helping. She just stood motionless, her eyes riveted to mine.

"You're looking well," I mumbled, which wasn't true. The scars would always be there, and she appeared thinner, with shadows under her eyes. All the mixed-up shame and hurt and love for this woman tumbled together through my mind, but this was a mistake.

"Hi, Lonnie." A frozen attempt at a smile twitched at her full lips.

I shuffled my boots around some more, wondering if I should leave. Nothing I'd planned to say would come to mind. I never would have had the nerve to come if I'd known it was going to be this bad.

Clarissa's eyes softened. "I do appreciate you driving up here. Please, come in." She held the door wide. I wanted to end the pain and refuse. Instead, I stepped over the threshold because it was the right thing to do, and sat in the offered chair at her varnished pine kitchen table. She edged into a chair at the other end.

"Would you like some coffee?"

"Sure, that would be nice." I didn't really want any, but at least there would be a few moments we wouldn't be fidgeting at the table, doing our best to avoid eye contact. She stood and stepped over to the kitchen counter to fill the pot, her right arm covered with a sweater and hanging useless. I stepped over, took the carafe from her, and ran the water into it. Both of us were careful to avoid any skin contact.

The coffee would be in the second canister on the counter. That wasn't something I had to ask. While I puttered with measuring four scoops of Nabob into the filter, I asked about her injuries, and the cougar attack. For both of us, that was neutral ground, and I listened, appalled as she told me all the details. It was my chance to sit and watch her—and get used to the scars.

"This guy that brought you down off the mountain. You said he's a preacher here in town?"

"Yes." Her voice took on a slight defensive tone, and her hands twisted at the pen she was again holding. "I think you would like him. He's the minister at Mountain Community Church, but he's a really neat guy. And his wife Darlene has been awesome. They've become very special friends."

"I'm glad he was there." There was a twinge of envy in my voice. I hadn't meant for it to come out that way, but at that moment, I would have settled for being even a tiny bit of a neat guy in her eyes.

"They're coming for supper tonight."

She gave me that serious, no-nonsense look I remembered so well. "You could stay, of course only if you want. You *might* like them."

Her sentences were short and nervous, and I took the 'might like' to mean I probably wouldn't.

"Oh, uh, thanks." I shuffled my feet under the table and cleared my throat. "I should get back tonight . . . have some things to do. I'll try to come up again before I have to go anywhere."

My lashing out against the verbal assault of some country preacher wouldn't likely bring any healing to our situation. It would only antagonize Clarissa. She needed my support; she didn't need me stomping on her religion.

"What rodeos are you working next week?" she asked.

"Uh, well, I'm not quite sure. We have some things happening. Brian . . . well, his plane . . ." My voice trailed away. I should have known she would ask. Why hadn't I thought this through? I jumped up to get another cup of coffee wondering how much of the Brian story to tell her. All I'd said on the phone from Inglewood was that he had been weathered in somewhere, so she had presumed that we'd connected later that evening.

"Something's wrong. What is it, Lonnie?" Her voice pitched higher. "Where's Brian?" My eyes slid away from hers, which was about the thirtieth time in the last half hour. What should I tell her? She had enough of her own problems, but the Bessers were like family. They treated her like their daughter, which was why my reception at the ranch last week had been a shade cool. Though it was difficult because of the limited telephone and mail service, she constantly stayed in touch with Brian's mom.

My chair scraped across the linoleum as I pushed it back. Carefully, I set my cup on the table while I stalled for time. This stupid spy business of Frederick's was over my head. Would he care if I let Clarissa know about Brian? I decided it didn't matter, and made my first agent-in-the-field decision— to tell her everything.

"Yes—something did happen to Brian." The worry on her face was instant, and I quickly tried to explain. "He's fine, or at least we think . . ."

"What do you mean, we think—?"

I held up my hand. "Brian's gonna be okay." I smiled, trying to gloss over my fear, but she knew me well enough to pick up the uncertainty.

"What happened?" Her eyes were wide with concern.

"I'm not sure how much anyone is supposed to know about what I'm going to tell you, but we think Brian was kidnapped."

"Kidnapped! Why would somebody kidnap Brian Besser?"

"We're pretty sure a Mexican drug cartel grabbed him. What we don't know is whether they just wanted the plane, or whether they wanted him as well."

The rest of the afternoon, I tried to explain what little I knew about a Mexican drug runner named Manuel *"El Lobo"* Lourdes, and a clandestine organization that billed itself as Stirling Associates. I'm not sure she believed it, at least at first, but the tale was too crazy to be made up, and we'd lived together long enough for her to know I was reasonably sane. She listened and asked an occasional question while she studied my face. Sometimes, I wished she would look away. It was as if she were trying to peer inside my soul, to see if there was any truth there.

"Have you talked to Bob and Anna?" she asked.

"Yes, I spoke to Bob last night."

I hoped the brief respite, talking about Brian's kidnapping had taken the focus off the problems between us, but now there was another protracted silence.

"Tell me, Lonnie." Her voice was low; the words dropped one by one like icy marbles of hail. "You've talked a lot about this other person. Who is *"we"*?" I looked up from trying to rub the varnish off the table with my left thumb and into the accusation that darkened her face. Instantly, I knew. She thought "we" meant my new woman. A wave of bleak dejection smashed me against some invisible wall. I held her eyes with mine, this time not wavering, and I tried to break through all the hurt and anger between us. "Clarissa, I want you to understand. I made a mistake that I will regret as long as I live. I am deeply sorry, and—there is no other woman."

Her answer was her silence, charged with all the bitterness of the past. We huddled at our respective ends, too wounded to move, as if the table between us were a vast battlefield. The pain was again raw, and our eyes escaped to the corners of the room to avoid contact.

My third cup of coffee and the afternoon were gone. Now I had to use the bathroom, but I didn't want to use hers. The familiar makeup, hairbrushes, and pink toothbrush would bring too many memories. No, I had better just go.

I stood, awkward, embarrassed, and dejected. The visit had been a mistake; painful—for both of us. I put my coffee cup in the sink and turned to Clarissa, pondering how to say goodbye. Our eyes met, and mine slid down the angry stitches in her face to the injured right arm she was holding close to her breast. She stood in the middle of the kitchen floor and blurted something about Brian's family. I told her to call me if she got a radio message from them, and promised to do the same as soon as I had any news of Brian. I'd made it to the door, and with my hand on the knob I turned toward her. What I wanted to say had to be now.

"Clarissa, I know it doesn't mean a whole lot coming from me, but you are a beautiful woman. Don't ever think those scars take away from that." I tried to smile; desperate to part as friends, but of course it didn't work. She wiped at her eyes, and I had to swallow hard and look away. I shuffled from one foot to the other while I waited for her to get her angry, bitter tears under control. The scars would never have mattered to me. I wished she wasn't angry. More than anything else, I'd wanted to . . . to help her somehow, even if it was too late to help us.

I cleared my throat. "I'll call you and let you know when I can come up again—if you'd like?"

She nodded, a lone tear tracking down her cheek, both of us knowing that it would be easier if that didn't happen. Prolonging this pain was useless. I would not see her again, and my whole chest contracted with a wrenching grief as I tore my eyes from her face, reached for the door and fumbled it open.

A hulking giant stood on the other side, an oversized, hairy fist nearly in my face as he prepared to knock. Behind the fist, there was a bushy brown beard, wire-rimmed glasses and fortunately, a contagious, silly grin. Beside him, an attractive, auburn-haired woman about half his size smiled and greeted me. I stuttered a vague reply. Likely, this was the preacher. If it was, I reckoned he had no trouble keeping order in church.

Chapter 14

LONNIE

THE GIANT AT THE DOOR dropped his hand and chuckled from somewhere deep in his massive torso. "I was just going to knock."

Clarissa stepped forward, quickly wiping at the tears with her sleeve.

"Clint—Darlene, you're early. Please, come in. This is Lonnie." The preacher couple stepped inside. The man held out his hand and encased mine in his grizzly-sized fist.

"I'm Clint Forsythe. Clarissa said you might come up today. I'm glad we finally get to meet you. She's told us so much about you."

Yeah, I could just imagine what she'd told them. I nodded a polite acknowledgement. Why were these folks back for a meal again? Somewhere in our conversation Clarissa had mentioned that they had been here Friday night for supper. This was all too rehearsed for my liking. It sounded to me like "let's convert Lonnie night."

"This is my wife, Darlene." The auburn-haired woman stepped forward and held out her hand. She and Clarissa could have dressed from the same wardrobe, with her well-fitting blue jeans, open necked yellow blouse, and thin gold necklace. Her trim feet were encased in open-toed leather sandals.

"Clarissa," Clint carried on as if he talked to red-eyed, flustered folks every day, which maybe he did. "We came early for a reason. I'm going to fix that standpipe by the fence. They had the parts at the feed store in town, so I grabbed a repair kit. I think we can make it quit spraying water all over the place, so I'll do that and Darlene can help you with supper." Clint turned to me. "Lonnie, you probably know all about how those work."

"More or less." How I wished I'd left five minutes earlier.

"They're all new to me. Would you be able to give me a hand before you go?"

I looked at my watch, not that I cared what time it was, then nodded and stepped into the yard with him. What else was I going to do? I could hardly tell him to shove off.

Together, we walked to the leaky standpipe. Clint asked questions about my rodeo career and various bucking horses. He displayed knowledge no preacher ought to have, and I warmed to him more than I intended. He was genuine, without pretense, and I'd found that to be an uncommon trait— in rodeo riders or reverends.

Between us, we replaced the faulty parts and ran the tank full of water, all the while talking easily. Finally, I had to ask. "How do you happen to know so much about bucking horse bloodlines?"

He released that infectious belly laugh. "That's a long story. I was raised up north, in the Dawson Creek area. That's big, open grass country, and as you probably know, there's a pile of horses up there, what with all the outfitters and ranches. After Darlene and I were married, we started a small church in a community west of there. My calling was to be a pastor, but I needed to do something else to pay the bills, so I followed my other passion. I bought horses that were destined for the dog food factory and gave them a chance to be bucking horses. It's a great life for a horse. Bucking horses work even less than preachers."

We both chuckled at that. I didn't have any knowledge of preachers, nor did I want any, but it didn't look to me like it was a ticket to Hollywood and cash.

"Anyhow," Clint continued, "I ended up with some good bucking mares and a stud. We sell a few older solid broncs every year. I lease the mares and some of the young horses to a stock contractor who puts on amateur rodeos up there so the horses get some seasoning. Many horses buck hard at home, but don't do well when you start putting miles on them. Some just don't have the heart for that steady traveling. So this gives the young horses a chance, and of course makes them more valuable when we offer them for sale."

We'd finished the repairs on the standpipe. Both of us leaned over the rail fence and talked, enjoying the warmth of the evening, the quiet occasionally broken by the distant sound of a car on the gravel road out front. Clarissa's gray horse stood next to me, hipshot, his head hanging over the low rail while he switched his tail at a pesky deerfly.

Clarissa hollered from the house that supper was ready.

The moment had come. Now I had to go say a polite, hands-off goodbye to her. I determined it would be better than the attempt this afternoon.

Clint turned toward me. "Lonnie, come eat with us. I'm sure there's plenty, and I know you're invited. Besides," he laughed, "it will be a long meal with two gabby women. Do me a favor and stay."

This was a setup if I ever saw one, but I was certain I could handle anything this preacher threw at me. Despite his ill-chosen vocation, I liked him, and I honestly did want to hear more about his bucking horse business.

"Alright." I shrugged my shoulders in resignation. "If it's okay with Clarissa. It's near dark anyhow, and another hour won't much matter."

Clarissa stood at the door as we stepped onto the porch that ran along the front side of the house. She arranged this. I knew exactly what was going through her mind, and I made a feeble attempt to look irritated.

"I've decided to stay for supper—that is, if I'm still invited?"

The eyes I remembered, the sparkly green ones met mine. "I don't know. Maybe we could find a place for you. You did help fix the standpipe, so I suppose we should at least feed you."

I tried my best scowl, but it didn't come off as any more than a sickly grin. I was glad to spend more time with her— even if I had to put up with a preacher.

I washed my hands in the bathroom, the one I'd so painstakingly avoided before. As I rolled my sleeves down, I couldn't resist a quick peek into the bedroom. The bedspread and decor were strange, and yet in a way it was the same as our bedroom had been. *Was there another man in the picture? Would I even know? Maybe not.* I muttered, cursing myself for a fool. I shouldn't have looked in there. It was none of my business. Reminding myself of the past had accomplished nothing, and now I had to go out and talk bucking horses with

Clint, and pretend this was a normal dinner party. Perhaps I could make up some excuse and leave. No . . . that would be too awkward. Now, I had to stay, so I took a couple of deep breaths, walked out into the little combination kitchen-dining room and sat at the table with the rest of them.

Clarissa placed Clint at one end of the table with me on his left. Darlene sat at the other end with Clarissa on her left, so either the conversation could encompass the four of us, or Clint and I could talk bucking horses while the women chatted about whatever they wanted.

After I'd parked in the only vacant chair, she looked over at the preacher. I knew what was coming. "Clint, would you . . .?"

"Sure." He smiled at Clarissa's hesitation.

Saying grace would of course be mandatory with a preacher at the table, so I bowed my head in the most reverent fashion I could muster as Clint started what was sure to be a five-minute monologue. "God, thanks for friends like Clarissa, and now Lonnie. Bless them God, as only you can. Let us all see Your glory in our lives. Thanks for the food. Amen."

I sneaked a glance over at Clint, maybe to see when the sermon would start, but all he said was, "Pass those potatoes." Too bad this big, bushy bearded guy was a preacher. I could get to like him. We all dug in. Darlene had done a great job on the Kentucky-baked chicken. She'd brought most of the food, and there was no doubt she could cook. The conversation wasn't bad either. Clint kept us spellbound with how he'd drilled that cougar.

"You know," he said, "I will never forget the terror when that cougar filled the scope on my .280 and I knew I had to squeeze the trigger. That rifle was sighted in at two hundred yards, and I was only a hundred feet away. Clarissa's face and upper body filled half the scope and that cat's chest covers the other half. If she moves, I'm going to hit her, and if I don't shoot, that cougar's next move will be to grab her by the neck or head to drag her off, which would have been fatal."

I kept an eye on Clarissa while Clint told the cougar story, but whatever trauma was happening inside, her face was calm. Mind you, I would have been surprised if it had been otherwise. She had a wide streak of fortitude in her, inherited I suppose from her grandparents. They were some of the first tough, gold-rush pioneers to come to Lillooet. That toughness could have some consequences in our present marital circumstances, which might not be in my favor. She was no wilting coward. For a moment, I panicked. Maybe she didn't want any support from me.

Clint continued with the story. "When the bullet slammed into that cat's chest, it was a far better feeling than if I'd bagged that monster muley buck that has eluded me. But when I ran up to her, it looked to be too late." He smiled at Clarissa. "There was blood everywhere, and I was sure you were gone. As I said before; God evidently had something else in mind."

I didn't think it was an appropriate time to argue the merits of chance versus divine intervention, and after all, what else would you expect a preacher to say, so I snagged another piece of chicken and let it ride. The important thing was that Clarissa hadn't been killed, and now she needed some support to get her life back together. The least I could do was contribute in whatever way I could, which tonight meant I should just keep my mouth shut.

The conversation moved on to other subjects. Clint and I talked more about northern British Columbia where he had spent a good portion of his life. We both were acquainted with a few of the same cowboy and ranch folks in the north, so overall, it was an entertaining evening.

Considering the company, the meal turned out better than I'd expected. I thanked Clarissa for supper, shook hands with Clint and Darlene and made my way to the door. Inside, I was an emotional wreck. A quick and public goodbye would have been the easiest, but she walked out on the porch with me.

"Lonnie, whatever else has happened, I want you to know how much I have appreciated your phone calls and support, even when we were at our worst. And—thanks again for coming."

I looked at her face in the light of the moon and wished I dared to kiss her. But that could be misinterpreted, something to avoid at all costs. Tonight was the first time we'd eaten together since the day she'd left. It was also the first time we had talked with anything more than a thinly disguised bitterness. Whatever that meant, I didn't want to ruin it. Overcome by emotion, I gently squeezed her arm. She stiffened, and I jerked my hand away, glad I'd had the sense not to be more daring. Hopefully, it was dark enough she couldn't see the instant flush that colored my face. "G'night. Thanks again for supper." I turned away and stumbled to my car, knowing I'd messed up the best thing that had ever happened to me.

Chapter 15

CLARISSA

Hot tears coursed down my face, and as much as I tried, I couldn't stop them. They were tears both of gratitude that Lonnie's visit had gone well, and a wrenching grief at the loss of the husband and friend I'd loved so much. Why had he betrayed me, and where did I go from here? Would divorce eventually extinguish the pain? The stars provided no answers. I mopped at my face with my sleeve and hollered in my best "everything's just fine" voice that I would be right in, then scooted down the hall to the bathroom. Cold water didn't make my flushed face look normal, but it helped. Again, I realized how thankful I was for Clint and Darlene, who had become such dear friends.

We ate blueberry pie with ice cream and drank cinnamon tea, all of which Lonnie avoided anyway. Clint devoured most of the pie, while we laughed and talked about people and events in the church, and the vibrant village of Lillooet. Like me, they loved the people and small-town ambience. In the end, the conversation inevitably turned to Lonnie and our soon-to-happen divorce. That wasn't as easy to talk about, but

I needed their advice, so I poured out my heart, avoided more tears, and listened to their combined counsel.

Though I didn't divulge any details, I brought up Brian and his missing plane. "The Bessers are such special people. Lonnie and I spent loads of time there. He and Brian have been friends and traveling partners for years, and Anna has been like a mother. She's helped me so much, just to get through the bitterness and . . . well, you know, everything with Lonnie."

Darlene put her hand on my arm. "Maybe it's time for another visit. It would give you a chance to visit, and perhaps just rethink your priorities for the next while."

"Yeah, maybe it would. It's just that with moving and work, and now this, I haven't had time to go anywhere." I cradled my arm against my chest. It had been a long day, and it was starting to hurt.

"I think you should go," Clint said. "Your being there would mean a lot to them. With Brian in trouble, they'll need some support. It sounds like you might be the one to provide it."

Clint was right. Besides, a trip to the ranch was appealing. To talk with Anna, and be with her in this time of need in her life would be wonderful. Mostly, the pain was now manageable, and my arm and face would heal just as well there as here.

"I'm on sick leave anyway," I mused. "And it's a good time of the year to go. The water should be hardly more than knee deep at the Messue Crossing." In the spring, or during heavy rains, the crossing could be treacherous on foot, but October was a week away. The water was always low this time of the year. Besides, going to the ranch was so much fun. The isolation was like going to another planet. I pushed my plate away and waggled an index finger. "Life is difficult there. No computer, no cell phone, no television, no nada." Darlene laughed. "You'll survive."

I grinned. "Probably quite well." In my heart, I wished I could live in the peaceful isolation that surrounded Bob and Anna—without the hardship of course. A visit was sounding better all the time.

In the ensuing silence, we stared into the crackling flames of the little fireplace on the west wall. I considered the possibility of going to the ranch. *If I took another week off from work, I would have four days to travel back and forth and three days to be with Bob and Anna. The walk would be hard, and then there was the river crossing. Maybe I shouldn't do this. I was out of shape. What if I had medical complications way out there? What if for some reason, the river was high? Well, it couldn't be, not this time of the year.* "No. I'm going."

"What does that mean?" Darlene asked.

"I mean yes. I think a trip to see Bob and Anna is a great idea. They will be worried sick over Brian."

Clint turned from staring into the flames. "Tell me about Brian. I know he's a top bull rider, but what's he like?"

"Hmm, you should have asked Lonnie that question. They have been close for years. Let's see. He's about five-foot ten, very good-looking, in a rugged, cowboy way. When Brian walks into a room, conversation falters and everybody turns to look. He just has that presence about him. Within minutes, he is acquainted with everybody, and before he leaves he has at least three more lifelong friends. As crazy as it sounds, he never seems to engender envy or jealousy. Women swoon over the guy but he doesn't appear to notice. I have never understood whether he's that way because of his faith, or in spite of it. Sometimes," My face flushed. "I wish Lonnie was more like him." *There—I'd said it.* Maybe if he'd been more like Brian, we wouldn't be getting divorced. Now I'd started unloading, it seemed I couldn't stop.

"Brian wouldn't have fallen for a one-night stand with some tramp . . . no, I didn't mean that. Sometimes I'm still so angry. I know it shouldn't be like this. I'm a Christian. I'm the one who is supposed to forgive."

"That is true." Darlene patted my good arm. "But as you surrender your rights to God, he will take away the bitterness and anger against Lonnie. And Clarissa, don't think that it's a one-time decision. You may have to give that anger—and Lonnie to God twenty times a day. He can take the bitterness away, but you have to be willing to let it go."

I sat frozen, while the pain stabbed like a slashing machete. It seemed not a place on my body was free from the bleeding agony.

"It hasn't been easy, has it?" Darlene put a gentle arm around my shoulder.

"No, I don't think anyone can understand this pain. Someday, maybe I will be able to forgive Lonnie, but it's going to take a while." The tears threatened to spill over again. It seemed all I ever did was cry.

"You will have to forgive another person as well," Darlene continued. She paused and looked away, like she was exorcising something far in the past. "That will be the most difficult." Her eyes filled with compassion as the tears course down my red, blotchy face.

"Clarissa, you will need to forgive the woman who was involved with Lonnie."

"I can't! I will never do that!" Just the thought of that woman still started uncontrollable tears of anger. I would never forgive that marriage wrecker! That was a nonstarter.

Darlene covered my hand with hers, and slipped her other arm around my shoulder. Her eyes filled with compassion.

"Clarissa." Her voice was gentle. "I truly understand the agony you're going through."

Through my tears, I looked deep into her eyes. For a moment, they revealed a dark window from the past. Somewhere, Darlene had seen great pain. She did understand. Maybe God did too.

Chapter 16

LONNIE

At the pavement, I turned and glimpsed Clarissa's silhouette against the porch light, but it was dark, so perhaps I was mistaken. Everything we'd had together was gone. There was nothing more I could do, and loneliness settled over me like a nuclear blanket. I couldn't stand the thought of that sterile, empty condo in the city, at least not tonight. Whatever Lillooet had to offer was better than what awaited me in Vancouver. I'd drive back in the morning, then call a real estate agent. It was time to break the last of the ties we had together.

I pulled up to the Concord Hotel. Even if this wasn't the best that Lillooet offered, it was good enough. Maybe I'd be lucky, and they would have a room that wasn't right over the bar.

A dried-up codger with washed-out blue eyes and a drooping handlebar mustache leaned a skinny elbow on the desk and watched me enter the lobby. He looked like he might be a leftover from one of the gold rushes. I walked up to the counter. "Could I trouble you for a room, sir?"

He gave me the once-over, slowly straightened up, and grinned. "Why sure, Lonnie, I think I can find a room for *you.*"

"Friend, you have the advantage of me." I gave him my best crooked grin. "How do you know me?"

"You're the cowboy from Okanagan Falls. I saw you win the bronc riding last year at Williams Lake. What brings you to our part of paradise?" He shoved a check-in form across the counter.

I wasn't about to tell this stranger what I was doing in town. "Well," I stumbled, trying to devise some generic cowboy lie. "Sort of a vacation. Just seeing the sights. The river's pretty low. Maybe I'll pan a bit of gold, or at least see if I can turn up any color." I gambled that if he recognized my name and face, he'd be more interested in the rodeo side of me than my credibility as a gold-panning tourist.

To my relief, he dropped the subject. I filled in the registration card. He stuck it in a file box, gave me a key, and stuck out his hand. "I'm Ezra Parker. Let me know if I can do anything to make your stay more comfortable, Lonnie. It's a pleasure to have you."

I shook his hand while repeating his name, so I would remember it.

"The room is up the stairs and to your left at the end of the hall—as far as you can get from the zoo." He nodded toward the bar, and we both grinned.

"Thanks Ezra, I appreciate that."

The bed was saggy, but there wasn't any noise from the bar. The following morning, I woke with only the usual hurt from old breaks and banged up joints. More mornings than not, I was reminded of my fading mortality.

The splash and shave routine over, I wandered downstairs to find a young woman on duty at the desk. She informed me I had two options for breakfast; either the hotel coffee shop to my right, or the Miners Café down the street. The morning outside looked promising, so I strolled down to the Miners Cafe. Old tools and knick-knacks decorated the walls, and I picked a window table, as far as I could get from the rest of the early morning crowd.

The waitress took my order. The bacon and eggs were too greasy, not that it mattered. My mind was far removed from eating. *Unfortunately, she'd manage just fine without me. Was she seeing somebody else? Probably. Why wouldn't she?* The thought tied my stomach all in knots, and I pushed the greasy plate away.

"Lonnie, this is a surprise. I thought you were going back to Vancouver last night."

I looked up. Clint, the preacher from last night, stood over my table.

"It was late, so I decided to stay, then drive back this morning."

Clint didn't seem inclined to leave, so I politely gestured to the chair across from me. "Sit—if you'd like."

"Sure—be glad to join you."

The waitress immediately brought him coffee and greeted him by name, which deep-sixed any doubts I might have had about the spontaneity of our chance meeting. He was obviously an early morning regular here.

"What brings you out this morning?" I asked, idly making conversation.

"I do some janitor work at some of the businesses around town." He grinned. "A country pastor has to have another source of income, and my evenings are generally busy with church functions, so I have to tend to my broom business early in the morning."

"Oka…ay? Let me get this straight. You do janitor

work—so you can be a preacher?"

Clint just smiled at me, kind of like I didn't understand something that basic—which I didn't. "Yeah, I know that may sound dumb, but this is where God has called me to be. And I learned a long time back that arguing with Him doesn't work all that well."

I raised an eyebrow but choked off a sarcastic reply while I concentrated on ingesting my early morning quota of caffeine. Chatting before my requisite two cups of coffee was more than I could abide—at least civilly. Clarissa and I sorted through that issue early in our relationship. My morning truculence was trying to her. She jumped out of bed happy as a meadowlark, chattering like a squirrel on speed. Eventually, she learned to give me my space, and I did try to upgrade my morning communication skills, with limited success.

The waitress refilled our cups, and Clint leaned forward. "Darlene and I have had the privilege of getting to know Clarissa quite well. She has shared some about your relationship—in the strictest confidence. She needed help, and after the cougar attack . . ." Clint shrugged. "Well, we just kind of took her in as part of the family."

"Yeah," I nodded slowly. "Thanks for all you've done for her." I stared out the window at the muddy pickup trucks, each of them scurrying to their respective stations of hard-hat drudgery. Clarissa had probably blabbed our whole story, so Clint would know everything about that stupid fling in Fort Worth. My fingers tightened on the cup, and I felt the too-familiar rising heat in my face. "We've had our bad times." I again stared out the window as another pickup sped by, probably driven by some guy who worked all day and then came home to a wife and kids. Suddenly, that didn't seem like drudgery. The guy had a lot more purpose in life than I had.

"I wish we could go back and do things over again." I shrugged. "That's a chapter that is . . ." I hesitated, not wanting to finish the sentence. Last night, Clarissa had carefully wrapped and hidden the hurt after Clint and Darlene had arrived, but it changed nothing of the volcano of boiling anger beneath the surface.

Clint nodded. "We'll be praying for wisdom, for both you and Clarissa."

I didn't know how to answer. Besides, what kind of religious solution was that? We were both finished, so I stood and paid for my breakfast and his coffee.

Outside, I hunched my shoulders against the snow-tinted breeze tumbling down from the nearby peaks.

When we'd reached the steps of the hotel, Clint turned to me. "I think I understand how you feel about preachers, but if there is any way Darlene and I can help, please let us know."

Don't wait by the phone! That's what I wanted to say, but instead I just nodded. This preacher didn't need to meddle any more than he already had.

Said preacher stuck out his over-sized paw, but I got a firm grip, so he didn't maul mine too badly.

"You know," he said. "Nothing is so damaged that God can't put it back together again."

A tugging desire in me wanted to believe that putting our marriage back together was possible. Clarissa maybe didn't know it, but I would go a long way to atone for the heartache I'd caused.

"Let's get together again." His eyes twinkled behind the wire-rimmed glasses.

I nodded warily. Religion had never done anything for me, and I had no intention of getting mixed up with this preacher, even if he did know a bit about rodeo.

On the way back to the city I analyzed every word Clarissa had spoken. Four hours later, on the outskirts of Vancouver, I'd found nothing that offered encouragement. Five months had passed since I'd seen her. It was doubtful anything had happened between us to slow the divorce process. She'd been grateful I'd made an effort to help; nothing more.

When I opened the door to the condo, the faint smell of dirty laundry wafted into the corridor. I set my hat on the kitchen counter and again resolved to call a real estate agent. The only reason this place had ever been home was because she was here. There was no reason to keep it any longer. I walked to the phone. The light on the answering machine was blinking. Four messages. Three were from bill collectors. They, at least, would be happy now that I had a steady paycheck. The last message was from Frederick. He'd left a callback number. I pulled the phone over and punched out the number, apprehensive, but hopeful there would be news of Brian. He answered on the first ring.

"Roseman here."

"This is Lonnie."

"Where have you been?"

"Lillooet. To see my wife." He asked a few other rapid-fire questions about my activities in the last forty-eight hours and listened quietly while I answered. Then, he abruptly cut me off.

"Be at the airport at seven tomorrow morning. You have tickets on Frontier Airlines flight six twenty-four to El Paso. Pick up a car at the Hertz counter. Your hotel reservation is at the Holiday Inn on Lincoln Avenue. Call this number when you arrive. Any questions?"

"Nope." I decided to be just as curt. He didn't give me the chance. The immediate dial tone baptized me into Stirling Associates, and I was irritated. Taking orders was a new experience for me, and I wasn't sure I liked it. Nevertheless, I'd do it for Brian. "It won't be for long," I growled. Neither Roseman nor his clandestine company had any part in my long-term plan.

The rest of the day was taken up with pacifying the power company, the phone people, and the strata manager. I was anywhere from one month to seriously behind in paying all three, and it took a while to convince them I wasn't a total deadbeat, that I now had a real job, and if they would just take a token payment, I would have the rest by the end of the month. That might not happen, but at least I could give them all a bigger chunk and hold them at bay until I either took more of Stirling Associates' cash, or won some bronc riding money. That of course depended on whether I could get Brian untangled from whatever mess he'd landed in so we could enter some rodeos.

***

MORNING CAME TOO EARLY, but I made it to Vancouver International on time. I walked up to U.S. customs with my fingers crossed. Those people have nervous moments when even Saint Peter wouldn't get through without a half-hour hassle. This was one of them, and I made it to the plane only seconds before they closed the doors.

Stirling Associates apparently didn't want agents sitting around in airports. I changed planes in Denver and was in the

El Paso Holiday Inn by early afternoon. Anxious to discover what Frederick had found out about Brian, I dialed the number immediately and got a first ring answer.

"Hi, Frederick. This is Lonnie."

"Hold the line for a minute." Silence. Stirling Associates didn't even have canned music. I waited for at least ten minutes while I doodled on the monogrammed hotel writing pad.

"Lonnie?" Frederick was back on the phone. "I want you to sit tight. Be a tourist for a few days, see the sights. If you leave the Holiday Inn, stay in cell range."

"What have you found out about Brian?" I asked.

"I will have the information we need within a day, maybe less. We have the location narrowed to a couple of different sites. You will know, the minute I have something concrete. Keep in touch." The line went dead.

I swore at my own stupidity. Why had I gone to work for these incompetent idiots? I could have stayed in Vancouver, maybe worked on my crappy marriage, anything other than sitting in a hotel room waiting for these clowns to make something happen. What was I going to do now? Be a tourist? Yeah right! I scrolled through every Texas friend I ever had, but produced none who would love to see me. How about friends who would just tolerate me? Zero again. Then I remembered Rock Esfalan.

Chapter 17

LONNIE

ROCK ESFALAN AND I had been first-year rookies in the Professional Rodeo Cowboys Association, both of us young and ambitious, trying to claw our way into the big-time. We lived close to each other, so it made sense for us to travel together. In those early years, we were a frequent team, and it was during those long, boring road miles that Rock taught me Spanish.

However, one day he decided he'd done everything he wanted to do in the rodeo business. He moved to Lordsburg, New Mexico, got married, and found a real job. For years, he'd worked as a deputy sheriff, and now he was the "big enchilada," the sheriff of Hidalgo County. We'd kept in touch off and on over the years, mostly through Christmas cards and the odd phone call. Visiting Rock would sure beat a motel room, and Lordsburg wasn't that far away. The more I kicked the idea around the better I liked it, and I was certain the pleasure would be mutual.

I scrolled through my contacts and found the phone number. Rock's wife Dora answered, with her faint Mexican accent. Though I had never met her, it didn't take more than about thirty seconds for me to figure Rock had done well in that department.

"He will be so excited to know you called." Her voice had a soft musical tone. "We got your Christmas card. We always look for the one from you and Clarissa. Rock will never forgive you if you don't come visit. He's just coming in the door." She gave Rock the phone.

"Lonnie, what a pleasant surprise."

"Rock, I'm in El Paso, for a day or two. I'd like to come up for a visit—if that works for you?"

"What are you doing in El Paso? Never mind. If you don't come, you're crossed off my friend list." He laughed, and it was as if we'd never parted company.

"Well, in that case I'll leave here in the morning. I should be in Lordsburg about noon."

"Good. Come to the office. It's on the north side of the interstate. You'll find it easy enough, and when you get here we'll go for lunch."

The fast way to get to Lordsburg from El Paso is straight west on I-10, but I got an early start and drove my rented Chrysler the long way, down the old state highway to the desert-killed crossroads of Hachita, then turned north on some used-up county pavement to Rock's town. The country was wild and desolate, and I reckoned there were more rattlesnakes than humans on these far-flung ranches.

The red-brick sheriff's office and police department wasn't hard to find. Sandwiched between the Bootheel Museum and a construction company, it was probably the most imposing structure on the north side of the tracks. Rock met me at the door with a big grin, and we clasped hands. Other than gaining a little weight and considerable notoriety in the years since I'd seen him, he hadn't changed. This desolate county attracted a tidal wave of illegal immigrant and drug problems, and Rock's no-nonsense approach to law enforcement ensured he hit the national news more often than he likely wanted.

Rock was everything you could ask for in a sheriff. Even though he was a short five-foot-seven, nobody ever messed with him. The few that did, found out there was more in this tough little package than they'd bargained for. Quiet and watchful, Rock could read bad guys like a worn-out comic book. And his Mexican ancestry gave him a rare empathy for the burgeoning immigrant crisis that festered between his native America and the Mexico of his heritage. Hidalgo County would have been hard-pressed to pick a better lawman.

We left the office in Rock's police-issue pickup and pulled up in front of a green trimmed little restaurant on Main Street. The six tables were as deserted as the street outside. Rock steered us to one by the window.

"It's good to see you, Lonnie."

"Likewise. What's it been? Five years?" We both grinned like two kids at a Christmas party. There was so much ground to cover, neither of us knew where to start.

A lilting Spanish floated from the kitchen area behind the high-top counter. "You want the special, Sheriff?"

"What is it today, Carmen?"

"A grilled tuna and cheese with split pea soup."

"Uh," Rock hesitated. "Yeah, sounds good."

"What about your friend?" Still no body appeared to connect with the voice.

"Double it, please," I hollered.

"Both of you want coffee?" The musical accent suddenly

appeared around the corner . . . in a wheelchair equipped with a special tray to hold customer's orders. The tiny woman filled two glasses with ice water, poured two cups of coffee and expertly wheeled them over to our table.

"Carmen, I want you to meet an old friend of mine. Lonnie—Carmen Meza, the best cook in Lordsburg—after my wife."

"I'm pleased to meet you, Lonnie." She flashed a sunny smile and slid the cups and glasses onto our table.

"The pleasure is mine," I replied, and truly meant it.

We talked about Rock's family, and laughed together while we ate. I gave myself a gold star for remembering the names of his two kids. Christmas cards are worth something.

The soup and sandwich arrived, so we started tucking it away.

Rock looked up from his soup. "How's Clarissa? You haven't even mentioned her."

My spoon paused midway between the table and my mouth. I'd expected the question, but it was still hard to answer. "We're separated, Rock. Have been for five months."

Rock dropped his eyes to his sandwich. "Another one, and sorry to hear it. Rodeo marriages crumble faster than the wedding cake." Both of us concentrated on the food to cover the awkward moment.

I nodded. After the other night at Clarissa's, it was too painful to talk about, even with Rock. "You heard about Todd getting killed?" I asked.

"Yeah, it was on the news. I really liked him. Everybody did."

We finished lunch and talked quietly of other old friends, places we'd been together, and those mutual acquaintances who still followed the rodeo trail. After an hour, we left the café and got in his pickup to do a quick tour of the town. I scrutinized the big canopy in the pickup box.

Rock noticed, and inclined his head toward it. "My portable jailhouse. We spend most of our time dealing with illegal aliens. They're a huge drain on the county resources. Still, it's hard to send them back. They're fleeing the poverty of their homeland, and by the time they get here, paradise is within reach. However, we don't have a choice. Then there are the drug smugglers. They're getting more brazen, and harder to stop."

"Rock," I turned in the seat. "You remember Brian Besser, don't you? That Canadian bull rider."

"I met him once or twice, but I think he started riding in the States the year I hung up my saddle. He was a nice guy, and he wasn't packing an oversized ego which was always . . . uh, refreshing in our business. Why do you ask?"

Our conversation stopped for a minute while Rock answered a call from the dispatcher. One of his deputies had apprehended some illegal aliens south of Animas. They had eluded the Border Patrol and scattered into a Manzanita choked canyon. The deputy had found one of them, a middle-aged woman lying in the desert with what sounded like acute appendicitis. He needed to stay with the sick one until medical assistance arrived. In the meantime, he was requesting help to apprehend the other three.

Rock muttered something a sheriff probably shouldn't say. "Sorry, I booked the afternoon off so I could spend it uninterrupted with you. However, this isn't unusual. The border problems never end, and the county gets stuck with the fallout—and the bill."

"Hey, don't worry about it. I'll find something to do."

"Would you care to come with me?" Rock barked some terse orders over the radiophone to another unseen deputy.

"Sure, I'd love to."

"It'll just be a routine trip. We'll make a run down the highway to Animas, then head south to the Adams Ranch Road and through a back road up to Highway 9. By the time we get there, we won't find anything, but we have to try." The edgy bitterness in Rock's voice said volumes about the whole Mexico, U.S. border problem, and I decided that would be a good issue to avoid, at least for today.

The Agave and Soaptree Yucca marched past us like long forgotten Indian sentinels. The land we traveled was lonely, drenched with history, but devoid of humans.

Rock hung the 'mike' back on its clip. "Anyhow," he said, "we got interrupted. You were telling me about Brian."

"Right. He lives up there in the bush country, way north of the Canadian border. His family has a wilderness ranch, and he flies a Cessna 180. We've traveled together the last few years."

Rock laughed. "And how did he get you into an airplane? You and flying didn't used to be part of the same sentence."

"Nothing's changed. I still hate it, but I guess now I dislike the highway miles even more. Besides, Brian's a first-rate pilot. Anyhow, his plane disappeared about ten days ago."

"Bad weather, or did he fall asleep?" Rock shook his head. "Planes. None of you guys should fly. Deadlines and bad weather don't mix well. Did they find him?"

"He didn't crash."

Rock's head snapped around.

"We think he was abducted—by a Mexican drug cartel."

"Oh-h-h?" Rock's eyebrows shot upward. "You said he was flying a 180?"

"Yeah, he's had this one for a couple of years."

"Hmm, interesting. Drug cartels usually go for the bigger 206s and 210s, or so my Border Patrol friends tell me. They grabbed the plane—and Brian?"

"Yeah." I slouched down in the seat and propped one knee against the dash to get more comfortable. "At Puyallup, Washington. Brian went to the airport after the rodeo. That's the last anyone saw him. They grabbed him there, or at least, that's what we think."

Rock glanced across the cab. "So, what are you doing down here?" His sideways glance was filled with suspicion.

Rock and I had always been close friends, and I hadn't any reason not to trust him, but I still didn't feel comfortable enough to volunteer the fact that I was on Stirling Associates' payroll.

"I don't know," I hedged. "I thought I would come down and nose around. Maybe talk to the Border Patrol people, take a Mexican vacation up in the Sierra Madre and see if I can find something." It wasn't even a very good lie, and I squirmed.

"If you did find him, what makes you think you could get him out?" Rock snapped. "Those drug cartels are a tough bunch of lizards. They have enough political clout, you'll get no help on that side of the border."

I straightened up in the seat and stared out the windshield. "Well, maybe . . ."

"Maybe, nothing. Lonnie, it's almighty near impossible to get any information down there, because either people are on the cartel's payroll, or they live in mortal fear of them. The minute you ask your first innocent question, you are a marked man. Generally, they just give meddling gringos a quick bullet in the back of the head. You're dark enough they may give you the preferred cartel treatment for Mexicans. To have body parts cut off, and stuffed in your screaming mouth before they kill you is painful—but effective. They do that to send a warning to others who would be so foolish as to intrude in their affairs. You don't want to go there."

I squirmed, and glanced sideways at Rock. He grinned, and slapped my shoulder. "Hey, sometimes they just cut off fingers. Depends on the circumstances."

A beginning fear sent icy, probing tentacles into my belly. What if I couldn't find Brian? How would I get him out? Suddenly, I was glad I had allies. Not that Frederick Roseman and Stirling Associates were good ones, but right now, they felt better than none.

We idled through the two-street village of Animas while scanning the surrounding farmland for any sign of fleeing Mexicans. The cultivated fields gave way to the more typical desert manzanita and ocotillo, and my conscience prickled. *What if I told Rock about Stirling Associates? He was a lawman; on our side. Besides, Rock dealt with drug-runners almost every day. What would Frederick think?*

Finally, I turned toward him. "Rock, I didn't tell you all the truth about what I'm doing down here."

"I know." He turned and grinned at me. "We spent too much time together to be able to lie to each other with any success. So . . . what's the part you *didn't* tell?"

I started back at that rodeo in Dillon where I'd first met what I thought was only an overfed tourist who liked rodeos. By the time we turned west on the Adams Ranch Road, I'd reached the night in Inglewood when Brian never showed to get on Popeye, and Frederick Roseman threw the pitch for me to join their organization. Telling the story to Rock helped, because I began to see more than ever that I needed Stirling Associate's intelligence network.

Rock listened, with only an occasional question.

We'd reached the interstate and were headed back to town before I reached the end of my long tale. Rock drove with both hands on the wheel, hunched forward to peer at the smooth sandy meridian for tracks. Now and then, he slowed, still hoping to apprehend the man and two teenagers.

Once, in an interval when there were no tracks, he spoke. "So now you're waiting for answers from Frederick Roseman, but you're afraid he may have a different agenda?"

I glanced sideways, but Rock's face revealed nothing. "Why do you ask?" I'd revealed nothing about Stirling Associates contract to kill Manuel Lourdes, and I was sure I'd never mentioned Frederick's name.

He shrugged, his answer evasive. "Oh, I don't know. Just a hunch."

I stared through the windshield. How much did Rock really know about what happened across the border?

CHAPTER 18

LONNIE

WE PULLED INTO LORDSBURG without any illegal aliens in the back of Rock's pickup. The Border Patrol would have to catch the three escapees.

Rock slowed as a harried young mother pushed a double stroller across the street in front of us. "What're your plans? You're stayin' with us, aren't you?"

"I will if you have room, but I can stay downtown. It's not a problem."

"You, my friend, are staying at my house." He looked at me sideways and grinned. "Maybe it isn't the Western Trails Inn in Yuma, and there won't be room service, but it's cheap."

I shook my head and chuckled, still embarrassed at the long-ago caper. "You had to bring that up."

The Western Trails Inn had been a welcome respite at the end of a long run. For three weeks, we'd flown all over the country, caught rides with other cowboys, and even hitch-hiked, once again chasing that road to fame. Our delayed flight had landed in Phoenix after midnight from some rodeo in the Midwest. We needed to catch another early flight to Yuma, but we had no money for a room, so we dozed the rest of the night in airport chairs.

The next morning we arrived in Yuma, weary, and in no shape to ride. We only had a few hours before the afternoon performance. Nevertheless, Rock ordered the taxi driver to take us to the classiest hotel in town. He hopped out of the cab and waltzed through the lobby like his uncle owned the joint. I assumed he knew some rich, successful cowboys that had a room. They'd maybe let us crash for a couple of hours and use their shower.

I scampered up the plush carpet stairs after Rock, hoping they didn't throw us out of those ritzy digs. Rock swaggered down the hall and pushed through the first door left ajar. My jaw hit the floor. Two queen-size beds graced the room, only one used. The rightful residents had of course just vacated, but it wasn't five minutes before a house maid showed up. "Are you gentlemen checking out this morning?" she asked. With more brass than a Mexican fighting bull, Rock stuck out his chest and with his best British accent told her that yes, we were going to check out in a couple of hours. The maid left, and we flipped to see who had to sleep in the 'used' bed. I lost, but they must have been nice clean people 'cause I didn't get any cooties or anything a shower wouldn't wash off. And did that bed ever feel good.

Memories flooded back from all the years we'd traveled together across the United States and Canada. We were young, inexperienced bronc riders, and we had to pay our dues before the winnings became regular enough to ward off a steady diet of cheeseburgers. Through it all, Rock Esfalan and I became closer than brothers.

We stomped into his house, still chuckling over other

scrapes we'd been in through the years.

Dora met us in the kitchen. She was a vivacious Indio woman, with the raven hair and expressive eyes of her people. Rock had done well to find her, and I was happy for him.

We sat down to a black bean and chicken dish topped with fiery chilies and mounds of crema mexicana. I ate more than I should have, plus had a generous helping of Dora's apple torta that was way too good to pass up. She said it was the kid's night to help with the dishes and shooed Rock and I out to the rocking chairs on the back porch.

The evening had that enveloping dry warmth that only happens in the southwest. We sat in the shadows, and watched the open desert darken to a deep lavender as the sun played hide-and-seek with the far blue peaks of the Peloncillos. The distant tire-whine from the Interstate blended with children's voices and the chirrup of nearby crickets. A hotrod with straight pipes broke the comforting silence, but it only added to the small town ambience, and I resolved again to ditch that Vancouver condo. I'd had enough of the city. This was what I wanted, a small town like the one Clarissa had chosen, which reminded me I'd promised to call her with an update on Brian.

"Rock. If you'll excuse me for just a minute, I need to make a quick call to Clarissa."

He looked across at me, and I could see one eyebrow raised. "If you're still talking, there must be some hope."

I shook my head. "Hardly. But I do try to check on her now and again. And she's always been close to Brian's folks, so I need to call and let her know what's going on."

"Use our land line. It's in the living room, unless Dora has it."

"As long as I can pay you." I grinned. "I'm sure you can beat the forty bucks the Canadians would charge me."

Rock waved a hand and chuckled as I walked into the house. "Don't worry about it."

I punched in the number, and that infernal answering machine immediately started its generic spiel. "Hello. You have reached Clarissa Bowers at Guardian Insurance. I'm sorry I've missed your call, but if you will leave . . .

"Hello?" Halfway through the spiel, Clarissa picked up the receiver.

"Hi, how you doin'?" Cautious optimism surged through every part of my body.

"I'm glad you called. What's the news?" Her voice was warmer than the usual freezer burn, but still reserved.

I told her what little I'd found out about Brian, which of course wasn't much, and that I was visiting with Rock and Dora while I waited for instructions and more news out of Mexico.

"I'm going up to the ranch for a few days to see Bob and Anna."

"You aren't healed up enough. You shouldn't be that far from medical help. There might be complications—infection, or who knows what. Besides, how are you going to get from the Blue Road into the ranch? That's pretty near five miles."

"I know how far it is. I'll walk in." I could feel her resentment building. When she got something in her pretty head, there wasn't anything I could say that would change it, especially now.

"It's too far. Call Bob. He'll meet you at the corrals," I fumed.

"Oka-ay. I'll call and let them know I'm coming. I'm not going to do it all in one day. I'll stay in Vanderhoof, and then travel out to the ranch the next morning. I'll be fine."

"Well, be careful. The crossing should only be a foot deep. Bob will come get you with the wagon, but it would be better if you just stayed home."

"Well, of course, Dr. Lonnie. Stupid me. Why didn't I ask?"

I clamped my mouth shut. I'd gone too far. Now she would hang up, and I'd feel worse than ever. For a full ten seconds, neither of us had to worry about call quality because there was only silence.

Finally, after a long sigh, she spoke. "Oh—and I'm praying for you and Brian."

"That's good. Brian will appreciate that," I stuttered. "Won't change much—but thanks anyhow."

"And Lonnie—I've been praying about . . . well, about us."

I swallowed twice, unable to articulate a flippant comment or any worldly advice for that. Praying about *us* wouldn't do any good, but if she were talking to God about us, that might mean she wasn't talking to her lawyer. That could be a positive sign—at least I was going to hope for that. "Sure—thanks. I suppose it can't hurt." But my disdain for anything religious came through way too loud and clear. On the other end of the line, the silence was again deafening. I could well imagine the compressed lips and deep frown lines.

I told her I'd call again if there was news about Brian. Then I got off the phone before we had a real argument. For a moment, I leaned against the living room wall wondering why I hadn't asked more questions about her, and how she was feeling. Why hadn't I been more compassionate? However, it was too late. Once again, my big mouth had driven us even further from any reconciliation.

CHAPTER 19

CLARISSA

THREE DAYS LATER, against my doctor's advice and Lonnie's uninvited instruction, I loaded my green Jetta. Even pared to the bare essentials, my backpack was still too heavy. When I hiked into the ranch, every pound would feel like five by the time I reached the Blackwater River. And cross it I would. There was no need for Bob to harness a team and come way out to the corrals on the Blue Road to pick me up. I could easily make it.

As I ticked off last minute items, I considered a pair of ancient, green hip waders. Lonnie had bought them at a garage sale one summer when he'd had to take some time off because of an injury. He'd flirted with fly-fishing, a venture that lasted long enough for him to lose most of his expensive hand-tied flies, and all his patience before he was ready to ride again. The waders were too heavy, so I threw them back in the closet. Lonnie had said the crossing was only a foot deep. I could easily wade through that. Sure the water would be cold, but so what. It wasn't that far from the river to the ranch. Even with wet feet, I'd be fine.

I slid awkwardly behind the wheel, trying to protect my injured arm and shoulder. Now that I was actually going, apprehension clouded my euphoria. Maybe I should have called Bob and Anna to let them know I was coming. I scowled. If Lonnie hadn't demanded it ... . . I tossed back a lock of hair, shoved the Jetta in gear and hit the highway north to the ranch on the Blackwater River. I could certainly do this without his interference.

The miles slipped under my tires, and white line monotony made my mind wander. I had much for which to be thankful. Most of all, just that I was alive. And now, visiting the ranch was the right decision. Perhaps I could return a small part of the support Bob and Anna had given me throughout the last months. My separation and coming divorce were a raw wound, but every day was a small victory, and a step forward. I reached up to my face and touched the prickly stitches. It was becoming a habit to trace the jagged lines with my fingers. How would I look when the stitches were gone and the bite marks healed into long, angry red tracks? Lonnie had said I was still a beautiful woman. Nevertheless, what did that mean? He'd already proven his deceit. Probably after driving away, he had cringed with horror, glad to be free from this disfigured woman.

I jerked my hand away from my face, and sat taller behind the wheel. I'd tobogganed from thankfulness into fear and anger? If I was going to encourage the Bessers, I needed to think about something other than my own self-centered problems. Later, there would be time to work through *my* feelings, *my* scarred face; all those issues for which I had no answers. Now, Anna and Bob needed to be my focus.

The sleepy little ranching towns of the Cariboo country

gave way to the frenzied logging cities of the north. Maybe tonight there would be some further news from Lonnie to take to the Bessers. Darlene had promised to check my message machine while I was away.

Sprawled along the banks of the Nechako River, Vanderhoof was my final stop before heading into the wilderness. This would be my last look at civilization for a week. A quick reconnaissance convinced me that the motel on the hill south of town would be the most suitable for the night. I rented a room, carried my backpack in, and then walked down to the restaurant for an early supper.

The evening special was veal cutlets. I hurried through them, hoping to have a few minutes before dark to go for a walk. After I paid the bill, I drove into the main area of town and parked on a quiet side street. The sun still held in the western sky as I strolled along the evergreen-shaded streets. The girdled sigh from the rows of lofty spruce whispered mumbled secrets of long-forgotten scandal and intrigue. Aromas of spicy sausage and tangy barbecue wafted from the unseen backyards, sweetened with the laughing voices of children. Later, I drove back to the motel on the hill, tired, but more content than I'd been in a long time.

***

DAYLIGHT was still an hour away when I crunched my way over the frosty gravel to the restaurant. I pushed open the door and entered the already noisy warmth. The comforting scent of pancake batter, eggs, and frying bacon overlaid the good-natured bantering and loud arguments emanating from the crowded table next to the door. This café was the obvious morning coffee choice for a bevy of loggers and early-rising farmers. A steady stream of grizzled newcomers pulled up chairs, hunched over their coffee while they exchanged the day's news, then departed. I envied their camaraderie and sense of belonging.

When I paid at the till, I asked the waitress if she knew whether the Kluskus Road was open and passable for a small car. To my chagrin, she hollered over at the table of loggers.

"Ross, what's the Kluskus like?" Every head at the table turned toward the till while Ross answered.

"The back end is rough, but they're hauling logs over it," Ross answered quietly. He turned his attention to me with a modest grin. "Should be okay. Lots of trucks though, so be careful."

I thanked him, scrunched my stitched up jaw farther into my olive green turtleneck sweater, and scurried for the door.

A sandwich from the restaurant and my backpack were all I had to load in the car. Before eight, I turned south onto the infamous Kluskus Logging Road. At first, the gravel was wide enough to easily pass the ponderous loads. Farther south, the road narrowed, increasing the danger. Each driver waved cheerfully to this white-knuckled newbie bug, and though I panicked and dived toward the boulder-strewn ditch every time one of the monsters appeared around a dust-choked corner, they never seemed startled. Somehow, three hours later I made it to the Blue Road without being squashed like a pesky mosquito by the giant rolling tires. When I sighted the familiar corrals that marked the Messue wagon trail it was nearly noon. The heavy truck traffic had made the trip longer than I expected. I nosed the Jetta into a wide spot in the woods and stepped out feeling a sense of accomplishment, but relieved that the logging road experience was behind me.

The tart smell of the endless pine forest filled the air around me. Digging through my backpack, I found a brown scrunchie, pulled my hair into a ponytail, and made three quick twists to hold it. My pack fitted awkward and heavy on my left shoulder, but it was as light as I could make it, so I started down the trail. Not wanting to waste any daylight, I munched on half the roast beef sandwich I'd bought that morning in the restaurant. Twice, I tore off a piece of the crust and left it for the bold and inquisitive Gray Jays that flitted silently beside me.

From the corrals where Bob loaded cattle to take to market, the land sloped downward until it reached the winding river. I followed the deep-cut tracks of the old wagon road, which eventually led me to the grassy hillside overlooking the crossing. I stared at the rushing current, and gasped. The water was running fast and turbulent, washing far up the south bank, much higher than usual for this time of the year. Lonnie had said it would only be knee deep. I walked down the hill and across the small meadow to the bank. The dark water rushed past, before it emptied into the lake only a few dozen yards away. What now? Go back to Vanderhoof and call Bob to come get me? No. I'd get to the other side, in spite of Lonnie. Knee deep. Yeah, right! Anger strengthened my resolve as I hitched the heavy backpack higher on my uninjured shoulder, took a deep breath and stepped into the glacier-cold stream. The icy pain was instant. I stared at the dark swirling water ahead of me, fear of the current adding to the already numbing cold. However, there was a big warm cook stove ahead of me. And it was a hundred hard miles back to town.

I hitched my pack high on my shoulder and plunged

deeper. It wouldn't be more than thigh deep. By the time I was halfway across, the water lapped around my waist, the current wild, tugging at my feet. I glanced back, my teeth now chattering. It was too far. But if I tried to turn around, I would lose my footing, so I forged ahead. Panic sucked my belly against my backbone. My legs no longer had any feeling. Suddenly, I stumbled into a hole and went down. My pack slid off my shoulder. My breath whooshed outward as the sudden icy water soaked my upper body. I flailed at the sucking current, scrambling to regain my feet. Desperation and fear drove me forward. If I were swept out into the lake, I would drown for sure. Sobbing with fear and pain, I floundered to my feet and scrambled forward. When I stumbled out of the water and collapsed on the gravel, the top of my head was the only part of me not soaked. I glanced back and watched helplessly while my pack floated out toward the lake, then disappeared into the depths.

When I struggled to stand, my wooden legs buckled underneath me. The gravel cut into my knees. If I stayed where I was, I would die from exposure, probably before nightfall. Lonnie's warning came back to mock me. I should have listened. Somehow I made my hands push my body upright until I could stumble forward. A gust of wind drove the cold deeper into my bones. My mind didn't want to focus, but if I was to survive, I had to think; push away the fog that threatened to overcome. Somewhere far away a voice spoke quietly to me. *Concentrate. Move or you will die!* Panic forced one rebellious foot to move forward, then the other. My movements were slow and awkward, my legs unwilling to follow the commands from my foggy nerve center. My dripping, icy clothes clung to me. I couldn't stop the violent shivering, but each step was a victory. Slowly, the wooden stumps below my waist clumped forward. My socks squished inside my hiking boots, but it didn't matter. I couldn't feel my feet anyway. Halfway to the top of the ridge a prickling sensation worked downward toward my ankles. A small thrill coursed through me, and I laughed with relief. I would make it—unless I met a bear.

At the top of the ridge, the southbound trail intersected the ancient westbound Indian Trail to the Pacific. My eyes darted into the surrounding dense forest. In this area, bears, especially the surly grizzlies, were a constant worry. Bob always said black bears kill more people than grizzlies? That was small comfort, and I sent up a prayer they'd all stay on the other side of the mountains.

Farther on, the narrow wagon track that led to the Besser ranch dropped away from the Indian Trail and angled toward the southwest. Two miles later, it broke out at the top end of the verdant, natural meadows that had drawn a younger Bob Besser to file a deed on this remote wilderness ranch.

My violent shivering had stopped, now replaced by a mind-numbing drowsiness. I was so tired. The ranch house with its new shiny metal roofing was so far away. I wanted to rest. My hands were blue. My legs again wouldn't cooperate, and I stumbled. My injured arm swung uselessly at my side. *How very funny. The pain has gone away.* My mouth opened to laugh, but the sound that came out was strange and shrill. *My arm has healed.* Somewhere on the far edge of lucidity, a voice mocked me. I was going to die.

In the distance, somebody was hurrying toward me. I laughed as Anna approached. Why did she look so worried? I'd made it. Through the haze in front of my eyes, I heard her scream for Bob. Why was she doing that? I was so happy to see her . . . but I just needed a little rest. I'd set my backpack down . . . now where was it? Never mind, I could find it later. But why was Anna shaking me and slapping my face? Bob's face swam in front of my eyes, and I tried to smile. It was so good to see them. He picked me up and carried me. There was no need for that, but I was too tired to protest.

In the guest bedroom, Anna peeled off my wet clothes and wrapped me in hot water bottles and a warm blanket. Somewhere in the distance, I heard her cry of alarm at all the stitches.

"Clarissa, what happened?"

"I—I had an accident with a cougar."

"What do you mean? How did that happen?" Anna kept talking to me, shaking me to ward off the drowsiness, making me talk. I wanted to sleep, but she wouldn't let me. As if in a dream, I heard my slow disconnected voice answer her repeated questions.

"I was riding up on the mountain behind my house. The wind was blowing . . . I guess Monte never smelled him . . . he jumped right in the saddle with me."

Anna put her arms around me, and I hugged her. She was my mother. No, actually she wasn't, but I didn't care. I loved her. I winced at the pain in my shoulder. The hot water bottles were doing their work, and now I realized how close I'd been to hypothermia and a quick, silent death.

Anna sat on the edge of the bed. "Don't you ever do that again. I am so glad you came. It means a lot to us. However, we will always meet you at the corrals." Anna squeezed my arm, and I hugged her even though I again winced at the pain.

"So—what about this cougar attack?"

"Let me get out of this bed. I can talk just as well by the kitchen stove."

Anna agreed, and found some dry clothes for me. They weren't a good fit, but everything else I owned was at the bottom of the lake.

Though I could usually talk about the cougar attack with little emotion, I finished by blubbering all my fears about the scars on my face. That sweet woman with the craggy, seamed face and work-roughened hands made a cup of tea while we sat and talked. I gave Lonnie's last report on Brian, and soaked up heat from the venerable black and white cook stove.

"So what happened at the river?" Anna poured more hot water in my cup. "And why didn't you call so we could meet you?"

"Lonnie told me the water would only be a foot deep."

"It was, when he was here. But we've had more rain than we ever have this time of the year."

"The water was so cold, and I tried to hurry. I stumbled into a hole and fell, and with only one good arm, I couldn't hold onto my pack, so it went down the river." I shrugged. "Now I don't even have a toothbrush," I finished lamely.

"I think we can manage to find enough to keep you clothed and combed." She smiled and shook a finger at me. "But, don't you dare do that again. Not the river—or the cougar." She patted my shoulder as she stepped by me to get more wood for the fire.

Later, Bob came inside and joined us in the warmth of the kitchen. Together, we watched the weakened October sun sink behind the craggy, western peaks. Bob's first question was about Brian, and I retold everything I could remember. While they listened, Bob reached over with his gnarled, wind-darkened rancher's fist and enveloped Anna's hand.

How long did it take to make a marriage as committed as this one? What ingredient had been missing in mine?   Lonnie and I hadn't made the five-year mark before our commitment had melted like rotten ice. Was it ever possible to regain a broken trust; to heal the wrenching hurt?

I helped Anna put on the roast beef and new potatoes, the last Swiss chard from the big ranch garden, and some sliced tomatoes from the greenhouse. We sat at the hand-finished birch table and bowed our heads for Bob to say his short, simple grace. He asked God to take care of Brian, wherever he was, and his voice caught before he could finish.

What if Brian was . . . no, I wouldn't go there. Brian was coming home. Wherever he was, Lonnie would find him.

By eight o'clock, my hurt arm was throbbing, and my eyes were closing. I was still weak, and of course falling in the river and getting hypothermic hadn't helped. My shoulders sagged. I'd come here to help, to try to be an encouragement to Bob and Anna. So far, all I'd done was add to their burden.

Anna gently took my arm. "You're completely done in. Come. We've kept you talking way too long." She steered me toward the small guest bedroom down the short hallway, but I stopped for a moment to admire a recent family picture. Brian was in it, as well as his sister Brenda, and her husband, Tom. There were recent photos of Brenda's two children as well, both bright-eyed little blondies. They lived far away in Alberta. Neither she nor her accountant husband had any interest in a life as rugged as the one in which his wife had been raised.

"And how are they?" I asked sleepily.

"Oh, they just bought a small acreage west of Calgary. Brenda's thrilled to be twenty minutes from the mall. She loves being around people. This never was the life for her."

Anna lovingly fondled the picture of her two grandchildren. "I miss them so much. Those kids are the only reason that would make me leave this ranch. I don't get to see them except for a short time in the summer, and oh, that is hard."

I squeezed Anna's arm in sympathy and stumbled into the bedroom, completely exhausted.

"Lonnie was the last to use the guest bedroom," Anna said.

There was no sign of his presence. This would likely be the closest my estranged husband and I would ever be to sharing the same bed. The night air made me shiver, and I wasted no time donning the flannel nightgown Anna found for me. I pulled the giant comforter up to my neck and drifted toward unconsciousness. A faint odor, spicy and sweet, all mixed up with the scent of pine needles wafted from the comforter. The smell reminded me of Lonnie, but then maybe that was just one of the dreams.

Chapter 20

LONNIE

Rock's boot scuffed against the plank floor of the porch as he changed position. "Lonnie, I've been thinking about your friend, Brian." His voice pitched lower, and I settled back on the cushions, comforted by the night sounds, and the rhythmic squeak of the rocker.

"I ran into an old sheepherder the other morning. He told me a story that may be of interest."

I stopped the rocker in mid-glide. "If it has anything to do with Brian, I'm interested."

Rock shrugged. "Don't know whether it does or not. I'll leave that call up to you. Anyhow, I met Julio down in front of Carmen's—you know, where we ate lunch. He's a good friend of mine; known him ever since I came here. He works for the Paloma Ranch, south of Hachita. They have a government lease where they summer about five thousand ewes. Their range runs into the Big Hatchet Mountains, so it's rugged and remote country. Anyhow, last Thursday I was leaving the café when I ran into him. After we'd gotten our greetings over with, he tells me we need to talk. It was a quiet afternoon at the shop, so we went into the café for another cup of coffee. Julio told a story I haven't heard for a while. He claimed he was sleeping in the sheep wagon, when about midnight, a plane came in low over the bed ground. The sheep panicked, and scattered all over the valley, so of course he spent the rest of the night gathering and calming the herd. Three nights later, it happened again. The plane wasn't as close this time, but it still spooked the sheep. This time he watched it land on a flat ridge about two miles away. The next afternoon he grazed the sheep over that way, so he could take a look. Sure enough; a short strip had been rough-carved out of the desert flat. It probably took two or three guys half a day to clear the rocks and fill the worst of the holes. Julio says there were at least eight different sets of people tracks, and that they're running cocaine. Don't ask me how he knows that, but I'm inclined to take his word."

"So . . . the cartels probably do this all the time. Why are you telling me this?"

"Actually no, it doesn't happen all the time. Our borders are nowhere near secure, but they've developed easier ways to transport their evil product into the country. Don't get me wrong. Flying drugs into remote areas of the country still works. It's just that the big cartels have developed more efficient ways to move multi-ton loads of product. Drug mules, tunnels, and submarines have taken over from the airplane. Part of the reason for that is the lack of pilots with the audacity and skill to do night landings with a Cessna 180 or its equivalent in the desert. I'm not saying this has anything to do with Brian Besser. However, what's happening is different from the normal drug pipeline; which means a new operation. You might find it beneficial to drive out and talk to Julio."

"What do you mean a Cessna 180? How does a Mexican sheepherder know a Cessna from a seagull?" Rock just looked at me, and the hint of a smile touched the left corner of his mouth.

"Go and talk to him tomorrow. The ranch headquarters is five miles south of Hachita, on the highway to Antelope Wells."

"Rock, I don't want to go clear down there to talk to some dumb sheepherder. Just tell me what you know."

"Uh-uh, you need to talk to him. Go to the ranch headquarters. They'll tell you where to find him. Supper will be ready when you get back." Rock got to his feet. "And for dessert? More of that excellent apple torta. Or for you," he murmured, "perhaps pie would be more fitting."

I thought he muttered something about humble, along with the pie, but the subject quickly changed, and I neglected to ask what he meant. It was a slip I shouldn't have made.

Chapter 21

LONNIE

When the sun painted the tops of the Pyramid Mountains a soft lavender, I tiptoed out of Rock and Dora's house. A café out by the interstate looked good enough for breakfast, and after two cups of coffee, I was ready for the trail. Highway 10 took me east to the Hachita exit. I growled at the stupidity of what I was about to do, then resigned myself and turned south for my meeting with a sheepherder. My fist tightened on the steering wheel. I shouldn't have let Rock talk me into this. On the other hand, the weather was beautiful, and I certainly had no other way to pass the time until Frederick Roseman called.

Ground down by time and bad luck to a few ramshackle houses, Hachita still supported a small grocery store and bar. A restaurant looked like it might be open some days. Today wasn't one of them, so I walked into the store and bought a cup of coffee that appeared to have originated in the Alberta tar sands.

On the other side of the pavement, three strands of rusty barbwire surrounded a weathered gravestone. In no rush to meet my sheepherder, I strolled over and peered down at it while I sipped the steaming coffee. A hundred years ago, W.H. Arnold died at the age of twenty-three. What had snuffed out this young man's life, and why was he buried here? Maybe Rock would know. I walked back to the car and headed south toward the mountains to meet my sheepherder.

Five miles down the road, the weathered Paloma Ranch sign appeared on my left. After a mile of bad gravel, I arrived at a collection of neat, but cash-starved buildings. Another wind-scoured sign at the gate identified this as the Paloma Ranch headquarters. Hopefully, I could get directions to Julio's sheep camp.

The work-lined face that answered my knock belonged to a woman. Her sun-darkened visage appeared ten years older than she probably was, but that didn't take anything away from her warm greeting. She informed me that Julio was with one of the sheep bands on the east side of Big Hatchet Mountain. After detailed directions, she wished me well and sent me on my way. The woman reminded me of Brian. Just meeting her made your day better, and I drove out of their cobblestone road whistling and thinking kind thoughts about a world that likely didn't deserve it.

Spanish bayonet and ocotillo, interspersed with the never-ending juniper and mesquite, marched in ragged ranks, south, and then east through the sprawling valley ahead of me. The boulder-strewn trail hugged the side of the mountains, and each time my rental car scraped through the bottom of one of the rock-filled washes, I winced, and wished I'd rented something more appropriate.

There seemed no end to the countless brush-choked canyons and faint game trails that stretched deep into the Mexican interior. It was easy to see why the army of border police and federal agents were only occasionally successful at slowing the flood of drug smugglers and illegal immigrants. Stopping them altogether was an entirely different matter.

When the road angled toward Thompson Canyon, I started seeing more sheep signs. However, another hard mile scraped under my soon-to-be rent-a-wreck before I spotted the woolly critters. I nosed the car into a wide spot in the road and hiked along the side of the mountain, searching for the sheep wagon. It appeared as I rounded a shoulder of rock, down next to a dry wash. Two border collies stretched in the sparse shade underneath it. A slight, Mexican looking fellow sat next to one of the wagon wheels repairing what must be a leather bell collar. I knew he'd seen me, so I just walked up and said hello.

He looked up and studied me for a moment. Then in a low, barely accented voice, he said, "You are Lonnie Bowers, the bronc rider."

"Guess I am." I turned on my "I'm a star," grin. Recognition never hurt, especially if you needed information. I wasted no time. "Rock Esfalan sent me out to talk to you. He's an old friend of mine. Said you might know something about a plane flying in at night, and maybe dropping some drugs."

The herder studied me with a quizzical smile before he stood and extended his hand. "I am Julio Fernandez. Would you like some coffee?"

Again, I heard the slight accent, as if it came from a mother tongue learned in the distant past and seldom used.

"I made it this morning, so it should still be drinkable." His smile was slow, but welcoming.

"Sure, I'll have some coffee." I side-kicked a rock out of the way, and pulled up a piece of firewood for a chair. If I could just get whatever information this Mexican herder had about Brian, I could get out of here. The whole camp had the disagreeable odor of sheep.

The herder stepped from the wagon with two cups of coffee, passed one of them to me and returned to his repair task. The silence dragged on, broken only by his quiet efforts to make the ripped bell-collar serviceable. Occasionally, he sipped at his coffee and glanced out at the moving sea of blatting wool.

The guy had obviously already forgotten the subject, so I started again. "Rock says you saw a plane."

"Yes, there was a Cessna, a 180 with the Continental O-470-S model engine."

"Hold it!" I set my empty coffee cup on the ground in front of me, frustrated that Rock had thought this sheepherder's crazy story made sense. I'd have been impressed enough if he'd said he'd seen a small high-wing plane. However, this nonsense about engine size and type was ridiculous. I leaned forward and emphasized every word. "This could be important." My voice crackled with at least part of the built-up anger and tension of the past week. "I have a friend whose life may be at stake. I'm not sure how you would even know what a Cessna looks like, never mind what type of engine, but I need to know exactly what you saw; nothing more."

While I talked, he gazed out at the sheep. A silly half-smile lit his dark, expressive face which only made me angrier. Rock had sent me out to talk to some half-wit. Anything this old sheepherder told me would be highly suspect. The guy was about as bright as a five-year-old flashlight. However, I wouldn't get information by losing my temper. Besides, his intelligence level wasn't likely his fault.

"There's more coffee in the wagon. Help yourself, if you would like." The sheepherder's voice was still friendly, the inflection unchanged.

"Thank you." I picked my cup off the ground and sauntered toward the wagon door of his mobile shanty. I'd seen these old herder wagons before, often in the high desert of Nevada. They're the mainstay of the sheep industry, though they usually pay scant homage to modern convenience. Rubber tires had replaced the old wooden-spoke wheels on this one. Plastic barrels had taken the place of the heavy oak water kegs, and the roof hoops were covered with mostly waterproof canvas. Entrance was gained through a rickety two-piece door that opened to the acrid aroma of spilled navel-dip iodine and day-old coffee. Inside, a scarred counter shared one side with a one-legged fold-down table. On the other, a wood heater held the soot-blackened coffee pot. I poured a cup and returned to my upended block of firewood.

The sheepherder sent one of the dogs out to bunch some wanderers. In spite of my sour mood, I watched with admiration. The dog moved the truant ewes into place, and loped back when the herder whistled. He flopped under the wagon, but his keen eyes never left the herder, eager for more instructions.

"That's a good dog," I said.

"Yes, Chico is small, but very brave and willing.

"What about the other one?"

"That is Alonso. In the Spanish language, Alonso means 'ready for battle.' For him, it is fitting. He was born with anger in his heart. Always, he is ready to pick a fight."

I turned to look at Alonso lying off to the side by himself. His head had snapped up from between his black and white paws when the herder spoke his name.

"Alonso has so much talent. He is a much better stock dog than Chico, but he is often distracted from his work by his jealousy of Chico, and his dislike for everyone around him. He has a hard life, but only because he makes it hard. Chico is different. He has only a little natural ability, but he wants so much to please, and he is happiest when he can work the sheep. Though he has less talent, I think his life is much better than Alonso's."

I watched the dogs while I listened to the herder. Though he might make up stories about airplanes, he sure enough was savvy with dogs. We both sipped our coffee while the sheep grazed up one side of the sloping canyon. A few minutes later, the herder sent Alonso out to turn the leaders on the left side. He whistled to signal the dog left, then right, walk up, back off, all of it pure ballet. Even my untrained eye could see that Alonso had unusual talent. He eventually trotted back, growled at Chico as he went by, then flopped down under the wagon.

"You see?" The herder smiled as he looked over at me.

"Yeah, I do. There's a considerable difference in their ability—and attitude."

The herder surveyed the sheep, then squatted, his back against a wagon wheel. "May I ask what is so important to you about the plane?" he asked.

I weighed the consequences of telling him about Brian and the abduction at the Puyallup airport. There couldn't be any harm in relating the major details, and it might impress on him the need to stop embellishing whatever he'd seen.

"I have a friend, a bull rider from Canada who we think was kidnapped by a drug cartel.

Apparently, they grabbed him with his plane and took him into Mexico. We're looking for any clues which might help in finding him—or what's left . . ." My throat tightened. That couldn't happen. I swallowed the rising panic at the thought that Brian might not be alive.

"So you think this plane might be your friend's?" His voice gently broke through my fear.

I shrugged. "It might be, so I would appreciate if you told me exactly what you saw. Don't add any details unless you're absolutely certain of them."

The sheepherder nodded, then poured the dregs of his coffee in the dirt. He had that slow-witted smile on his face again. "I would first like to tell you about my life. Would that be alright?"

Instantly annoyed, I stood and stared out at the moving herd while I got a tight grip on my anger. I couldn't believe this. Why had Rock sent me out here? Other than a scenic trip, this had been a total waste of time. Sure, it wasn't the sheepherder's fault he had an IQ in the negative zone, but Rock should have known. Nevertheless, he'd been hospitable, and the coffee was drinkable, so. . . .

"Well sure, why not?" I glanced pointedly at my watch.

However, time didn't seem to matter to him. He picked up a chunk of greasewood and whittled on it with a worn pocket knife.

I waited.

Finally, he started to talk in his low, drawly voice. "I was an Air Force pilot for much of my life; two tours in Vietnam. However, my first love was always small planes. So after Vietnam I left the Air Force and went to work as a test pilot for Cessna. Many times I have flown the Cessna 180 Skywagon.

The basic airframe varied little over the years, but Cessna did change the engine configuration. Every plane was thoroughly tested. I know the sound of a Continental O-470-S. I flew the first 180 with that engine—and many afterward."

He sent Chico out to the herd, which allowed my burning face to regain some natural color. His story had the ring of authenticity. This man was telling the truth.

"I don't understand. What is all this? Why are you here?"

"Ah, you wonder why a former test pilot would be caring for sheep." His weathered, mahogany face softened as he chuckled. His laugh was infectious; enough I had to join him. After all, it seemed bizarre that somebody who had enjoyed the income and prestige of a test pilot would be herding sheep.

"Many strangers ask that question. I could tell you that I do it because I like working with the sheep and the dogs, and that is true. However, there is more." He waved a hand out at the sheep. "This peace and serenity replaces my life-long lust for danger. In a strange way, it becomes the antidote for the adrenaline I crave. All my life I have lived on the thrill of uncertainty, first as a jet pilot, and later testing new and different planes. You, perhaps better than most, understand that crazy need. You have lived in the rodeo arena since you were a young man. However, adrenaline is addictive, and it can destroy your life. Many cowboys, long after age and injury have robbed them of their ability to win, find it difficult to walk away and start a new chapter in their lives. They just keep reliving the same old scene in a new town and another dusty arena. Only they don't win anymore. Eventually, desperation and bitterness drive them to drown their impotence in a different drug, or a new relationship."

Pictures kaleidoscoped through my mind while I listened to Julio. I'd won Inglewood, and I warmed inside to the memory of the cheering fans and fat check. But Cotton Ginny had been a cream puff, easy to ride, and nobody knew it more than me. What about Air Wolf? He was a horse that never could have bucked me off five years ago. At Dillon, he'd done it easily. Was I losing that necessary competitive edge? Was it time to hang up my saddle? Could I move on, or was I trapped as well by the adrenaline of danger, and adulation of the crowd?

Julio threaded the bell back on the collar he'd finished, then buckled it. "You know, fighter pilots face the same problem when it's time to step out of the cockpit. Maybe that is why I'm here."

He paused to reprimand Alonso, who was bullying Chico over who got the shadiest spot under the wagon.

"That Alonso never quits." He shook his head. "He is at peace with nobody. Always, he has a fight going. If it isn't with Chico, he will choose a cantankerous old ewe and pick on her, and if that doesn't work, he will battle with me over who is the boss. His is truly a hard life, but I have learned much from him. I am grateful for my dogs. Sometimes, they teach me more than I could ever teach them."

Julio pushed away from the wagon wheel he'd been squatting against, and I stood as well. It was time to go. If I hadn't found out much about Brian, meeting Julio and listening to his wisdom had been well worth the trip.

"So, you wanted to know about the airplane?"

I nodded; a humbler man than I'd been an hour ago.

"The second time it came, I saw it against a full moon. I think the plane was blue and white, but that is difficult to tell in the moonlight."

If Julio thought the plane was blue and white, it was good enough for me. I'd loaded my saddle in a Cessna with those familiar colors more times than I could count.

As I reached for his hand, a lump rose in my throat. What I said was as much of an apology as I could make. Then I thanked Julio Fernandez—for everything.

CHAPTER 22
CLARISSA

BREAKFAST WAS NEVER LATER than six-thirty at the ranch. I loved the early morning routine after I'd braved the cold, and shivered into some clothes. The crackling fire had already warmed up the sides of the antique cook stove, and I huddled next to it after exchanging a warm hug and cheery good morning with Anna. Bob had gone out to pitch some hay to the yearling colts and the three other young horses he was training. Anna poured a cup of coffee from the ten-cup pot on the back of the stove, and set it in front of me. I wasn't usually a coffee drinker, but at the ranch, it tasted good.

Cup in hand, I walked to the living room window to watch the sun paint the treetops. A dozen geese flew overhead, honking their cold weather warnings. The poplar leaves rustled and whispered, as if they were yellow flags of caution. Within a few weeks, the deep freeze of a British Columbia winter would turn the land white and still, except for the howl of wolves, and occasional warble of the garrulous black ravens.

When I walked back into the kitchen, Anna was breaking eggs into a hot skillet.

"Can I help?"

"Sure, if you want, you can slice some bread for toast."

I pulled a half-loaf out of the bottom drawer, and painstakingly ran the bread knife through the loaf while Anna talked.

"Clarissa, what about this company Lonnie is working for? Did they think the kidnappers would release Brian?"

"Maybe," I hedged. "He . . . I guess he didn't really know."

"But last night you said Lonnie thought they might let him go?"

"Yes, he said it was possible."

Bob stomped inside and hung his hat and coat on a peg by the door. He huddled up to the cook stove, rubbing his red hands together. "It's frosty out there this morning. There was ice on the stock tank." He squeezed Anna fondly, and offered a cheery good morning while he held his gnarled hands over the stove. "You two look pretty serious. Do I need to leave?"

"No." Anna poked at the hash browns. "We were just talking about Brian."

Bob's face sobered.

"I asked Clarissa whether the company Lonnie is working for thought the drug cartel might release him."

Bob turned toward me. "What did he say?"

The truth wasn't good, but it wasn't right to cover it. That wasn't why I'd come. "Lonnie said he thought the cartel had grabbed Brian with his plane because he's an exceptional pilot, and they might not turn him loose. That's why they're going in after him."

Bob poured a steaming, black cup of coffee. "And what else?"

I took a deep breath. "They thought . . . if he wouldn't fly drugs—well, they would make him." My gaze darted back and forth between Bob and Anna. That wasn't exactly what Lonnie had said. Apparently, this Frederick had been blunt. "If he won't fly—they will kill him." It wasn't necessary to tell them that, at least not yet.

I put my arm around Anna as fear flooded into her eyes. She leaned into my shoulder, and I held her close, glad I'd not told her all of what Lonnie had said.

"Did Lonnie have any idea where they might be holding him?" Anna asked.

"No, only somewhere in northern Mexico. He said the company wouldn't send him in until they were sure of the location."

Anna spooned the eggs, hash browns and bacon onto a platter while I put the silverware and plates on the table.

Bob closed the damper on the stove. We moved to the table and sat in our usual places. Then he reached over and put his hand in Anna's. "Let's put Brian in God's capable hands and eat this before it gets any colder."

Bob asked the blessing, and prayed for Brian. His worry was like a building storm cloud, but both he and Anna seemed to have a peaceful assurance that whatever happened, God was in control, and even more amazing—they were sure Lonnie would do the right thing. Wow—that would be a first!

Breakfast was always marvelous at the ranch. The good part was I never had to worry about a weight-loss program here. The daylight-to-dark labor burned off any excess calories. Table talk centered on ordinary ranch events. It wasn't that Bob and Anna weren't still worried. It was apparent by their sudden silences, and the difficulty of concentrating on the simplest of chores. We discussed the things ranchers everywhere talk about; plans for selling the calves, and how many cows hadn't come in from the range area yet, what they planned to do with the weanling colts; anything but Brian's dangerous situation.

Horses were a major addition to the Bessers' income. Every year Bob sold some of the young horses as weanlings or yearlings, but most were kept until they were well-started two- or three-year-olds. His horses were in high demand from other ranchers, both for their cow sense, and because of their high level of training.

After washing the dishes, Anna and I walked down to feed the chickens. The grass, wet from the heavy morning frost swished against our black rubber chore boots as we finished and hiked to the lower meadow. The early morning sun had burned off the wispy fog in the low places, enough so we could see a cow moose on the far side of the meadow. She decided we weren't a huge threat to her calf and continued searching for the greenest of the sedges.

When we got back to the house, Anna poured coffee and stoked the fire in the kitchen stove. "Lonnie was here with Brian. That must have been just before your accident. They spent three days up at the Kushya camp."

A flash of resentment bolted through me. We used to do that together. "Believe it or not, he came up to Lillooet last weekend to see me." I made a conscious effort to keep the sarcasm out of my voice, with little success.

Anna's eyebrows rose, but she just nodded and waited for me to continue.

I took a deep breath. "He stayed for supper. That pastor and his wife were there too; the one who rescued me from the cougar." I dropped my eyes to the table. "I hadn't seen Lonnie since . . . well, the day we split. Actually, we had a good evening together."

The heat from the crackling pitch-pine fire caressed us with its warmth. Anna still didn't say anything, but she studied my face as she cradled her cup of coffee in both hands.

"Anna, I really need your advice. What should I do . . . I mean . . . about getting a divorce?"

She thought a moment. "What do you think God is telling you to do?"

"I'm not sure."

"You need to learn to listen to His voice, in every area of your life. He knows what is the very best for you—and for Lonnie." Anna reached over and squeezed my hand.

"What if I'm supposed to divorce him?"

"You will know—at the right time. Trust Him to show you the way."

"I hate Lonnie for what he did. But the other day when I opened the door, and he was standing on the veranda, twisting his hat in his hands and shuffling from one foot to the other like an eight-year-old kid, my heart went out to him, and I wished . . . for a moment, I wished things were different. Ever since he left he's called me, just to make sure I'm okay. And all through the visit with Clint and Darlene, he was the perfect gentleman, and that's saying a lot for Lonnie when there's a preacher, or for that matter, a Christian of any stripe to bash around."

"And the scars on your face?" Anna asked.

"I will never forget what he said. He was so sweet. He said, 'Clarissa, you are a beautiful woman. Don't ever think those scars take away from that.' I couldn't take it anymore. I just started bawling. I know if he had reached over and touched me, I would have fallen into his arms."

Telling Anna about it made me cry all over again, and she set a box of tissues in front of me.

"Is that what you wish would have happened?" she asked.

"I don't know. Is it possible to love someone and not forgive them?"

Anna thought for a moment. "No, my dear, it isn't." Anna reached over to the end of the table and gathered up her tattered old Bible with both hands, opened it to the Gospel of John, and laid it in front of me. "Read verse sixteen of chapter three."

The underlined verse was familiar, even to me. I didn't need to read it. God loved, and reached out to offer forgiveness—to every person on the face of the earth. Perfect love probably meant I had to forgive Lonnie—regardless of what he had done.

I squirmed. "I suppose I could forgive Lonnie, if he were truly changed." Then, Darlene's words came flooding back to engulf me. *"Clarissa, you need to forgive the woman who was involved with Lonnie."*

Angry tears tracked down my face. Maybe someday I could forgive that woman, but it wasn't today.

Chapter 23

LONNIE

AFTER I'D SCRAPED OVER what seemed like every rock in New Mexico, I turned my abused rental car north onto the pavement. Next time the company was going to have to shell out for a suitable vehicle. This mid-size compact would be lucky to make it back to El Paso with a muffler.

The sun had slid into the Peloncillos when I pulled off the interstate and into Lordsburg. I parked on the street in front of Rock and Dora's gray brick home and walked up to the step. Rock stood at the screen door.

"You're just in time. Dora fed the kids, but we waited to eat with you. Grub's on the table."

I washed up, and we sat at the table, chatting about the country I'd seen during the day. Both Rock and Dora proved knowledgeable about the different mountain ranges, as well as the history of the area, and I remembered the grave I had seen that morning. After the food had all gone around, I turned to him.

"Rock, I stopped for gas down at Hachita this morning. Across from the store, there's an old grave. A young fellow who died way back around the turn of the century. Just curious. Do you know anything about it?"

"Yeah, I know the grave. W. H. Arnold on the headstone. Hearsay has it that young Willy Arnold was a miner. He worked a claim southwest of there, up in the foothills. By all accounts, he was a decent fellow, and had no trouble with any-body. One Saturday, Willy decided to come to town. He picked up his supplies, and then stopped at the saloon to tip back a few cool ones. He got into a quarrel with a fellow who was trouble and quick with a gun. Tough talk turned into gunplay, and when the smoke cleared, Willy lay dead on the floor. They buried him there by the road." Rock shrugged. "To send a message, I guess."

I was busy tying into Dora's roast and mashed potatoes, but still fascinated by Rock's account of Willy Arnold. "What do you mean? What's the message?"

One corner of Rock's mouth turned up.

"That the good guys don't always win. Double that in Mexico!"

Dora put down her fork and turned to Rock, her face in-stantly dark. "Lonnie isn't supposed to try to rescue his friend? You would do the same thing. Stop being such a hypocrite!"

I clenched my jaw. Obviously, my friend had spilled my whole story to his wife. I dropped my fork on my plate, irri-tated and angry that he had betrayed a confidence. Rock just sat there with a pained look on his face, seemingly unsure which arrows to deflect first. His head swiveled from one to the other of us while he tried to chew his way through a tough piece of roast beef. For a moment, there was silence. Then Dora giggled, and that made me grin, and the tension defused.

Rock finally got the roast beef down, and held up his fists, both still clenched around his knife and fork.

"Alright! Lonnie first. Yes, I did tell Dora. I told her because she's my wife, and I trust her—one hundred percent. However, I also told her because Dora is more Mexican than Pancho Villa. She has a million relatives in northern Mexico, even some good ones." He ducked as Dora playfully threw a potholder across the table at him. "If you have to go over the border, there may be some help you can trust. I still hope your people find another way to do this, but if they don't, you may need better inside help than what the Stirling people provide."

I nodded. "Okay. I'm sorry. I shouldn't have gotten mad."

But Rock's feathers were still ruffled. He turned to Dora. "Now you. Mexico is a dangerous place when you start messing with the drug cartels. You know that. But yes, I guess if it were Lonnie, I'd go drag his worthless carcass out of there, but . . . I would just like to see them explore every angle before they send Lonnie in to be cartel road kill."

Dora's eyes flashed, and one of her dark eyebrows arched. Rock mumbled something about women, but his voice petered out like a run-down razor. I grinned at his discomfort. There was no doubt in my mind that if I was down there, he would come with guns blazing. I'd do the same for him.

We pushed back from the table. "Dora, thanks for another excellent meal."

"You are so welcome. I hope you can come—"

The phone interrupted her. Dora answered, and handed it to me. The gravelly voice on the other end was becoming very familiar.

"Be in El Paso tomorrow night. You have a room at the La Quinta Airport Inn. I will meet you there at seven." The line went dead.

I grimaced. Frederick didn't waste your time with small

talk. Rock stared at me, and I shrugged. "I have to go back to El Paso tomorrow morning."

Later, we moved to the porch, and again reminisced about rodeos, cowboys, and all the places we'd traveled together, from the San Francisco Cow Palace to Jacksonville, Florida. The evening was spent thumbing through the pages of our past, rediscovering the good and the bad, like old trophy buckles to be polished and treasured. Even though the remembering helped to bury some of the worry of tomorrow, it didn't completely cover the growing worry that Brian was gone, and maybe in the biggest trouble either of us had ever seen.

Before Rock and I turned in, he handed me a small card. He'd printed a name and town in black ink. No telephone number. "Genaro Chacon is a rancher in the mountains north of Madera. Lonnie, if anything goes wrong, find this guy. He's Dora's cousin. You can trust him."

I didn't see where a Mexican farmer was going to be of any help, but I'd had recent experience with judging folks who didn't fit my preconceived notions. I thanked Rock for the card, and said I'd be real careful. We shook hands, and like old friends do, we made sincere promises to stay in touch, pledges we'd probably never keep.

Chapter 24

LONNIE

The drive to el paso was long and hot, but I had much to plan—and worry about. An hour before sunset I drove up to the soaring columns in front of the La Quinta Airport Inn. My current financial status would hardly allow these digs, but if Stirling was paying the bill, I'd be happy to be their guest. I checked in, then wandered down the street to a chain restaurant. Not that I was hungry, but it would kill some time until my meeting with Frederick.

Mechanically, I chased some kind of fancy-name spaghetti around my plate. What would Frederick have for me? Would he have a way to get Brian out, so I wouldn't have to be the one to poke a stick into that Mexican wasp nest? Though I was loathe to admit it, Rock had scared some caution into me. These drug cartel people were powerful, smart, and armed to the eyeballs. They could easily reach out and waste anybody who messed up their sandbox. Nobody was going to waltz into their base of operations and pull off this sort of stunt; which was . . . ? I hadn't a clue. I really hoped Frederick and company had that part covered.

After corralling the last of the spaghetti, I paid the bill and sauntered back to my room. I pushed the door back against the wall and surveyed the room. I half expected Frederick would be sitting in the chair at the end of the desk, but it was empty. Ten minutes later, he knocked like a normal person, which he wasn't.

I opened the door, and stepped back.

"How was your New Mexico trip?" His curt question was devoid of any welcome or greeting, but I was beginning to understand the man. It wasn't that he didn't care or lacked manners. He just didn't have time for the social warm-up that most of us depend on to start a conversation. His eyes flickered over each corner and entrance to the room before he gave me any attention.

"The trip was fine. I've got an old rodeo buddy in Lordsburg—he's the sheriff there."

He nodded, then lowered his bulk into the one and only chair before he leaned forward, his eyes intent on my face.

How much of my visit with Rock and Julio should I divulge? My decision was instant. I was going into Mexico on a suicidal mission. I had no choice but to trust him and his organization, so I blurted out everything about Julio and the Cessna 180 landing in the desert.

Frederick asked an occasional question, and after I'd finished, he sat staring absently at the far wall while he did his usual 'tap index finger on desk' routine.

I waited, then cleared my throat to remind him I was still in the room.

His eyes shifted back to me. "We think we've found their base. What you have told me confirms our intelligence. They're running an operation north of Madera up in the Sierra Madre."

Madera. Where had I heard that name? Then I remembered. That relative of Dora's that Rock had mentioned lived somewhere north of here.

"Manuel Lourdes," Frederick continued, "is operating on a concession from the Sinaloa cartel. They own the drug routes from Juarez to the California border. What Manuel is doing is out of the ordinary. That's why the Sinaloa people made a deal with him. They will be watching to see how successful he is, and if he continues to elude the border authorities, all the cartels will duplicate his operation."

"Isn't it a bit late to do anything about this Manuel? You said this had gone on for months, so the cartels already know how successful he's been."

Frederick nodded. "Yes, they do."

"Aren't you doing the Sinaloa cartel a favor by eliminating someone they may want to get rid of anyway? They've seen him implement a strategy, which has been hugely successful. Now you guys go in, eliminate Manuel, and hand the whole operation to them."

"Yes—and no," Frederick replied. "But good thinking." His voice was flat, and the comment was only an observation, not a compliment. "Let me explain the politics of the drug trade." Frederick stood and paced back and forth. "Right now, the border, from the Gulf of Mexico to Tijuana, is divided among five major cartels, with a couple of smaller ones fighting for a larger share. Any of these five will sometimes grant a concession to an operator like Manuel Lourdes, for a price. Manuel carries on his business, and as long as he pays his bills, everybody is happy. Remember, he is not a principal player, nor is he part of any of the five cartels. By eliminating Manuel, we can send a clear message, with a minimum of fallout."

"So what's the message?" I was discovering that Frederick reasoned on a completely different level, and I listened with new respect.

Frederick leaned forward in his chair. "We've lost the drug war. That's a given. All we do now is attempt a degree of control, and try to keep the number of bodies at an acceptable level, if there is such a thing. When we wipe out Manuel Lourdes, it sends a message to the big boys. It's our line in the sand. If you use planes to fly drugs across our borders, we will come to wherever you are with every bit of the considerable firepower we can muster."

"So why don't you go after one of the really big sharks? Wouldn't it be more productive to take out, say—the head of the Tijuana cartel?"

"That's a valid question. However, if we eliminate the guiding hand behind one of the five families, it creates a void. A savage, brutal war erupts to control that lucrative section of the border. Hundreds of people are killed, and to make it worse, we lose control of intelligence channels that sometimes have taken years to build. So, if we take down Manuel Lourdes, which I might add is long overdue, we avoid an all-out war. But the cartels will know who did it—and why."

"Okay." My respect for Frederick Roseman had just ratcheted up another notch, and I pulled out some hotel stationary. "How do we proceed?"

For two hours, I scribbled notes while Frederick Roseman outlined every detail of my itinerary into the Sierra Madre. "Here, you're going to need this." Frederick handed me a sheaf of papers when he'd finished. "One of the reasons Lonnie the rodeo cowboy has decided on a holiday in Mexico is because of his long-held interest in his Indian roots."

I sat back in my chair and raised my eyebrows. There was little in life in which I had less interest.

"Hey," Frederick held up a hand, stifling my protest. "Studying your roots is a very contemporary thing to do. Who knows, you might learn something." He rummaged in his briefcase and shoved another bundle of papers at me. "Study these. You'll need to have some knowledge about the ancient Paquime and Anasazi."

"Who are they?"

"Read the papers—and try to look less like a cowboy, perhaps a bit more scholarly." He grinned at his poor attempt at a joke. Then he squared his shoulders and scowled, as if he'd just breached the strictest code of behavior. "And—while we're on the cowboy subject, your role may change. You have the language and complexion to blend in as a national. Do that when and where it's required. You can also just be yourself. But be careful. Playing two roles can come back to bite you, though there are occasions in short-term operations where it can work to your advantage."

After he'd finished, and my fingers were numb from writing, he pulled out a miserly bundle of peso notes and handed them to me. I counted the bills. "What's this for? Lunch?"

Frederick's mouth tightened. "You will be able to replenish those when necessary, but don't carry large sums on your person. An American-size wallet will attract attention you don't want." Abruptly, he shook my hand, wished me well, and left. I resisted the temptation to look into the hallway for his two muscular refrigeration experts.

Two hours later, I was still memorizing my notes. Frederick's attention to detail was remarkable. He'd left nothing to chance. Every item, each circumstance was covered. Tomorrow morning, instead of heading for Kansas City and one of the last big rodeos of the year, I'd be on a Mexican bus. The thought did nothing for my frame of mind, but I decided Brian likely wasn't rapturous about his circumstances either, so I buckled down to commit the rest of my notes to memory before shredding them.

Or, that's what I should have done. Instead, though it would be late on the West Coast, I decided to call Clarissa. For some reason, I needed to hear her voice once more before I disappeared into Mexico. I pictured the phone ringing at the end of the counter in the little yellow house. If she hadn't gone to bed she would be sitting in the brown leather recliner, maybe having a cup of chamomile tea. I hoped she'd answer. She didn't. Instead, I got the cheery Guardian Insurance greeting. I left a message, trying to convey how things were going in the search for Brian without blabbing anything over the phone that could be used by the wrong parties. Frederick had already pounded phone protocol into me. I was learning.

The looming danger ahead sapped my antagonism toward her faith, enough so that I asked her to say another one of those prayers. If she'd been on the phone, I probably wouldn't have said that, but the prayer would be more for Brian's benefit. Not that it would do any good, but . . . hey, it couldn't hurt anything.

I told her how much the dinner and the evening had meant, which just embarrassed me, then said a quick goodbye and hung up the phone, before I babbled anything more she'd laugh at. My face burned. I shouldn't have called. Everything I'd said was going to sound particularly sappy to her.

"Yeah, Lonnie. You liked the dinner and the time together, did you? Then why did you wreck it? That used to happen every night!" I had

no answer to that charge.

I spent the hours until midnight again poring over every detail Frederick had given me, then shredded my notes, and went to bed. Tomorrow would be the first step toward bringing Brian home.

Chapter 25

CLARISSA

Bob harnessed the team by lantern light. He and Anna would take me out to the Kluskus corrals where I had left my car. I wanted to make it all the way home today, if I could. Lonnie might have called with information about Brian, and I did have to go back to work sometime, and start physiotherapy.

After a hurried breakfast, we bundled into the wagon, and crossed the frigid water at the Messue well before eight o'-clock. The river had dropped, but now ice clung to the banks. A cold gray sky threatened snow, and I shivered under the blanket Anna had draped over our legs. The willows along the river, shrouded in satin, stood silent, their hoarfrost branches like waving sparklers.

When we started the long climb up the north side of the canyon, soft, pillowy flakes of snow floated onto the steaming horses. They leaned into their collars, digging hard, panting with the exertion. Bob rested them at the top before we moved on through the last few miles of jack pine forest to the corrals.

When we started again, Bob let the horses pick their own pace up the narrow, winding trail. He turned to me. "Clarissa, we're going to move into town later this week. The communication at the ranch is too sketchy, and we need to know what's going on with Brian."

"Will you stay at the Martins?" I snuggled up closer to Anna, trying to stay warm.

"Maybe for a day or two," Anna answered. "We might look for a place to rent. Alex will stay at the ranch while we're gone."

Alex Baptiste was an Indian friend who lived seven or eight miles east of the Bessers. "Why don't you come and stay with me in Lillooet?" I asked. "Then you wouldn't have to rent anything." I squeezed Anna's arm. "To have you be there would be marvelous, and you could get the news right from Lonnie. Then when Brian and Lonnie come home, we'll have the most gigantic party you could ever imagine. Besides, I may have to be in Vancouver at our corporate office for a few days, so part of the time you would have the whole place to yourselves."

Anna glanced at Bob. He thought for a moment, and then nodded. "I suppose we could do that, if you're sure we wouldn't be too much—"

"Don't even go there. I would love to have you. Please come."

The snow was heavier now, and the flakes started to pile into a white carpet ahead of us. Suddenly Bud, the offside black gelding, snorted. Both horses stopped, splayfooted, wanting to spook. Bob sawed on the lines and spoke softly to them, holding them steady. Three wolves, two big blacks and a gray, loped across the trail and disappeared in the trees a hundred yards in front of us. Bob moved the team forward, but stopped where the wolves had crossed. He peered at the scuffed moose tracks under the muddy wolf prints, and shook his head.

"Will the wolves get her?" I asked.

Bob shook his head. "No, they'll not likely get the cow. But they'll run her until her calf can't run anymore. Then they start eating on the calf. They might kill it first, and they might not."

I shivered and peered into the dark forest on each side of the wagon. My arm suddenly ached from the cold, and I was glad for the protective presence of Bob and Anna.

The mud-streaked Jetta, now partly obscured by the falling snow, was as I had left it. My car keys were in my backpack at the bottom of the lake, but I kept a spare in a magnetic box under the front bumper. Bob brushed the small accumulation of snow off the hood and windshield while I retrieved the key.

I started the car, gave them both my best one-armed hug, and repeated my invitation for them to make my house a head-quarters during the search for Brian. Then, I maneuvered onto the fast disappearing road and headed north. Before the falling snow obscured the steaming horses and the two waving figures, I stuck a hand out and waved. Later, when I caught up to a loaded logging truck, I fell in behind it and let it shepherd me the hundred miles to town and civilization.

***

THE SUN had long set before I turned into my driveway. The house looked forlorn and dark, but it was still a welcome sight. The long drive from the ranch had been exhausting, but before falling into bed, I checked the message machine. Ben Thomas had called, "just to see how my injuries were progressing." I suspected the real reason he called was that he was swamped with insurance claims, and needed me to get back to work. I smiled at his roundabout method. However, it was comforting to be needed.

Darlene had called to see if I was home yet. She had come yesterday to water my plants, feed my cat, and fill the water tank for Monte.

The other message was from Lonnie, and was two days old. I played it over twice, listening to his voice, trying to understand.

"Hi. I'm in El Paso tonight at the La Quinta Inn. When you get in tonight, call me. I am going into Mexico tomorrow. Things look very promising there, if you know what I mean. Do pass my regards to the Bessers. Um . . . it wouldn't hurt to, well, kind of say a prayer for Brian and me."

I couldn't believe he'd said that. Lonnie, the man who scoffed at any mention of God. He went on. "Thanks again for dinner the other night. That was real special, and . . . well yeah, I just wanted to tell you that. I will call you the minute we're out of Mexico. Anyhow . . . goodbye."

"Goodbye!" What a lame ending. Couldn't he come up with something better than that? My index finger stabbed at the 'delete' button on the answering machine, and I flounced off to bed. I was angry and disappointed, but couldn't pinpoint why. Or maybe I just wasn't ready to go there yet.

CHAPTER 26
LONNIE

THE TAXI DRIVER who stopped in front of the hotel lobby the next morning was Mexican-American. "Hola, Señor. Cómo está?" Spanish was nothing new for me in this part of the country. My skin was the same shade as his, and if I were careful, my speech wouldn't betray me.

"Quiero ir de Los Angeles-El Paso el servicio de limusina." I spoke as correctly as I could. He nodded, commented on the weather, and asked where I was from; the usual cab driver openers.

Where I needed to go was the Los Angeles-El Paso bus terminal, in the old downtown section of El Paso. For a middle-class Mexican with no wheels, that was the best way to get to the main bus station in Juarez, and for the next while, it looked like Frederick would make sure I was very middle-class.

I'd asked Frederick why I couldn't just take a taxi across to the Juarez bus station. That was after we'd argued about me taking a reliable jeep into Mexico. His straight-faced answer had been, "No. Rich gringos take taxis. For now, you are neither rich, nor a gringo!"

Everything I spent now had to stand up to any possible outside scrutiny. Apparently, what I'd won this year riding broncs would not support a high-flying tourist trip to see the Paquime and Anasazi ruins around Madera, so I'd have to go in less style.

The driver hunched over the worn steering wheel while he expertly maneuvered through the multiple lanes of traffic, all scrambling for the downtown area, all the while regaling me with a history of the city.

To the south, Juarez, the most dangerous city in the world crawled helter-skelter up the far hillside toward a jumble of white-painted rocks. I tried to make out whatever message Juarez had for the world.

As if he'd read my mind, the driver pointed at them. "Do you know what those words say?"

"No." I was tense and edgy, and really didn't care.

"It says, 'The Bible is true; read it.'"

I snorted. "Really?"

He nodded seriously, like he'd just shown me the Magna Carta of Mexico. I had little use for Bibles or anything connected with them. However, maybe some religion wouldn't hurt. Brian and I could both handle some extra mojo on this crazy morning, so I said nothing more.

We arrived at the Los Angeles-El Paso Terminal, and I knew by the throng around me that I'd entered old Mexico, even if I hadn't crossed the border yet. The faces reflected the shade of my own skin, and the air was saturated with the liquid tones of rapid Spanish.

Tourists definitely did not arrive at the Mexican border from here, and as I clambered on the bus with a couple dozen others, more of Frederick's advice came rushing back, enough to make me wish I was going the other way. If it hadn't been for Brian, I might have turned around and headed for the rodeo in Kansas City.

Listen carefully, Frederick had said. *Do not make any notes or carry any phone numbers related to Stirling Associates—or anyone else. If you're caught, it's much easier if you have no family.* That was simple. I had no relatives, or at least none that would pay to get me back.

The cartel will kill you, regardless of whether a ransom is paid, so don't involve family. It will only cause more pain for them. I fidgeted, remembering Rock's graphic narrative of dismembered body parts.

The bus stopped at the border. All passengers had to get out and go through customs with their luggage. If you got the green light, you got to go through. The red meant you really got torn apart. I approached the light, my clothes bag at my side. Two guards scrutinized me, their rifles at the ready. For a moment, I wished that my face was lighter, that I looked more like a harmless gringo tourist. I walked forward and put my finger on the button. Red. No, I didn't need this. The older guard with the hard face beckoned me forward. *"Documentos. Pasaporte."* His hand beckoned impatiently.

I fumbled in my shirt pocket. I'd hoped to at least get over the border without betraying for all who cared to see that I was not Mexican, just in case I needed to play that role. I handed him my Canadian passport. He scrutinized it, and then my face while the younger soldier unzipped my clothes bag and satchel and pawed to the bottom of both. They found nothing more dangerous to Mexican citizens than a penknife. The older tough-looking guy handed my passport back and waved me through. I let out my long-held breath, walked by the guns and into the terminal.

The cavernous Juarez bus terminal made my spine prickle, but I made an effort to walk through, as if armed guards and federal troops with automatic rifles were part of the furniture. Was Frederick right about the bus to Madera? His instructions had been explicit when I had asked why I had to go to Chihuahua, a two hundred mile detour, rather than straight to Madera.

I peered at the schedule behind the counter. Sure enough, the one bus to Madera left at ten tonight. Frederick had told me he didn't want me getting into a strange town in the middle of the night, even if I did speak the lingo. So I followed the crowd to the Chihuahua-bound bus, surrendered my belongings to a pair of grasping hands, along with the necessary five peso *propina*, and found my assigned seat. The in-transit movie disqualified it as a chicken bus, but the second-string actors didn't do anything to loosen the tentacles of fear that gripped me as the bus rolled south over a flat, barren land, and toward whatever was to come.

The movie was beyond bad, and I turned away. The elderly rancher-looking gentleman across the aisle wasn't into it either, so I opened a conversation—in Spanish of course. That was what Frederick had told me to do, and by the time I got to the city of Chihuahua, I had a working knowledge of a Mexican rancher's cattle problems. A thin, fiftyish man with the remains of his sparse hair tied into a ponytail took the rancher's place. His mid-life crisis consisted of a hiatus hernia, and a new woman. Both sounded painful, and I was glad to see his ponytail exit in a small town on the outskirts of the city. Nevertheless, every interaction gave me added confidence that I might survive.

Get comfortable in your role, Frederick had said, *before things become critical, and don't let your guard down. From the time you leave this hotel in the morning, every word, each action, can get you killed.*

"I feel so lucky to be working for your company," I'd replied sarcastically. Apparently, that had been the wrong thing to say.

You can quit anytime—until tomorrow morning. Frederick hadn't smiled.

Quitting wasn't an option. Brian was somewhere down here, and if I had to, I would turn over every rock in Mexico to find him.

At Chihuahua, I changed buses. The Rapidos Cuauhté-moc bus was as good as the Estrella Blanca and there were times I almost forgot that I wasn't just an American tourist on a jaunt to visit some ancient cave ruins. However, I wasn't comfortable enough to forget Frederick's warning. Each choice I made could cost me my life, and if I missed one small cue or made one mistake, it could cost Brian's life as well.

"Remember who you are. Work on your role, every day, all the time!" Frederick had punctuated every word with an accusing finger aimed at my chest, but I knew it was for my own good.

Darkness had fallen when the bus disgorged thirteen Mexicans and me onto a Cuauhtémoc side street. Two taxis waited in the dark street, the drivers lolling against the fender of the lead car while they watched the bus passengers for a possible live one.

I walked across the street, my clothes bag slung over my shoulder. "I would like to go to the Hotel San Francisco. On *Calle numero tres.*" One of the drivers nodded, and opened the trunk. I threw my gear in, then slipped into the back seat.

"Make sure you have your own soap and towel, because those are extra there. However, the rooms are spotless, and breakfast is included.

You get all that for about seventeen bucks American. That's the level of
room where you should be staying."

Last night, I had spluttered at Frederick's seventeen-dollar
room, undoubtedly filled with cockroaches and cooties, but
like everything else that man did, there was a good reason. I
was beginning to respect his attention to the little details that
might keep me from getting killed.

When I stepped out of the dust-colored taxi, it was just
as Frederick had said. I signed the register, and trudged up the
concrete stairs to the third floor. Room number 302 had a lock
that any enterprising seven-year-old could have picked. The
one small window looked out onto the rooftop of the next
building. I opened it. Clarissa might have squeezed through,
but if there was trouble, my shoulders would never fit. I paced
around the room, then sat on the worn green bedspread and
listened to a slow heavy tread coming up the stairs. The shoes
padded across the hallway carpet and stopped. I crept to the
thin, wooden door, my heart hammering in my chest. Was
there only one of them? My long-held breath exploded noisily
with the sudden rattle of a key in the lock across the hall. I
shoved the only chair in the room against the door before I
went to bed, but with every sound, I was instantly awake. It
was a long night.

***

AT FIRST LIGHT, I swung my legs over the edge of the lumpy
bed, and immediately grimaced at the pain in my left shoulder.
There was more of that lately, and now it took longer to get
rid of it. A dozen times I stretched, trying to work the stiffness
of a thousand broncs out of my shoulders and arms. The time

was coming . . . no, I'd think about that some other time. Now, I needed to focus on the present.

Today, I would be in Madera, and that was when finding Brian would get dangerous. I worried about Frederick's man Felix. How reliable was he?

"Felix can take you to any of the ruins in the area," Frederick had said, *"and to Manuel's mountain hideout and airstrip."*

"He's trustworthy?" I asked.

His hesitant reply bothered me at the time. Now it seemed more ominous. The disconcerting memory of what had happened to Stirling Associates' last inside man weighed heavy, and I determined to be cautious.

That afternoon, I stepped off the bus and into a dusty street. Madera looked to be like any of the other midsized Mexican towns the bus had rolled through, but to me, the scent of danger was strong, like slipping into the saddle on a wild, crazy-eyed bronc. The driver set my bag on the sidewalk. I picked it up and walked to the front of the bus. Three multicolored taxis were parked on the other side of the uncharacteristically wide street. The drivers hunched in the shade of a pine pole shelter. Two of the *taxistas* toyed lazily with their cigarettes and eyed me as I approached. I scanned the three of them. The tall skinny one. That had to be Felix.

"Felix Santiestaban is a dark, Indio-looking fellow," Frederick had said. *"About six feet tall, long faced, . . . thin-bodied."*

I walked up to the shelter. "Felix?"

The man I'd picked, turned, and barely nodded.

"Your nephew sent me. I am in town to visit the ruins. Would you take me to the Motel Real del Bosque?" He stared at me, suspicion scrawled across every line of his face, the drooping cigarette now firmly clamped between nervous lips.

His eyes narrowed. Then he reached for the cigarette in his mouth, ground it into the dirt with the heel of his boot and nodded.

"Sì, por supuesto." Yes, of course. The other two straightened, no longer slouching, their eyes flickering over me, assessing my worth. They would undoubtedly question Felix about who his fare had been. He strolled over to the sidewalk, grabbed my bag and slung it into the trunk of his cab. I slid into the front seat, and proceeded to babble as much nonsense as I could dream up about the ancient cave sites. His only response to my running monologue was an occasional noncommittal grunt as we wound our way to the east side of town, and the motel. Now and then he looked at me sideways, rapid, nervous glances that worried me. At the motel, he pulled the cab onto the cobblestone courtyard, parked, and walked to the trunk to unload my bag.

This was my moment of commitment. I blurted the pass phrase. "Would you please help me check in? To room fourteen." My switch to English was like I'd hit him with a cattle prod. He froze, his eyes transfused with terror at the recognized words. My identity was no longer a question. He dropped my bag on the red paving stone courtyard and backed away. Then, he whirled, and bolted to the still open door of his cab. In seconds, he was gone.

CHAPTER 27

LONNIE

BETWEEN THE MOTEL COURTYARD and the office, I had to find a new plan. There was no doubt in my mind that the cartel had put the fear in Felix. Now our whole operation was in disarray, *and* we had a major security concern. My security—if I ever had any! What would Felix do now? I darted a quick glance at the street. I was caught. How could I get out of the country quickly? There wasn't any way because that jerk I was working for thought I shouldn't have wheels. I'd have to find a car, a used scooter, anything to get me to the border. If I stayed here, they could deal with me at their leisure. I stared at the blue mosaic tiles under my feet while I examined the few bad options I had. The immediate priority was to get out of sight, so I grabbed my bag and slipped through the plate-glass door and into the office.

"Do you have a room, please?" I used the most ridiculous tourist Spanish I could drum up. Right now, I wanted to appear anything but local. Rock's graphic description of cartel punishment for locals made me want to wave my non-Mexican passport like a flag. My attempts must have been acceptable, because the girl behind the counter had to smother a giggle at least twice while I mangled her language. Two hundred pesos bought a key, and I ducked across the courtyard to room number nine. The front window provided a view of the gate leading into the complex. At least I'd be forewarned, for whatever good that would do. Once again, the bathroom window at the back was way too skinny for my shoulders. My eyes ricocheted around the room, searching for a suitable weapon to take on a drug smuggler's machine gun, but the most dangerous thing I could find was a coat hanger. And room service probably couldn't supply anything more lethal than a long-necked Corona bottle.

Where did I go from here? I peeked out the side of the curtain. These dudes were tougher than a sack full of badgers, capable of everything Rock had told me. I paced the floor, and tried to control my fear. Would there be a sudden knock on my door followed by a spray of bullets, or would I get the Mexican treatment? Finally, exhausted from the horror of what was sure to come, I sat on the bed and tried to think through what had caused the sheer panic on Felix's face? Nobody had shown up yet. Did I really need to run, or was Felix just afraid that he might have been seen with me? Did they suspect him of being a snitch? And what would he do now that he knew I was working for Stirling Associates? I paced some more because I had no answers.

How I wished I could talk to Frederick, but he had given explicit instructions never to call unless I was requesting an immediate evacuation. Before I did that, I needed to understand this Felix guy. What was he thinking, and what would he do? Again, I edged back the heavy cotton curtain. Through the narrow slit, I watched the late afternoon sun beat down onto the vehicles in the cobblestone parking lot. A blue, late model Chevy pickup, a white Toyota, and on the far end, an older Nissan sedan. The white Toyota hadn't been there five minutes ago. My stomach contracted, my breathing suddenly shallow and fast. Were they already at the door, out of my line of sight? A minute went by—or was it an hour? I couldn't tell, but gradually I relaxed, sat on the bed again and wiped at my sweaty face.

What would I do if I were Felix? Would he tell the cartel about this Americano cowboy? That he worked for a clandestine CIA spin-off group? They would want to know where he had obtained all this information, and suddenly I started to chuckle with relief. If Felix opened his mouth, the cartel people would know the only way he could have that information was because he or somebody close had already spilled their guts—for money. Felix, if he had any brains, wasn't going to say anything. If he muttered so much as one word, the cartel would know he'd snitched, and they would kill him. The odds were at least even that I was safe for the moment. Felix might panic and run, but he couldn't voluntarily betray me without cutting his own throat.

So, what was I supposed to do next? The plan Frederick had given me was up in smoke. To find Brian and get him out, I had to have local help, somebody to act as a guide, to give me cover. Again, I peeked through the curtains and immediately stiffened. A short Mexican in a straw hat and pointy-toed boots swaggered across the courtyard, like a banty rooster on steroids. He had a gun in his hands. I stared at the figure striding across the courtyard, and what he carried in his right hand suddenly focused. It was only a pipe wrench. Carbon dioxide whooshed from my lungs like air out of a punctured truck tire. I slumped against the wall, relief flooding through every pore in my used-up body.

Maybe it was the banty rooster's hat that triggered my memory. Dora's cousin? Rock had said his name was Genaro Chacon, and that he lived in Vallacito between Casas Grandes and Madera. Maybe he would be a replacement for Felix. Probably he wouldn't, but it wasn't like I had any other options. That meant tomorrow I'd be taking another bus ride. Once again, I scowled and said some bad words about Frederick Roseman and his whole organization. Everything would have been easier, and likely safer, with some wheels. So far, what Frederick had set up, was a colossal failure. All I could hope for now, was that Dora's cousin, Genaro would . . . would what? Replace what was supposed to be a seasoned intelligence agent? That he would be willing to go through the charade of acting as my guide to the Paquime and Anasazi ruins while risking his life to take me to the drug smugglers' headquarters? That was a lot to ask for, and I wasn't hopeful. But of one thing I was certain. Tomorrow, everything I owned was going with me. If this Genaro was a bust, Frederick could stuff his operation. That thought lasted all of three seconds, which is how long it took for me to remember Brian. I was stuck with Frederick. And . . . I would be stuck with whoever I could find to replace Felix.

Chapter 28

CLARISSA

Sunday morning service at Mountain Community Church was not what I'd imagined. For one, I'd been the only woman under thirty in a dress. This was definitely not a city church. I'd hoped to slip into the back row, then leave unnoticed. Clint sabotaged that idea in the first ten minutes. After all the announcements of what was happening that week in the church, he'd looked at everybody with a big grin and said, "Now, turn around and shake hands with the folks around you. Welcome them to the house of the Lord."

Darlene, who was way up in the front row, turned and immediately noticed me. She scurried to the back of the church and hugged me. "Clarissa, I'm so glad you came. I hope you will always feel welcome here." Others also greeted me warmly and introduced themselves.

Church was a new experience for me, and wouldn't you know it, Clint's sermon was on forgiveness. He hadn't known I was coming because I didn't know until an hour before the service that I was going to work up the nerve. Nevertheless, it did seem like he'd planned it just for me. Maybe he had the sermon ready—in case I showed up. I knew better, but it did seem a strange coincidence.

I fumbled through the Bible, trying to keep up with all the verses he was quoting. If anybody had been sitting close enough to see me thumb through the index in a frantic search for the book of Colossians, they would have laughed at my inept clumsiness.

After the service I'd driven toward Farwell Canyon and home, mulling through Clint's words. Now, Monday morning when I needed to be concentrating on the claim I was working on, his sermon floated through my head, poking and prodding at my hoarded bag of prejudices. What were those verses in Matthew? "If you forgive men, then God will forgive you. But if you don't, then God won't forgive your sins." I leaned back in my chair and frowned. That was hardly fair. What if the person wasn't sorry? What if they didn't even want to be forgiven? Clint had used a quote from an elderly Dutch woman. She'd spent years enduring a German concentration camp. Her words were, "Forgiveness is to set a prisoner free, and to realize the prisoner is you."

I tried again to concentrate on the insurance claim in front of me, but that quote kept coming back. Every time it did, I had to blink back tears. I had some people I wouldn't forgive. Did that mean I was guilty—a prisoner?

Today was one of the first days my arm hadn't throbbed with pain. I was determined to make some progress on the three big insurance claims that my boss, Ben Thomas, had emailed to me. Life was returning to normal, whatever that meant.

I scooted my chair forward and peered at the claim in front of me. It was all mixed up. Let's see . . . our company would subrogate . . . forgiveness. What had Clint said? I doodled on a scratch pad while my mind boomeranged between the legal issues in the insurance claim and the sermon.

Again, I attempted to understand the intricacies of the client dispositions. Somehow, I had to resolve the very different stories the insured parties had told me. Any reasonable solution eluded me, and finally, completely frustrated, I shoved the papers aside, grabbed a jacket and walked out to the pasture. Monte shuffled over to get his neck and ears scratched. I wanted to ride, but with only one good arm, I wasn't sure I could saddle him. He was so gentle and well trained I knew I would be fine once I was in the saddle. However, we hadn't been out for a ride since the cougar attack.

I ambled toward the barn and pulled the lever up on the standpipe. Lonnie would be deep into Mexico, on his way to wherever he was going. As I stood watching the water cascade into the metal tank, I asked God to please watch over Lonnie and Brian, and immediately, it seemed He asked me whether I'd forgiven Lonnie—which was completely off the topic.

Chapter 29

LONNIE

THE FOLLOWING MORNING dawned clear and cool. I had no drug cartel bullets in me, which might mean I'd been right about Felix. It might also mean they just hadn't got around to killing me yet, which restarted the churning in my stomach.

I again used my worst broken Spanish to tell the girl at the motel desk that I'd decided to visit the cliff ruins, and that I wanted to keep the room for a few more days. That much palaver was a strain on my supposed tourist babble, but I hoped it would allay any suspicion if I had to keep odd hours pursuing other activities.

I walked down to the bus station and bought a ticket for El Vallacito, the pueblo where I hoped to find Genaro Chacon. The bus didn't leave for an hour, so I walked over to eat at a nearby rustic restaurant. Photos of Pancho Villa competed for wall space with mining relics, rusted rifles, and ancient radios. In this area, Pancho Villa seemed to be more folk hero than bandit, a Mexican Robin Hood who robbed from the rich and gave to the poor. I stared at proud pictures of his last days of mayhem, next to grainy photos of his bullet-riddled body, while I chewed through chorizo, frijoles, and Mexican scrambled eggs. The stark pictures spoke of national pride and death. Maybe it was the Indian in me, but I neither understood, nor had come to terms with either.

On the way back to the bus station, I bought a pair of leather *huaraches* with tire-tread soles. These Tarahumera Indian tennis shoes would be more practical than my boots if I had to do any hiking in the mountains.

Scarcely a half-hour later, the northbound bus deposited me and a dark, stocky woman with two little kids at the dusty intersection into El Vallacito. She wore the bright, colored skirt of the local Indians, and we exchanged polite nods before she shuffled down a trail to the east. I set a brisk gringo pace up the already hot, dirt road to find Genaro. Two miles later, the first buildings came into view. By then, the heat had turned my brisk pace into a Tarahumara Indian shuffle. I stopped at an orange-painted store that had 'mini super' emblazoned in blue across the front and bought a bottle of water. The woman behind the counter took my ten peso coin. I made an instant decision to abandon my short career in tourist Spanish. In this small town, a guy who looked like a Mexican but couldn't speak Spanish would attract way more attention than if I were just a cousin from the coast. In my very best Spanish, I informed her I was from Mazatlán, here to visit my cousin, Genaro Chacon.

"Do you know where he lives?" I asked.

She gave me a long suspicious appraisal before she handed me five pesos in change. "Of course I know where he lives. Up the canyon." She pointed toward the end of the dusty street that wound past the store.

"How far?"

"Oh, maybe one kilometer."

I thanked her, and she pushed the bottle of water across the counter, all the while searching my face. I left the store with a sinking feeling that the cousin lie had been a really bad idea.

Turning toward the canyon, I trudged along a dusty riverbed hemmed by Creosote and Mesquite to find the house of Genaro Chacon. Twenty minutes later, I rounded a bend to see what must be Genaro's Rancho. Three strands of rusty barbed wire defined the grass-challenged yard. Beyond the fence, a worn trail led to the open emerald metal door of a one-story adobe house. Several red chickens pecked at unseen bugs, and a massive black pig rooted around in the side yard. Parked on the east side of the house, a derelict Ford pickup with a definite list to starboard took up what passed for a driveway. Sometime in the late sixties, the pickup had been red and white. Today, there were several other colored body parts, all of them liberally dusted with the burnt ochre of the road.

I rapped my knuckles against the open, green door. Nothing happened.

"Hola?" Is anybody . . . My voice trailed off as a ponderous, wary-eyed woman swayed around the corner and into the breezeway. A dark-eyed little pixie, thumb in her mouth, peeked shyly out from behind the woman's voluminous red skirt.

"Buenos dias." I said my cheeriest good morning, hoping to impress this female battleship with my harmlessness. "Is Genaro at home?"

"He is out back." Her eyes appraised my scrawny frame, as she pointed a sausage-sized thumb toward the backside of the house.

"Gracias." I thanked her and walked through the yard. The huge, black pig lifted her massive head and glared at me.

Warily, I sidled by her, but she only grunted her displeasure at my uninvited presence.

A wiry, light-skinned man of medium height eyed me as I approached the block wall he was building. I searched the high, questioning eyebrows and unsmiling lean face. "Genaro?"

He nodded.

"My name is Lonnie Bowers. I am a friend of your cousin Dora, and her husband. I have come to visit the ruins."

Genaro nodded and muttered a generic Spanish welcome. He seemed unimpressed with my stated objective.

I looked outside the yard, wondering how to continue. "You have a very nice ranch." This produced more warmth, so I questioned him about his agricultural enterprise. He apparently ran a few cows, and kept a small herd of goats. His wife, Teresa, made cheese from the goat's milk and sold it at the central market in Madera, along with a few eggs from her flock of chickens. At the proper intervals, I nodded sagely, feigning a knowledge of goats and chickens which I certainly didn't possess. Twenty minutes later, I cautiously broached the subject of business.

"Genaro, I would like to see the Anasazi and Paquime ruins, but I need a guide. Would you be interested in doing that for me?" He hesitated, perhaps appraising my monetary value. I smiled inwardly. This guy wasn't going to turn down a cash job that just strolled into his yard. Later would be soon enough to discover whether I could trust him with more than a trip into my Indian past.

"I have done that before," he replied. "I could take you in my pickup. However, you must understand, it takes several days to see them all." He paused, likely assessing the most he could charge this supposed friend of his cousin. I waited for the pitch, desperate to make this work.

"I would have to have six hundred pesos for each day. The Anasazi ruins are on a very rough road, and it takes much time to get there."

Six hundred pesos was exorbitant. It was obvious he expected me to beat him down on the price. I kicked the dirt with the toe of my boot, and shoved my hands deep into my pockets, letting the moments drag. Finally, I spoke. "But that is just for the pickup and gas. To have you as a guide, I would certainly have to add another two hundred and fifty pesos. Would that be reasonable?" I asked.

"Yes, yes, of course," he spluttered, overwhelmed by this idiot who had stupidly offered a sudden gold mine. "I had forgotten to add my services as well." A polite and formal handshake sealed the deal. He knew he was being paid a handsome price for his services, and I hoped I'd bought some loyalty, at least until I knew where he stood.

We arranged to meet the following morning at my motel, and I left to flag down the next Madera-bound bus. Tomorrow, we would drive north to Cuarenta Casas to explore the ruins of a people long vanished. Maybe I would get to know the real Genaro Chacon. I had no doubt what the outcome would be if this was a mistake. A quick bullet, if I was lucky. There would be no negative press reports, and everybody, including Stirling Associates would deny I ever existed. That part I knew when I signed on. Brian might then be deemed too great a risk, and he would walk the same plank.

When I arrived back at the motel, I pushed the door to my room inward with a great deal of caution. The maid had been in, and I checked my clothes bag and satchel to see if anything had been tampered with. Everything appeared the same as when I'd left, but Felix still worried me. He was a loose end that could have fatal consequences.

After an early supper in the motel restaurant, I wandered over to the one-room museum next door. The usual pottery, pestles, and shards were on display, the same as one sees in any natural history museum, but the feature piece of this small gallery was the ancient mummy of a twelve-year-old girl. The desert air had dried and preserved the parchment skin, and I was mesmerized by the still intricate detail of her fingers and hands. What had she looked like in life? What had caused her death, and why had she been left unburied in the adobe dwelling where she was found nine hundred years later?

Uncomfortable questions about my own mortality filtered to the surface, and my mind skipped back to another grave I had discovered years ago in another cemetery. The marble stone, yellowed with age, had a haunting sentence carved into it. "As you pass by, remember that as you are, so once was I, and as I am, you soon will be. Prepare well." At the time, I'd stood over that faraway moldering grave, trying to picture the man laid beneath the stone. Who had he been in life? What made him choose that disturbing epitaph?

Contemplating the hereafter made me think about Clarissa, and of course, Brian. Clarissa had said she was praying for us. What did that mean? Did it count for anything? Neither Clarissa nor Brian had any doubts. None of the complexities of Christianity were a problem for them. I couldn't buy it, and I turned away from the dead girl, discouraged with the seeming futility of life.

Sobered by my visit to the museum, I hunched into the chilly mountain wind and walked quickly back to my room.

Still cautious, I unlocked the varnished plank door and peered inside. There were no intruders—yet.

I flipped through the few available TV channels. The only channel that worked carried an insipid movie in Spanish. Soon bored with the juvenile plot, I turned it off, undressed, and tried to sleep. That didn't work either. A raucous Mexican music channel on the TV next door competed with the squeals and laughter of a party well in progress. Things didn't quiet until close to dawn. I fell into a fitful sleep. I dreamed of Brian, and then it changed to Clarissa, or maybe it was God, slamming a varnished door in my face.

Even bad nights end, and I rolled out with a muttered curse at the folks next door who had partied all night. Stumbling through the shower improved my frame of mind. I grabbed some breakfast at the motel café, and by the time Genaro arrived, I was pacing the floor.

The inside of Genaro's five-colored Ford pickup looked better than the outside, and I reckoned we had at least an even chance of making it to the Cuarenta Casas ruins. North from Madera, the desert foliage gives way to the Piñon Pine and Encino forests of the Western Sierra Madre. It was apparent why this wild mountain maze was appealing to Manuel Lourdes. The *barrancos* and canyons would hide a thousand drug smugglers, providing more than adequate cover from the prying eyes of *"la policia"* who often out of fear, and maybe greed, didn't want to stop the flow of money anyway. Manuel flew drugs in and out of here with impunity.

While Genaro drove, I scrutinized the surrounding mountains. Where was Brian in this secretive wilderness? And how was the best way to approach this cousin of Dora's? But this morning, when I needed to see what I'd bought, the cousin was taciturn and silent.

I tried to break the ice. "Genaro, I stayed at Dora and Rock's house last week. They have two wonderful children." I gambled that the supposed Mexican importance of family would open the door to conversation. Genaro only grunted, while he hunched further over the steering wheel, doing his best to avoid the constant battery of potholes.

I settled back into my seat and pulled my hat down. *Good try, Lonnie. What's your next plan?*

My second try was no better than the first. "Genaro, what's your little girl's name?"

"Bonita."

"A pretty name." I waited, hoping he'd embellish his one-word answer. He never, so I soldiered on. "How old is she?"

"Four."

And that's how it was the whole trip. Except for terse answers, Genaro refused to talk, and unless I developed a sudden need to know about ancient Indian culture, I'd just wasted the equivalent of three hundred and fifty George Washington photographs. However, it was too late to change anything. I might as well enjoy the day. I'd paid dearly for it.

We arrived at Cuarenta Casas, apparently the most accessible of the ruins. In Spanish, the name means "forty houses." At one time, there may have been forty of them perched precariously along the cliffs. Nine hundred years later, there were only a handful. Genaro and I walked to the edge of the sweeping canyon redoubt that served to protect the ancient Paquime, and gazed across to the ruins. These people had the same skin, maybe the same heritage and traditions of my mother's people, and an eerie sense of kinship prickled through me.

We took an hour to pick our way to the bottom of the canyon, cross the nearly dry creek and wind our way up to the other side to the adobe structures perched under the cliff overhang. I asked Genaro the names and uses of the different plants. He had an intimate knowledge of each one. Mescal and Sotol were interspersed with Yucca and Spanish Daga. The trees were less varied: the Piño Real that we call Apache Pine vied for space with the leafy Encino. The trees and plants were interesting, but I was more concerned with finding some common ground to establish a relationship with Genaro. I would get nowhere in my quest to find Brian without a whole lot of mutual trust between us, and I had little time to make that happen. Though Rock had said Genaro was reliable, I could not take chances.

When we reached the dwellings, I reverently ran my fingers over the centuries-old adobe and stared awestruck at the squat labyrinth of shelters, all with the signature t-shaped doorways. Far below us the little ribbon of creek snaked along the bottom of the canyon. This center of Paquime commerce and trade was well chosen. A handful of defenders could hold off a small army, and I wondered what had caused these people to abandon their home. The canyon walls had no answer, and when I questioned Genaro, he only shrugged. I wished I'd read Frederick's papers on the Paquime and Anasazi instead of watching TV last night. I resolved to look through them when we arrived back at the motel.

Genaro and I spent two hours at the ruins before winding our way down to the creek and up the other side where he had parked the pickup. Several times I tried to start a conversation with him, and got nowhere. The day had turned into a real zero. Sure, the cliff dwellings were fascinating, and I found myself looking forward to seeing the others; but Genaro was not going to be the man I needed to find Brian.

We arrived at the motel, and I asked Genaro to be there at eight in the morning. I was tired and disappointed, but I might as well take another day to explore. Besides, the guy had already been paid, and no other plan came to mind. And to go back to Frederick, and wait for him to find a new inside man was unacceptable. That would take more months of gathering intelligence—way too risky for Brian. I needed to make something happen now.

Supper in the motel restaurant found me gnawing through the problem of Genaro. The more I chewed, the tougher it got, which seemed my fate, because the slab of Mexican steer on my plate was the same texture.

CHAPTER 30

LONNIE

MY USELESS GUIDE arrived at the motel a few minutes after eight. I slung my canvas mochila into the back of his pickup, and we set off for Huapoca Canyon to see the cave the literature called Cueva de la Serpiente.

After finding the least uncomfortable spot on the lumpy seat, I mulled yesterday's lack of response. He didn't appear any more inclined to conversation today, but it was worth a try. "So why do they call this place the Snake Cave?" I glanced sideways at his wiry form.

He shrugged. "Only because it is full of rattlesnakes. One must be very careful there, especially in the hot summer months. The name has nothing to do with the original people."

My skin crawled. What history I had with rattlesnakes had not been good, which engendered a huge dislike for the slithery reptiles. Suddenly, it hit me. This guy had just belted out a whole sentence. I sneaked a sideways glance at his impassive brown face. What changed? His one sentence was more than he'd said all day on the trip to Cuarenta Casas.

We bounced another mile in silence over that rocky excuse for a road. He maneuvered around an especially treacherous crater, then shocked me again.

"Last night after I dropped you at the motel, I called my cousin Dora. I thought you were just another rich gringo tourist, except you don't look very much like a gringo. You are an Indian?"

I didn't think this was the time or place to debate politically charged names for my ancestors. If Genaro was going to talk, I would be Indian, Mexican, or any other race he thought appropriate.

"I talked to Rock as well. He told me what you are trying to do. I am sorry. I did not know, and of course you could not say. I think I can help you."

The big load I was carrying instantly became a whole lot lighter. Right now, I figured I owed Rock and Dora more than I could ever repay. However, I still had doubts, and I needed to make sure of this guy. My life and maybe Brian's might very well depend on him.

"Thank you Genaro, but . . . why would you do that? You will be in great danger if you help me."

"Yes, I know well what the drug cartels do to people who talk, or get close to their operations, but I also know what drugs have done to my family." Genaro steered around a pothole the size of a Kenworth truck. "The lady at the store who you asked for directions? That is my little sister. I understand you are our cousin from Mazatlan." He gave me a toothy grin. "She said she did not know we had cousins in Mazatlan. I told her of course we did, so now she tells the busybodies in the street that our rich cousin from Mazatlan has arrived on a holiday. That is okay, but some of the words you use, they say differently in Mazatlan, so be careful."

This game I was playing was pregnant with quicksand. I could make a fatal slip just by opening my mouth, even if I did speak the language well.

"My sister's boy Alphonso spent much time when he was younger helping me with the cattle and the goats. He was like a son to me, but like many of our people, he wanted more, so he slipped across the border into the United States. Everything was good. He found a construction job in Los Angeles and sent money home to his mother. That is how she was able to start the store. Then, one day the money stopped coming, and there was no word from Alphonso."

"So what happened?"

"Many months went by before my sister discovered the truth. While Alphonso was working for the construction company, he started using marijuana. Before long, he was hanging around with bad people. He moved on to other drugs and got involved in a prostitution ring to pay for it. They used young women from our country, as well as Guatemala and El Salvador; girls who entered the U.S. without proper papers. Because they were in the country illegally, it was easy to force them into prostitution." Genaro held the wheel with both hands, his knuckles pinpoints of white. "In the end, he died from the 'crystal meth.' An overdose they said. Maybe it was, but I think it was on purpose. I think our Alphonso could not live with himself anymore."

The rattles in the dash covered the long silence. How many stories were there like Alphonso's sad tale? I stared out at the bleak landscape. The drug problems weren't my fault. Besides, they'd never stop them. There wasn't the political will on either side of the border. It was sad, but there was nothing

I could do about it. I'd come for Brian—nothing more.

Genaro spoke again, and for a moment, I wished for yesterday's silence.

"So Lonnie, I wanted you to know why I would risk my life. If I refuse to do what I can, the cartels will continue to kill our children, and the tears of more mothers will cry for vengeance, because—there is no justice."

I fidgeted and crossed my arms, the cab suddenly too small. "Why do you say there is no justice? I'm not sure I understand."

"Of course you understand," Genaro snapped. "Why are you here? Why didn't your people, or the DEA just call up the chief of police in Madera and say, 'Hey chief, we have a problem with Manuel Lourdes? He is flying cocaine into the United States, and we would like you to put him in jail. The chief of police would sound very sad and agree that, yes, Manuel is a big problem, while he smiles and counts the payoff Manuel sends him. "We have no system in our country that will deal with those as rich and powerful as Manuel. Someday it may happen, but not today. So in place of justice I seek retribution—for my country, my nephew Alphonso, and for my sister Julie."

I was both shamed and grateful. This man's loyalty was not for sale. He'd been baptized into the drug wars long before I ever showed up, and he likely would be in it after I returned to my simpler and safer world of broncs and bulls.

When we arrived at the trail head, Genaro parked his Ford with the nose pointing down the hill. "Sometimes it doesn't start," he apologized.

I didn't think it necessary to point out that I was amazed every time it did start.

We stepped out, and I lifted the sagging door and pushed it closed. The steep canyon trail that led down to Cueva de la Serpiente lay ahead of us, and we picked our way down the rocky slope. Halfway to the bottom we came to a flat spot. Several wheelbarrow-size boulders served as a cheap barrier to the precarious drop-off on our left. Genaro rested his foot on one of them while he gazed into the distance. "Rock told me about your friend. You think Manuel kidnapped him?"

"I don't know for sure, but we do know Manuel is flying cocaine into the Big Hatchet Mountains in New Mexico. Somewhere he's found an exceptional pilot to make that happen. It could be Brian. We know that Manuel is using a Cessna 180. Brian's plane is a 180, so it could be him."

"So how are you going to find out?"

"I'm not sure . . ." I hedged, worried that Genaro would refuse to help me. What I was going to ask was perhaps more than he was prepared to risk. Either way, I needed an answer. "I need to find Manuel's hideout, see if Brian is there, and gather the necessary intelligence so we can send in a team to rescue him."

"And this team? Their objective is to extricate Brian, and eliminate Manuel Lourdes? In that order?"

"Umm . . . I guess I don't really know about that."

Genaro looked me square in the eye, his voice soft in the canyon silence. "I need to know the answer, Lonnie. Probably both of us do."

My eyes wanted to slide away, but he held them, and I knew before we went a step further, I was going to have to tell Genaro everything. He deserved complete honesty because if he helped me and we failed, it could cost him his life.

We sat on a couple of russet boulders while I explained

that *my* first priority was getting Brian out, which probably differed from Stirling Associates' agenda. He listened without comment, but the uncertainty in his eyes was obvious. Abruptly, he left and padded farther down the switchback trail, hands in his pockets while he stared into the brushy bottom of the canyon. Heat waves radiated from the towering rock bluffs to the east; the afternoon silence unbroken except for the soft coo of a nearby dove. I waited, sensing there was more to Genaro's decision than I understood. Later, as he walked back up the trail, I watched his face, fearful of his decision.

"I think you understand what it means for me if I take you to Manuel's mountain drug operation. If anything goes wrong, I am a dead man. Maybe my wife and children also, as a lesson to others. I think you are a man of your word, but I do not know this Stirling Associates or Frederick Roseman. I want you to promise that no matter what else happens, the first priority will be to take out Manuel Lourdes. He cannot be left to seek revenge on my family."

I don't know how I expected Genaro to reply to my request for help, but I hadn't expected this. He'd cut to the core of the issue with knife-like precision. He was willing to do what he felt was right, but he wanted some assurance his family might come through this alive. How could I answer? There wasn't one chance in a million of finding Brian without Genaro, but if I used his help, then I had a responsibility to him, one which would weigh as heavily as my loyalty to Brian. It was my turn to mull through how I would respond. I didn't have so much as a slingshot to protect either of us, yet if we were to continue, I had to give some guarantees. How could I guarantee that Manuel Lourdes would be destroyed? Whatever I said now could affect the lives of this man and his family.

The rodeo arena had given me no preparation for that, and there was nobody to turn to for advice.

Frederick certainly hadn't given me the authority to commit to the decision I was going to make, but I did it anyway. Whatever the cost, we were going to protect Genaro. Brian would have made the same decision. He'd want it that way.

"You have my word." I stood, reached across the distance between us and gave Genaro my hand.

He clasped it, then spoke abruptly. "We can go to Manuel's mountain airstrip tomorrow night."

"You know where this hideout is located?"

He laughed contemptuously. "When planes take off in the mountains at night, it makes everybody curious. People whisper, everyone knows, but to talk is not a good thing, especially to strangers. The drug cartels have a saying. *Plata o plomo.* It means—take the bribe, or take the bullet. They have many bullets for those who would dare to speak of their activities. Manuel spends much money to buy silence from the people. We have many nice things in our village. Our church is grander than any of those in the pueblos around us. We have a new school building for our children. All of it is easy to justify, and we are quick to be blind to the source of the money. We shrug our shoulders, and pretend we have no choice. However, we are wrong, and unless we stand against the evil, it will consume us."

I squatted on my heels and sifted red dirt through my fingers. Stark restaurant photos of the bandit-turned-hero, Pancho Villa, paraded through my mind. This struggle of greed and power was as old as Mexico—as ancient as man. Nothing I could do would ever change it; but even if Brian wasn't here, or if he was already dead—it didn't mean I could walk away.

Genaro stared toward the caves while my fingers toyed with the earth running through my hands, both of us pensive, less than eager to step into the uncertain and dangerous future that lay ahead. His eyes flickered over my face, and he nodded toward the canyon. "Today we go down there to try to understand the Anasazi past. Tomorrow night, we will do what must be done to make a better future for our children."

I reached over and again took his calloused, farmer hand. It was a commitment that surely weighed heavy for both of us.

CHAPTER 31
LONNIE

GENARO AND I shouldered our packs, and for a short time tried to forget about tomorrow as we picked our way down the trail into Huapoca Canyon. For being just a mesquite goat rancher, his knowledge of the Anasazi and the Cueva de la Serpiente was more than respectable.

"Will there be rattlesnakes in the caves this time of the year?" I was already watching where I placed my feet.

He looked up at the hot sun, and shrugged. "We will see."

The ancient adobe dwellings were graced with the same t-shaped doors we had seen at the Paquime ruins. Again, I stared in awe, and wondered. Where had these people come from? How had they lived? Did they die from disease, or had a stronger tribe annihilated them? Were they the first, or were there others on the land before them? There were no answers to my questions, but it seemed likely these nomads had come to conquer and be conquered, as others had before them. I followed in silent awe, as the wind wailed and moaned through the rocks and canyons with a lonesome dirge to these people long vanished. But the kinship I expected to feel didn't happen; only curiosity, and a desire to know and understand the Anasazi's time on the earth.

"Where did they go?" My voice was a reverent whisper in the eerie silence.

"I am not an educated man," Genaro said. "But I have heard it said that the Anasazi didn't disappear, that they are the ancestors of your Pueblo cousins in the United States. I don't think that is so, because they and the Paquime we visited yesterday would never have abandoned their homes. They left in a quick and violent way. Another stronger tribe annihilated them, probably to control the trade routes. The conquerors assimilated the more desirable women into the tribe, and killed the rest. That is the way of war the world over. I do not think you red men were any nobler than the rest of us." He turned with a sly grin, but I found no argument against his reasoning.

At the first dwelling, I stuck my head through the doorway. The instant "chirr" of a coiled rattlesnake on the floor made me jerk violently away. I'd forgotten the snakes.

Genaro chuckled. "That is why they call it the Snake Cave. They are always here when it is hot." I had no more desire to see the inside of the dwellings. The rattlesnakes could slither around, undisturbed. We turned and faced the heat of the canyon and the long climb up to Genaro's rusted-out pickup.

The trip back to my motel room in Madera was spent planning the next night's trek into the mountain hideout west of El Vallacito. The time had come to search out the answers I had come to Mexico to find. Whether Brian was there or not, if Genaro and I were caught, we would disappear. There would be few if any repercussions for Manuel Lourdes. Even if there were, it wouldn't help us. We would be dead.

Genaro dropped me at the hotel with instructions to be

ready at noon. We would start into the mountains early to get the worst of the six-hour trip behind us before dark. Some of our trek would have to be by moonlight, and it would be hard going through that rough country, especially if there was substantial cloud cover. However, the last part of the trail was apparently well worn, pounded into the red earth by the *burros,* the peasant farmers who carried in the Columbian cocaine from the large ranch airstrip tucked next to the mountains north of Madera.

After picking up the cocaine, the *burros* were supposed to split up and wind their way alone through the mountains. That way, if there was a bust, *los federales* would only capture a small portion of the drugs. But Manual paid the right people and supported the right causes. Everybody was making money. The *burros* had been left alone, so according to Genaro, they all used the same trail. And why not? No local police would dare to mess with Manuel Lourdes. That would start a war local law enforcement had long ago lost. The cartels would make sure nothing changed.

I ate supper at the little motel restaurant and babbled to anybody who would listen about the magnificent adobe dwellings at Cueva de la Serpiente. I presumed that was what a tourist would do. My performance seemed to have made a suitable impression on the waiter and three other guests in the dining area, and I made sure they were well-informed of my plans for tomorrow. I would be leaving early in the morning for an overnight trip to Sirupa Canyon to visit more ruins. Where Genaro and I were going, we needed no suspicious outsiders.

CHAPTER 32

CLARISSA

TUESDAY MORNING, THE INSURED met me at the still smoking crater filled with the blackened appliances, charred beams, and ash of his once upscale home. I held out my hand. "I'm Clarissa Bowers with Guardian Insurance. I'll be handling your claim."

"Bruno Trembley." The handshake was awkward, flaccid, a complement to the narrow, weak mouth and furtive eyes.

I moved toward the remains of the burned structure. "I'm sorry about your loss. Fire destroys so many things one can never replace." I faced him, and tried to look past the gold earrings and other heavy male jewelry. "You were living in the house?"

"Yeah."

"Anybody else?"

"Just me and my woman."

"No children?"

"Nope."

I took notes as I ran through my standard list of questions. They were items I needed to know for the file, but more important; they gave me time to watch the client, to get a feel for the truthfulness of his statements. I ticked off three pages of standard answers. None of them were red flags.

For a moment, I gazed out over the gaping crater, my next question delivered in the same toneless vanilla flavor as the rest. "How did the fire start?" I listened for the smallest nuance, or change in tone or pattern. That question was often a trigger for the real investigation.

"It was a short in the electrical panel. I flipped a breaker, and poof—up she went." The response was immediate—and a lie.

I deliberately slid my pen into my clipboard, crossed my arms and let the silence drag to the uncomfortable stage. I closed the file and crossed my arms.

"I'm pretty sure that's what it was. There were sparks everywhere." His voice pitched higher.

I walked three feet closer to the open hole—and waited. His story still rang false.

"What—you don't believe me?"

"How soon did you want to start to rebuild?" I turned toward him and smiled as if I hadn't heard the last question.

"Well . . . what if we just took a cash settlement? We're thinking about moving away, so that's what we want."

"We don't usually do that, but . . ."

"We'd take a discount and . . ." his voice trailed off and his eyes shifted away.

"Perhaps we could . . . let's see." I opened the clipboard, as if I was referring to my notes, again dragging out the silence.

"How soon could you pay us?" He shifted from one foot to the other, his hands busy rattling loose change in his pockets.

Caution signals plinged through the insurance adjuster part of my brain. "Mr. Trembley, I can recommend our company pay that cash settlement. I can also deny the claim . . ."

"You can't do that." His face reddened, but his eyes were furtive, wide with fear.

I shrugged. "Your option then is to sue our company." I stepped back from the cavernous hole. "Mr. Trembley, this was not an electrical fire. And now I need you to tell the truth. Who torched your house?"

The red face in front of me paled. "I . . . I didn't do it. It wasn't me. How do you know?"

"My job is to know." I wheeled and walked to my car. Opening the door, I threw the clipboard onto the seat, and looked at my watch. "I'm waiting, Mr. Trembley."

***

CLAUSE BY CLAUSE, I slogged through the necessary paper-work to pay out the cash settlement the client had requested. Bruno Trembley was a drug dealer. For whatever reason, he was behind on his payments to the big boys. So as a warn-ing—they torched his house. Next, they would come for him. To survive, he needed cash, and a ticket to anonymity.

This claim was my closest exposure to the real drug world. I'd seen at least a half-dozen marijuana grow-operations, and the devastation they caused. But I'd never been exposed to the trademark violence and debilitating fear the drug trade ruthlessly maintained throughout their spidery networks. Since that afternoon with Bruno Trembley, fear for Lonnie and Brian gripped my every waking moment.

I shivered, though the afternoon sun had unusual warmth for this time of the year, as it streamed through the office win-dow. Enough insurance work. I closed the file and shut down my computer. Today I was going to ride, or at least try. I wondered. With only one usable arm, could I even get a saddle on Monte? It was time to find out.

Both horses ambled up from the pasture, and I caught Monte and tied him to the hitch-rail. He stood hipshot, half asleep, while I combed the tangles out of his mane and tail, then brushed the dust out of the rest of his coat. The saddle pad went on easily. The tough part would be to get the saddle situated properly. On my first attempt, I tried to hold the saddle with my left hand while boosting it up with my knee. I succeeded in smacking poor Monte a solid blow in the ribs before it slid to the ground. The pad slid off on the other side and Monte skittered away, no doubt wondering what he'd done to deserve that. I petted and soothed his hurt feelings. After two more unsuccessful attempts, I got the saddle in place and cinched up, still apologizing and trying to pet some good humor back into him.

As I led Monte into the yard, I remembered something a wonderful old friend had told me. Doc Stone had come out to tend to a wire cut on Monte. He'd stitched and powdered his upper leg, and while Doc was putting his needles and sutures away, he'd turned to me. In his gruff old voice, he'd said, "You don't need to worry about him. Horses are healin' creatures."

I slipped the bit between Monte's teeth and thought, *yes; horses are not only healin' creatures; horses are forgiving creatures.* Monte wouldn't hold a grudge against me for whacking him in the ribs with the saddle, not once, but three times. He wouldn't lash out in anger because I'd tightened the cinch too much, or maybe bumped his teeth with the bit. However much I'd wronged him, he just sought to understand, to do what pleased me, and to go where I asked him to go.

I picked up the reins and led him around the yard before hoisting my one-armed body into the saddle. Panting with the exertion, I pointed him toward the mountain trail where it all happened. But with each prancing step, I mulled through Monte's almost automatic forgiveness for my clumsy, inept saddling. He would remember what I'd done. He might sidle away the next time I heaved the saddle at him, but he would hold no resentment. There seemed a lesson there, but I purposed to leave that for another day.

CHAPTER 33
LONNIE

ELEVEN PACES WAS THE LENGTH of that motel room, and I figured there were at least that many things that could go wrong. The problem was I had little power to change the course of any of the coming events. If we were discovered, I had no weapons. If we had to run for it, I had to depend on Genaro to guide us out of the mountains. How loyal would he be if we ran into trouble? I hoped not to find out, but the whole plan was ludicrous. My life and Brian's were in the hands of a man I'd known for less than three days, a man on whom I had to depend on for everything. The whole concept ran contrary to my nature, and training.

About noon, Genaro's cranky old pickup rattled into the motel courtyard. After yesterday, it was down to half a muffler, but we passed half a dozen others just as noisy on our way through Madera.

I pulled my hat lower over my face, not that there was any need. My complexion was no different than a hundred other men on the street, and a good many of them wore the same boots and brand of jeans. I didn't have to pretend to be a cowboy, so I'd not drawn any undue attention. Frederick did have that figured right. And though my Spanish wasn't perfect, it was better than passable.

"The plan—it had to be changed." Genaro accelerated onto the El Vallacito highway. "We will wait until just before sunset to leave. We will have a guide for part of the way."

I swiveled toward him, instantly suspicious. "Why? And who is this guide?" I didn't need this last-minute change. The plan had been to leave earlier in order to get the worst of the trip behind us before darkness set in. And one more person knowing why I was here, and what I was doing, was one too many.

"My wife's cousin will take us part way. He says it is too risky to be on the trail in the daytime. The night belongs to the *burros*, but he says if we run into trouble, we will have a much better chance to get away without being recognized. Also, he knows that part of the mountains better than I do, so if we have to leave the trail, he would be able to take us another way. I could not do that."

That sounded reasonable. Genaro was probably taking care of us. I just hoped he was right about this relative. Though I would pay the cousin well, we had to hope he was helping on principle. If it was only cash he was looking for, we were going to come up on the short end. Manuel could and *would* out-pay us.

We arrived at Genaro's adobe canyon house and walked to the door. His wife blocked our entry with the ferocious black eyes of a mama grizzly. A work-worn finger the size of my thumb stabbed an inch from my face. Her face was dark with anger, and she started on me in rapid, bitter Spanish.

"You! You are bringing us much trouble. Do you think

the few pesos you have given to my husband will replace him after *El Lobo* kills him? You will get what you want and leave. And if Genaro survives, we will have to live here in this village always afraid that someone will tell Manuel who it was that betrayed him. Every night, I will worry. If my husband comes home late from the cattle, I will wonder if he is dead. If they cut out his tongue, if . . ." She turned away, unable to hold her tears. Raw terror lay behind her anger, and I began to understand the gravity of what I had asked. I walked to the door, sobered by the danger I'd brought to them. No one had the right to ask for the sacrifice Teresa might make. I would have to find another way.

Genaro held up his hand. "Wait. This is hard for my Teresa. Drugs have taken much from her. Please, excuse me for a minute." He followed Teresa inside, and I wandered out to the ramshackle corrals. I needed help. How would I find Brian without Genaro?

Three skinny crossbred Brahma cows were shaded up under a couple of gnarled Encinos. The herd of goats was nowhere to be seen, and the only other livestock was the giant black sow, tied to a tree by one of the ramshackle sheds. I found a sawn-off stump and joined the cows in the miserly bit of shade provided by the towering Encinos.

Later, Genaro walked down from the house. "Please, accept my apologies for our lack of hospitality. Teresa is very afraid and upset with what we are planning to do. She thinks it is too dangerous, but a man has to do what is right." He shrugged. "Nothing has changed. This is my duty."

In that sandy barnyard perched on the very edge of the Sierra Madre, I gained a lot of respect for a Mexican goat farmer. There were no words I could say that wouldn't embarrass both of us, but my hand rested briefly on his shoulder. If the world had more of this man's courage, there would be no place for the drug lords to peddle their white death.

"Come," he said. "Teresa has made some *horchata*. It is refreshing on a hot afternoon."

I followed Genaro inside, unsure of my reception, still ready to call everything off. We sat at the wood-topped dining room table. Teresa set tall glasses with a milky liquid in front of us. Silently, she averted her eyes, refusing to look at me. Slowly, I sipped at the sweet vanilla liquid. Concern for Genaro and his family were now added to my worry about Brian. If we were caught, all of us would die.

Genaro pushed his glass away. "We have a difficult night ahead. You should rest. We will have to push very hard to be back here by dawn." I drained the last of the *horchata* and stood. He led out to the breezeway which split the kitchen and wash area from the rest of the house. A hammock swayed between two wooden posts, and he gestured toward it. "There. No one will bother you."

I thanked him and eased onto the edge to pull my boots off. Sleeping in a hammock was not a skill I'd developed in my years of riding broncs and bulls, but I managed to get in the middle of it, and promptly decided the Mexican siesta in the heat of the day made a lot of sense.

I slept longer than I intended and woke up groggy and grouchy. That wasn't anything new, or so Clarissa would have said. She seemed a million miles away. I wanted desperately to talk to her before we started into Manuel Lourdes' stronghold tonight, but of course that wasn't possible. Again, a seed of fear stirred inside me, and I wiped my sweaty palms onto my pants. This was a hundred times more dangerous than the worst headhunter bull or chute-fighting bronc. These guys had machine guns, and I hadn't ever had to deal with them.

I rolled over the side of the hammock and yelped as it dumped me onto the floor. Teresa came around the corner and covered her mouth, trying to hide the mirth, but it broke through and we both laughed together.

"Come," she gestured toward the little dining area. "I have fixed *cena* for you and Genaro." We sat at their little kitchen table and tied into Maria's delicious *empanadas* washed down with more *horchata*.

As the hot Mexican sun flirted with the far blue ridges of the Sierra Madre, I strapped on my new Mexican *huarache* tennis shoes. We filled our light *mochilas* with water and a couple more of the *empanadas*, and because the mountain nights can be near freezing, I threw in my denim jacket.

Genaro led us through the corrals and into the bottom of a dry, sandy wash. "Pepe will meet us on the trail."

I didn't say anything. Teresa's cousin was a big concern. Could I trust Genaro's judgment? Though he'd given me no reason not to, I was jittery and uncomfortable with what might lie ahead.

Single file and quiet, we followed the west-running trail. Within the hour, dusk obscured the uneven track, and Genaro moved slower as he followed the dry wash into a canyon, then over the top and into another rocky creek bed. We took great care to stay off the skyline, especially when the bright three-quarter moon favored us with light. Occasionally the scudding clouds danced across the night sky and pitched us into blackness. Though Genaro knew the trail, the periods of inky blackness slowed our progress.

What we followed were the wandering trails of the desert-savvy cattle, tracks that mostly led to tiny springs, or mountain reservoirs of water. Without light, the rough and uneven track was difficult to navigate. Nevertheless, I was thankful we weren't out on the cactus-strewn flatlands. There, a misstep had immediate harsh and painful consequences.

After an hour on the trail, Genaro stopped, and we rested at the bottom of a sandy draw. He spoke, his voice little more than a whisper. "We will follow this about three more miles until we intersect the main route, the *burro* trail. Pepe will be waiting for us there. He will take us into the mountains, close to the hideout."

I nodded. There was little to say. I had to follow and trust, and I hadn't a good record at either.

Genaro shouldered his pack and we again struggled up the north side of a brush-clogged canyon. After another half-hour of climbing, he angled up the side of a wash. Though I could see no trail, he never hesitated. When we reached the top of the ridge, he held to a northwesterly direction, climbing always higher into the mountains. The canyons all ran nearly straight east and west, so with our northwest bearing, we had to descend into the brush-choked bottoms, and follow them until we came to a suitable route up the other side. Though the night was pleasantly cool at this high altitude, the work was exhausting. At one point, at the bottom of one of the sandy washes, Genaro signaled a short breather.

"How much farther until we meet this Pepe?" I panted.

"One more hour—maybe less," he replied. "Soon we will be on the plateau. It will be easier there."

Forty-five minutes later, we scrambled up the last shale slope and broke out onto the plateau. An old game trail, faint with disuse, made the travel easier. Somewhere ahead of us, a

fox yelped. Genaro went down on one knee and made a strangled sound, like a crying baby with laryngitis.

I chuckled, recognizing the cry of a wounded rabbit, an
old remembered sound from somewhere back when I was a
boy. I wasn't the only Indian on this trail.

"Shh…!" He held up his hand for quiet. The fox yapped
again, and Genaro moved ahead, alert and ready. A few hundred yards down the trail, a figure stepped from behind some
juniper, and we met Pepe.

Genaro introduced us. The man's only acknowledgement
of my presence was a curt nod. The moon sulked behind a
blanket of cloud, which meant I couldn't see the new face I
was forced to trust. Pepe and Genaro squatted in the trail and
talked. I tried to peer through the gloom while I listened for
any voice inflection from this Pepe that would warn of du-
plicity and trouble ahead.

"How far is the airstrip from here?" Genaro asked.

"Five miles, more or less," Pepe shrugged, "About three
miles from here is the start of what we call the cocaine trail. I
will take you to there, but no further. We have discussed this,
Genaro. I will not risk my life for an Americano."

I shivered with the cold and heightened tension. Good.
The sooner we got rid of Pepe, the safer I would feel.

We moved out with Pepe now in the lead. I glanced at my
watch. Ten o'clock. Genaro and I had been on the trail for
three hours. We needed to be at the site by midnight if we
were going to make it back before dawn. To have someone
see Genaro with me, a stranger, dragging into his Ranchita
after a night in the mountains would cause talk, which could
be fatal. I grumbled to myself, while I deliberated on the hundred ways Brian was going to pay for getting us into this mess.

Though I still had reservations about Pepe; hearing the conversation between him and Genaro gave me a better understanding. Pepe found no redemption in risking his life to slow the flow of drugs and death. He was here as a favor to Genaro, and of course—money. I understood. I just hoped he wouldn't sell us out. Pepe and Genaro might have been thrown together as relatives, but they were miles apart in conviction and courage.

An hour later, we hit the deep rut of the cocaine trail. Even a city Indian like me could see there had been a steady stream of *huaraches* up and down this track. We stepped into it and from there it was easy going. Within a mile, the trail snaked down into a deep canyon. It followed the bottom for another mile before moving toward the north side of the canyon floor where it hopscotched its way to the south wall, then zigzagged to the top.

Before we started the ascent of the north wall, Pepe stopped. He and Genaro whispered a few words. Pepe then turned and disappeared. We were on our own. I was glad to be rid of him.

"How much farther?" I asked.

Genaro put his finger to his lips. "Pepe says the airstrip is very near to the top of the rim."

The trail up the north wall looked to me like a planned suicide, with only the fickle three-quarter moon for light. Carved by wind, water, and perhaps the ancient Anasazi, it switch-backed up the face to the top, eight hundred feet above our heads. At the first switchback, I looked over the edge. The straight drop to the bottom made my stomach turn over twice, and I focused on the trail at my feet. We were silent, both of us cautious, not knowing how close we might be to the mountain hideout. Sound carried far in this high mountain air. Once, when the moon disappeared behind a cloud, I dislodged a small rock. We both froze while it bounced and echoed its way to the canyon floor.

Halfway to the top of the canyon wall, a guttural laugh broke the night silence. Panic gripped me. We stood rooted in the trail, frozen by the sound of the voices at the top of the wall. It had to be the *burros* making their way down the narrow trail in the moonlight. Once they broke over the top, they would instantly spot us. We were caught like two mice on a pool table, with not a pocket in sight.

Chapter 34

LONNIE

Genaro and I stared at the top of the cliff, then at each other. He signaled for me to follow—as if I had any other choice. We tiptoed down the narrow track, careful to make no sound that would carry on the clear night air. There was no way we could make it to the bottom. They'd pick us off as easy as two crows on a wire.

Fifty feet back, a small niche, hollowed out over the centuries, had widened the trail to maybe five feet. A few steps further, it abruptly narrowed again. Maybe . . . if there was no moon—which there was. Perhaps if there was heavy cloud cover? There wasn't. This was not going to work.

The niche was a crazy, dangerous choice, but we didn't have any other. There was no way we could get all the way to the bottom without them seeing us, and we sure couldn't go up. I inched my way in to the wide spot, both of us silent shadows, illuminated by that way too brilliant Mexican moon. To kick a rock loose now would be disastrous.

The *burros* started down from the rim, their progress marked by the occasional voice, clear in the mountain stillness.

I wished now we'd tried for the bottom. At least there, we'd have some chance of escape. Here, there was none, and each minute seemed an eternity. The wind-scoured rock gouged into my back. I was doing my best to become a part of it. If even one of the *burros* glanced sideways when they went by, we were done for.

I sneaked a glance up at the brilliant three-quarter moon, because our only hope was if a cloud obliterated it. There were some to the east, right in line, but they'd never cover that wretched moon fast enough to help us. As much as I tried, I couldn't drag my eyes from the stomach-churning chasm on the other side of the trail.

My mind raced in frantic, useless circles. What reason could we give for our presence? What could we say to keep them from shooting us, or throwing us over the edge? That terrifying fall would be a hundred times worse than being shot. Without a doubt, one of them would know Genaro. He had no business here, so it would go hard on him, and probably his family as well. How many would there be? Could we fight our way out? Some, if not all, would be armed. We didn't have much of a chance, but I determined if I went over that ledge, at least two of them were coming with me.

My mind darted to Clarissa. For the ten thousandth time, I wished I could go back and atone for those bad chapters in our lives. Everything I could have said at her house . . . I should have told her . . . the voices sounded louder, and I pressed harder against the rock at my back. I wondered. Had she said that prayer? Now would be an opportune time. Maybe I could make a deal with God. If He got us off this mountain alive, I would take a run at Christianity. But the words wouldn't come. It was too phony. How do you make a deal with a God who doesn't even exist?

I shivered with the tension and cold, more sure than ever we were minutes away from death. The clear sound of their voices floated down to us on the still mountain air. They were only yards away, and there were too many of them for us to have a chance. I stared at the moon, bright, and big as a beach ball. In that light, we stood out like neon cutouts against the brown sandstone cliff behind us.

Ten feet before they got to our hollowed-out recess, whoever was in the lead told everybody to stop, then said something about having to retie his *huaraches*. A good number of the Tarahumera locals still wore the old sandals that had a long crisscross lace to keep them snug. I sneaked a glance at the moon, and tried by force of will to speed the cloud cover. As a kid, I'd gone to Sunday school a few times. One of the stories I remembered had some crazy Israelites following a cloud and fire into the desert. We didn't have any fire, but if that guy would just take a minute longer to retie his sandals, we sure enough might have our own special cloud.

Hardly daring to breathe, I glanced at Genaro. Like me, he was spread-eagled against the rock; eyes riveted to the dark cumulus cloud as it obliterated the bright light of that tropical moon, seconds before eight *huarache* shod Mexicans trooped by us, all of them close enough to reach out and touch. They continued down the cliff trail and disappeared into the red pine at the bottom.

I exhaled and slid down the wall, drained by the tension. "Genaro," I whispered, "I don't know what you think, but that cloud cover saved our butts."

"No." Genaro breathed. He made the sign of the cross. "God saved us."

I wasn't sure about that, but neither did I argue. And in case it was Him that saved us, I muttered a grateful thanks.

Still shaky from the narrow escape, we edged our way carefully to the top. If Pepe was right, Manuel's hideout was close. There might be sentries, and I had no intention of running into one out of carelessness. I'd likely used up any credit or goodwill I had with whoever was up there on the other side of that moon. And the moon? It sailed across the night sky with not a cloud in sight, and had from the moment we'd been pinned to the canyon wall, which seemed a strange coincidence.

The trail from the top ran straight as an arrow along the side of a razor-sharp ridge, but we moved farther up the hill and Indianed through the prickly pear and catclaw, away from the trail and any watchful guards.

A thick band of pine at the end of the ridge almost hid the entrance to a long box canyon. The ground lay flat in front of us, smooth enough to be an airstrip except for the scattered brush that ran most of the length of it. Excitement shot through me at the possibility of being close to Brian. If I could find him tonight, maybe we would get out of here. However, there wasn't a building in sight, and certainly no plane. Puzzled, I glanced at Genaro. He nodded at my whispered question. Yes, this was exactly where Pepe had said it would be.

We made our way further toward the head of the canyon, then bellied through the rocks to a brush-covered mound. The still night air brought no sound other than the odd small desert animal, and far off, a yappy coyote. I scanned both sides of the canyon for a partially hidden building. A major drug operation was supposed to be working out of here, yet there was nothing except that long stretch of flat brush-clogged ground. For a half-hour, we laid on that mound, listening for any unusual sound, watching for movement or lights in the distance.

Weariness crept into me. The fast pace through the brush-choked draws compounded by the heart-stopping stress of meeting the *burros* on the canyon trail had sapped my last bit of energy. But what now?

Suddenly, the deep thrum of an airplane engine broke the stillness. I grinned at Genaro. We were lying right on top of a hidden airplane hangar. Below us, a pair of well-camouflaged doors ratcheted away from the base. They were decorated with the brush the Mexicans call Tascate. A familiar Cessna 180 taxied outside. The dash panel lights were bright enough to silhouette Brian in the left-hand seat.

It took all the control I had not to run down to that plane and hug the guy. I don't know why. Maybe it was just because he'd had the good sense to stay alive. A swarthy Mexican filled the right-hand seat, a stubbed-off AR15 propped on his lap.

When the plane turned toward the runway, Brian looked right at me, though I know he couldn't see us on the mound. His face was vague and indistinct against the shadowy lights from the cabin. He looked tired and the chiseled planes of his face seemed sharper, but it was hard to tell in the darkness. I clenched my fists in the dirt, reminding myself to keep my head down and stay calm. I wouldn't do Brian any good by running out in front of a machine gun.

The plane taxied out onto the long flat. Immediately, dim lights flickered down the runway. While I'd concentrated on the plane, the scattered brush had disappeared. It was all fake, probably nothing more than cardboard cutouts to disguise the strip from the air.

Within seconds, Brian had the plane off the ground. He banked north, then headed through a gap and disappeared. The runway lights were extinguished, and we could hear voices coming toward where we lay on the mound. I counted eight men moving through the darkness. Was that everybody on the site, or were there more? Before the men reached the hangar doors below us, they veered into a clump of thick Manzanita and disappeared. There had to be an entrance behind that wall of brush, because they didn't show again, and the voices faded to nothing.

I glanced over at Genaro and whispered, "I need to see what's down there."

Genaro shook his head. "It's too dangerous."

"Yeah, but I've got to find out if there are any more men, and how well they're armed."

"Alright," Genaro shrugged. "Let's go, if we must."

"No . . . you stay here. If there's trouble, somebody needs to go for help."

Everything in me screamed not to go into whatever was behind that wall of brush. But my job was to give Frederick's team the best chance I could give them to extricate Brian. They had to know what they were up against; the precise layout of the facility. I had no choice.

I scooted closer to Genaro. "Listen, if I'm not back within thirty minutes, get out of here as fast as you can. Call this number. A man will answer. You will give him a code number and identify yourself as 'Felix Two.' Then say, 'Come for supper. Tonight, the quail are ready.'"

"That is all?" Genaro asked. "What does it mean?"

"It's a coded message for them to bring in the big guns as quick as they can get them here. They'll tell you what to do from there. Now, repeat the phone number and the code." The phone number was easy for him, because he could say that in Spanish, but the code had to be repeated in English. There was only one 'r' in it, so the way he said it was recognizable, but even in our present danger, I couldn't help but grin at his version of the unfamiliar American words, and for a moment, it eased the tension.

I slid my pack off and crawled down the slope. At the bottom, the hangar doors were still open. I eased inside, hoping to avoid the brush entrance to the right.

The room was typical, wide enough for a small aircraft, and of course empty. At the back, a closed man-door led into what must be another room. I held my ear against it. No sound. I eased it open a crack. A murmur of distant voices echoed from somewhere ahead. I placed each foot carefully as I moved forward in the darkness. My eyes adjusted to the gloom, enough I could see the plastic bags stacked against the walls like common bags of cement powder. I ran my hand over one. They were undoubtedly filled with cocaine.

A wider entrance at the far end revealed a large natural cavern. The voices, now louder, indicated they were directly ahead of me. I slid closer to the doorway, every nerve screaming danger. But, I needed one peek around that corner.

The rock wall was rough on my face as I slid my cheekbone an inch at a time until I could see into the room. At its widest point, it was probably forty feet. The length was at least the same distance. The mottled, rusty rock floor had an occasional sparkle of perhaps richer metals embedded in its surface, but what held my attention were the men sprawled around the room. Again, I counted eight; four of them playing cards at a trestle table, the others hunched around a smoky fire flickering on the far side of the room. The only other lights were a few candles. Farther back and against the left wall, several hammocks were strung between a half-dozen army-issue metal bunks. I scrutinized them for more bodies. There were no others. But where would they hold Brian? There must be a secure cell farther back in the cave. My eyes darted back and forth. That would be difficult for the commandos to reach. The safest for Brian would be for them to neutralize this bunch when Brian was gone with the plane. When he landed, they could easily take out the single gunman who flew with him.

I'd seen enough. It was too dangerous to stay longer. I slid back along the wall. A massive shadow blocked my way. I tried to duck away from the movement I sensed in front of me. I was too slow. Pain blasted through my head—and that's the last I knew.

CHAPTER 35
CLARISSA

MONTE TOSSED HIS HEAD and pulled at the bit, wanting to run, but I held him to a steady trot up the first part of the Farwell Canyon trail. When we reached the fork that led to Cinnamon Gulch his ears twitched, swiveling to pinpoint the slightest sound. Nostrils flared, he tested the wind for any scent of his feared enemy. He hadn't forgotten. Neither had I. We both had some spooks to exorcise, an important process for me, but just as essential for Monte. The trail narrowed as we switch backed higher on the mountain, and the afternoon breeze calmed to a whisper, for which I was thankful. The last time we had been here, there had been a high wind blowing straight away from us, enough that Monte hadn't caught the cougar scent until too late. This, our first return to the mountain, was much easier without added weather complications.

Monte snorted a protest, and probably my uneasy laugh did nothing to quiet him. The issue was clear in his mind. He wanted nothing to do with this trail. The fear was still fresh enough that now, each step I coaxed him forward, became a small victory. A big rock ahead of us worried him. He stopped, front feet ready to whirl, every sense alert for danger. I petted his neck and let him stand. After a few minutes, he moved ahead a few steps without any urging from me. It was as if he was saying, "I don't know why you want me to go here, but I will trust your judgment—for now."

Even as I tried to encourage him, my rein hand trembled. He warily scanned every tree and rock. How could I blame him? *I* was afraid of this trail. It was like we were pointing fingers at each other, blaming the other one for not seeing the danger in time. Monte had been walking along, trusting me, when suddenly his most feared enemy leapt out of nowhere. I had trusted his superior senses to warn of danger. We both had much to rebuild.

The dreaded tree with the big overhanging branch was now in sight. Despite my urging, Monte would only consent to a few steps before he again stopped to test the wind. Then, he would hesitantly move ahead, a few feet closer to the tree. I could feel his tension between my knees, and the muscles along his neck were hard under my hand. He wanted to bolt from that place of terror and pain, so we stepped ahead only as his fear subsided. An hour later, we were ten feet away from the gnarled, twisted pine. The thick, deformed branch that stretched over the trail made it look like a hanging tree of judgment, but with gentle firmness, I held his head so he had to face the place where it all happened. This was not a time to hurry. Even if this took hours, it was time well spent, and while we stood through the countless minutes and faced the tree of danger, my mind wandered back to when Monte had become mine.

I had ridden him for the first time at the Besser ranch when he was a barely started three-year-old. Monte had been my ranch horse during those two days, and I fell in love with him. We were riding through the big meadow, heading for the ranch after an overnight trip to the Kushya Creek camp. I turned to Bob and hesitantly asked if Monte were one of the horses for sale. The Besser horses were always in high demand, and I feared he might already be sold. Bob didn't answer for a while. He just continued riding until I thought he'd forgotten the question.

A full minute later, his gruff voice broke the silence. "Nope," he said, "he's not part of the sale string. I might keep him. We're running short of good, broke horses on the ranch."

I was disappointed, but I understood. Bob spent months with these colts, and they brought high prices. Everybody wanted a Bob Besser trained horse, and would pay handsomely for one.

The last night at the ranch, Lonnie and I turned in early. We both loved these working holidays at the ranch, but we were always exhausted at the end of the day. As we undressed, I noticed a plain white envelope propped on the nightstand on my side of the bed. My name was on the envelope in bold black ink. Perplexed, I opened it. Inside, a single sheet of unlined paper was filled with strong, masculine printing. It read, "Sold to Clarissa Bowers. One gray gelding with a right hip brand, rafter seventy-seven. Paid in full. Signed, Robert Lewis Besser."

The gift was beyond generous, and there were no adequate words for the thankfulness in my heart. After I quit blubbering I put on an old housecoat and went out to the living room. Bob and Anna were still reading by the fire. I hugged them. I knew the gift was from both, because they did everything together. I loved them, not for the gift, but because they were the most caring, selfless people I had ever known.

Monte backed away two steps. I waited for a full five minutes before asking him to move forward again. We were only two steps away from the tree. Now, he stood splayfooted, his nostrils distended, ready to instantly run. I smiled. Probably that was how I looked to God; wild-eyed, ready to run from the fear and pain in my life. But He could see what I couldn't see, and there under the cougar tree, I began to understand. If God had seen fit to save me from a cougar, then it must mean He had a purpose and plan for my life. Did that include Lonnie? I wasn't sure, but when Monte conquered his fear and stepped under that gnarled overhanging branch, my bitterness melted like a late winter snow. No longer would it drive my decisions. Whatever happened with Lonnie and my future was up to God. To walk away forever from the man I'd loved would be the most difficult thing I'd ever done, but now I knew, if that was the right thing to do—I had the strength.

CHAPTER 36
LONNIE

AFTER THE COBWEBS of unconsciousness cleared away, my eyes focused on a well-exposed black hairy chest ornamented with a chained gold eagle medallion. A long way above that barrel chest, two cobra eyes over top of a flattened, mottled nose belonged to one of the biggest Mexicans I'd ever seen. Nobody had to tell me. I'd just met Manuel Lourdes.

They'd trussed me up like a bad Christmas package, and dragged me into the flickering light of the small blaze at the back of the cave. Manuel eyed my inert form with disinterest until he spied the big trophy buckle. A rumbling snicker choked back to a sneer. "Another Americano cowboy, only this one's useless." He turned, and a little crazy-eyed bozo rattled away in Spanish. They didn't know it, but I understood very well what he was saying.

"Would you like me to shoot him, boss?" the short gun barrel pointed at my head jerked in time with his rapid Spanish.

"Yes," Manuel growled, "but take him outside to do it. I don't want blood in here. It draws too many flies."

The little guy grabbed my tied wrists and started dragging me toward the outside entrance. I fought through the pain to stay conscious. My life was over. I'd failed Brian just like I had everybody else. Now my night with a woman who wasn't my wife was not just a casual slip. It was a broken vow. And my single-minded pursuit of buckles and fame seemed more like selfish vanity than following my dreams.

The jagged rock floor of the cave scraped against my back. The little Mexican panted with the exertion of dragging my hundred-and-seventy-pound frame. *What had I left to make the world a better place? Nothing. My time on earth had been little more than an ugly scribble of self-indulgence.*

The card players snickered in the background at the little man's efforts. Not that I was doing anything to help him. Two of them sauntered over to cheer on their struggling accomplice. Fear added strength to my weak resistance. I struggled and kicked out against my captor and the bullet that would take my life away.

Was I going to Hell? Purgatory? Heaven was probably not an option. Or was there only the oblivion I'd always believed in?

Suddenly, Manuel shoved the little Mexican back, and stood over me.

"How did you get here?" The question was soft, brooding.

My eyes rolled upward, and through the pounding pain, I focused on Manuel's face. That I would never answer.

"Paco, there may be some juice to squeeze out of this lemon." His words were clipped, dangerous. I didn't have to guess. I knew what that meant, and my stomach tightened with fear.

"Someone betrayed us; someone betrayed us," the little monkey-face shrieked, jumping up and down, all the time pointing the pistol in my face. He was screeching like a cockatiel with a diaper rash, so I laid still and made sure he had no excuse to pull the trigger.

Manuel's voice hardened. "Throw what's left of him in the jug. You can shoot him tomorrow." His expanding belly jiggled with sneering ridicule at my obvious relief. I didn't care. I'd been given a reprieve, however small, and I thanked my lucky stars, or Whoever arranged it. Now I didn't have to die—at least not today. That seemed like the most awesome gift on earth.

Paco started dragging me toward the back of the cavern. Manuel ordered one of the card players to help him. They dragged me into a room with a bed in the far corner, not that they bothered with that. The floor was jagged gravel, and that's where they dumped me. Pain lanced through my skull when I attempted to roll onto my side. A canvas bag with an embossed leather nameplate blocked my vision. The blurry name looked like Brian's, but my eyes wouldn't focus. A lock snapped shut behind me, and then the darkness again beckoned.

***

A HAND ON MY SHOULDER shook me awake. "Lonnie!"

"Yeah, Brian. I'm coming." Early morning. We needed to get in the saddle . . . cows to gather today. I was so tired. Perhaps if I slept a few more minutes—

"Lonnie!" Brian leaned over me.

This was embarrassing! I should have been up first to get the fire going. I felt the cool morning air against my cheek. The weather was always cold at the Kushya Creek cabin this time of year. I opened my eyes . . . not the cabin . . . pain . . . another concussion, one of too many. That big Mexican had sucker punched me so hard, and my head ached, and . . . once again I let myself slip into that peaceful oblivion.

***

THE NEXT TIME my eyes opened, I looked straight into Brian's face. This time I could see his grin was real. My hand shook as I reached up and touched his shoulder, just to make sure. Then it came back to me. This was my last day on earth. I struggled unsuccessfully to sit up, the pain in my skull like a dozen sledgehammers. Whatever was wrong with my pounding head, it couldn't have been that big Mexican. There's no way he could have hit me hard enough to do that much damage. Then I remembered where I'd been standing when he rang my bell. When that moose punched me, I'd had no time to brace or move with the punch, and my head had cannoned into the rock wall.

Brian grinned. I tried, but my mouth wouldn't cooperate. It seemed as if he'd been gone a year.

"You've got a golf ball sized knot behind your right ear, and it looks like it bled a fair amount. Can you talk?"

"Yeah, but I'm still woozy. When did you get back?"

"Just before dawn. This morning when I landed, Manuel was waiting for me. He told me I had a new cell mate and when they shoved me in the door, there you were. They're not stupid, especially Paco. He's sadistic and twisted, but he senses things others don't see, and he started that wild giggle of his because he could see right away I knew you." Brian smiled again. "Maybe it wasn't that hard. Another cowboy looking guy with a big gold buckle probably didn't just get lost in the Sierra Madre."

"Paco. The yappy little guy with the evil eyes?"

"That's him," Brian nodded.

"He's the one who was going to shoot me last night. They put it off until today." Dejection and fear coursed through me.

Brian stood and glanced at me with a worried frown. "God willing, we're going to make them change that plan. How'd you ever find this place?"

In normal circumstances, Brian's "God willing" would have elicited a snide comment from me. Today wasn't anywhere near normal, and I hoped God or somebody was half as willing as I was to get us out of this place alive.

"I was in El Paso for a few days with some time to kill, so I called Rock Esfalan. You remember Rock? That bronc rider from Omak?"

Brian nodded. "Sure, I remember him. Didn't you guys travel together a few years ago?"

"Yeah, that's the guy. Now he's the sheriff in Hidalgo County, which is right on the Mexican border. So, I went over there . . ."

Brian interrupted me, his voice tortured. "Hidalgo County? I know it well. That's where they make me land with the cocaine."

"Yeah, that's what Julio told me."

"Who's Julio?"

My head was pounding, and it was difficult to stay coherent. "I told Rock that you'd been kidnapped by a Mexican drug cartel."

"How did you figure that out?"

I held up my hand. "I'll get to that. For now, we need to just stay alive for another twelve hours. If Genaro got out of here last night, help will arrive—maybe tonight."

Brian's eyes brightened, but then dulled, as if he didn't believe me. "You've lost me again. Who's Genaro? You were visiting with Rock . . . where does this Julio come in?"

I knew I wasn't making much sense. "Genaro is the Mexican fellow who brought me in here last night, and if . . . well, if I don't make it, do your best to take care of him. He's risked his life to get you out of here, and to burn these killers. You can imagine what they'll do to him if he's caught."

"Alright. But we're both going to get out of here!" Brian's jaw was set hard. "And who is Julio?"

I reached over and grabbed the little table beside the bed, then tried to pull myself up to a sitting position. The room swirled, and the hollow pounding started in my head again, but with a little help from Brian, I sat up, my back against the rough planks of the bed. Eventually, the room quit spinning enough that I could relate what Julio had told me.

Brian slid down the wall and sat across from me. "The sheepherder makes sense. On one of the first runs we made into the Big Hatchets, the *burros* had the lights all set on the edge of my runway. I'm down to fifty feet off the ground, when suddenly there's panicked sheep all over the place. I'm sure your Julio had an awful time rounding everything up. I felt bad about that . . . ." Brian's voice trailed away, and I glimpsed the same haunted look on his face that I'd seen in the lights from the cockpit. He was tortured by a guilt most people would shrug off, knowing he was flying loads of cocaine to people it would maim and kill. That knowledge would eat at him every waking moment. In the rodeo arena, there wasn't anybody tougher, but deep inside, he was as tender as a two-day-old pup. Now, a week-old black stubble was dark against his haggard face, and his clothes hung loosely on his usually muscular frame.

"Brian." I reached over and put my hand on his shoulder. "You can't help it. They'd have killed you if you refused to fly, and you know it. Let it go; you have to. We're going to get out of here, one way or another." How I hoped that was true.

"I don't know, Lonnie." He wiped a hand across his tired face and shook his head. "At first I refused to fly, and then I really thought I heard God say to do it, that there would come a time to resist, that He had a plan. Now I'm not so sure. Maybe I was just scared. They threatened my sister. If I refused to fly, they would kill one of her kids. They even knew where they lived, and where her kids went to school." Brian stood, his shoulders slumping from the pain and weariness.

I ran my hands over my aching head again and wished mightily for some painkillers—for both of us. My watch said it was near nine o'clock. If they were going to execute me at dawn, they had already missed the deadline, so I was grateful I could still feel a headache.

Now, my head felt like somebody was driving a nail through my temple. I tried to shift into a more comfortable position. It hurt just as bad, but I kept talking about Frederick Roseman and Stirling Associates while I tried to scrub the pain away.

Brian interrupted. "So back in Inglewood when this Frederick dude came to see you. How did he know I was here?"

"I'm not sure. Maybe the Feds were tipped off by some air-traffic control system. Also, Stirling had a man down here. He may have sent word you were here before he was caught and executed. It was still a miracle we found you."

One of Brian's eyebrows shot upward, and I knew I'd said the wrong thing. "A miracle? So you're saying God had something to do with this?" His face momentarily lit with the old grin when he had me in a corner.

My face reddened. "Honestly, I don't know. The last few days there have been too many strange coincidences. Let's just say I'm trying to keep an open mind."

Brian pushed himself off the floor and started pacing back and forth. "This Genaro; who is he?"

I signaled him closer, pointed toward the door, and lowered my voice to a whisper. "He's a cousin to Rock Esfalan's wife. Rock said if I got in a jam and needed somebody I could trust, I should call him. He knew exactly where you were at."

I didn't think it would add to Brian's peace of mind if I told him how little faith I had that Genaro would actually get to a phone and give the right code message to Stirling Associates. Brian didn't need to worry about that, at least not yet. Frederick had said that when I used the code, they would have a team on site within six hours, which could put them here by early afternoon. It had better be soon. The only thing that might keep me alive was Genaro's name. That information I would not give them, but before they killed me, I wished I could have lined up just one hard right to Manuel's jaw.

The lock rattled open, and a light-skinned fellow with slitty eyes and a limp dropped a couple of plates filled with some red and brown Mexican concoction, along with two cups of coffee on the rickety deal table. The same ornery little Paco-weasel that wanted to shoot me last night was with him. He waved his big pistol around like it was a fairy sparkler stick, and I had no doubt he was itching for a chance to pull the trigger. Paco made me nervous, but he didn't seem to bother Brian. Occasional flashes shone through of the friend I knew so well; the happy, love-everybody guy he'd always been. Anyone else would have hated these perverts. Brian greeted them like they were brothers.

"Hey, Herme," Brian asked. "How are you doin'? Is that ankle any better?"

"Ah—Brian, eet ees still very sore, but not as bad as yesterday," he added, his eyes glowing with warmth.

"Come back after breakfast," Brian said, "and I'll wrap it for you again. Paco, you look as mean as ever. Lighten up with that gun before you hurt somebody." Amazed, I watched the barrel of his gun drop—at least a bit. Paco's trademark scowl turned into a leer, which was probably as close to a smile as he could manage. I turned away, disgusted. These guys lived to kill. They were the scum of the earth, and yet Brian treated them as if they were normal, caring human beings. I didn't understand, and didn't want to.

They fed me, I suppose because they had to feed Brian. However, the respite was short-lived. After we had finished the tortillas and frijoles, the man Brian called Ramon, and two others, came for me. I recognized him as the man who had been in the plane with Brian. He stepped into the cell, silent, almost apologetic. Though he was unarmed, the other two carried AK47's. I supposed that if I were going to work for Stirling Associates, I would have to learn more about those kinds of guns. Then the thought hammered into me that there wouldn't be any other mornings, and I wasn't going to need to learn any new stuff.

Chapter 37

LONNIE

Ramon gestured toward me as he spoke to Brian. "He's your friend?"

Brian nodded.

"The boss says he must come with us." Ramon's eyes darted around the room as he struggled with the unfamiliar English words.

"What's going to happen to him?" Brian's voice was icy and quiet.

Ramon spread his hands and shrugged his shoulders. "Maybe if he tells who led him here? I don't know. Nobody knows what Manuel will do."

A jittery silence dominated the room while Brian searched Ramon's face. I sat on the bed; rigid, waiting, while I listened to the exchange between them. The two enforcers outside the door edged closer, probably not understanding the foreign words, but feeling the rising tension.

"Ramon, tell this to Manuel. If anything happens to Lonnie, there will be no more flights." Brian stood with his hands on his hips, his face dark with an anger I'd never seen.

"Can you fly up those canyons?" Brian's voice cracked in the silence.

Ramon's eyes jerked up to Brian's face, like maybe it was a tone he'd never heard before. "No." His voice was barely audible.

"Does Manuel have anybody else that can fly up there at night without crashing?"

"No."

"Tell him, Ramon. If he takes Lonnie down the canyon to die, then he might as well take me because the flights will stop! Manuel will have to find some other way to pay the Colombians for the cocaine."

If I hadn't known it before, I knew then that I would never have a closer friend than Brian Besser. Ramon shrugged, then signaled the goons to escort me out. As I passed Brian, I squeezed his shoulder and tried to convey in a brief glance the gratitude I felt for what he'd tried to do.

Ramon and his troops muscled me out the door and through the main cave, then shoved me outside into that hazy, beautiful fall morning. There is no good day to die, and though I didn't expect to return, I—like all men who face death— held on to hope. Maybe Brian's ultimatum would work. Perhaps I could make a deal with them. But the only bargaining chip I had was Genaro's name. That would never be on the table. I could only hope that none of them were real professionals, because if they were very good, I knew they could extract any information they wanted. A strong man can control his spirit, but my long-ago training had taught me that well executed torture can make the body of any man a betrayer. The only hope was to last long enough for help to arrive.

If I could last for a reasonable time there was a chance

that Brian would survive. Frederick's combat team should arrive before any final confrontation over the flights. And Clarissa . . . yeah, she was always there in my mind. I hoped she had forgiven me. I wished I could hold her one more time, maybe wipe away some of the tears I'd caused. As we shuffled away from the entrance, jumbled thoughts ricocheted around my still aching head. Clarissa would probably marry again. Down deep, I hoped she would miss me—at least a little.

They walked me a hundred yards down the trail to another small cave which wasn't much more than an indentation in the rock. One of them tied my hands behind my back. Then they started to break me down—one punch at a time. Manuel and his crew weren't innovators in that arena, or it didn't seem so to me. At first, it wasn't too bad. Three of them took turns, but I'd been hurt worse in bar fights. They tried to keep me conscious, because of course they wanted Genaro's name. The questions came, one after another.

"What is your name?"

"Lonnie Bowers."

"Who brought you here?"

Silence. The beating got worse. A punch ripped into my jaw and I went down. They jerked me to my feet.

"Do you work for the DEA?"

"No." Smash—into the ribs. Big pain.

"Who brought you here?"

Silence. One eye swelling shut.

Always, they came back to Genaro. "What is his name?"

Silence. I groaned in agony as another rib broke. A fist punctuated every question, while Manuel sat against the canyon wall, his cobra eyes watchful and alert.

After what seemed like hours one of them hit me too

hard, and with the blood running out of every orifice in my head I passed out, but not before I heard Manuel yelling at the ham-fisted incompetent who had hit me too hard.

***

WHEN I WOKE UP, I was back in Brian's cell. He'd wheedled some water out of them, and had cleaned me up as best he could. The cool cloth on my forehead cut a little bit of the pain and as my swollen eyes focused, Brian's worried face came into view. I moved my hand far enough to touch his arm. "Thanks, bud." My face was swelling like a watermelon, and my voice came out raspy. They'd broken my nose and at least two ribs. But I'd not given them Genaro's name.

Probably because he was trying to keep me conscious, Brian rambled on about everything that had happened since they'd grabbed him back in the States. I hurt all over, and the best I could do was grunt a few replies, but it helped to take my mind off the present, and whatever was to come next. They wouldn't waste much more time. Genaro was a loose end and Manuel would know that could be trouble.

In the afternoon they came back for me, three new ones, meaner and uglier, if that were possible. They jerked me off the bunk and shoved me out the door. The adrenaline of fear ate through me, but I was already hurt too bad to resist. This session would be my last. I wouldn't wake up from this one.

They dragged me down to the small cave. This time they tied me to a small pine tree so I wouldn't fall. The same questions started again, and this time the pain seemed a hundred times worse.

"How did you get here?" A solid left to the gut.

"Who led you here?" A kick in the groin. Unbearable pain. Both lips were soon split, my nose smashed over on the side of my face. More broken ribs, but they took great care to keep me conscious. Eventually, my body betrayed me, and as much as I had determined never to utter Genaro's name, my swollen bleeding lips spilled the words. My eyes filled with bitter tears, not at the pain, but that I somehow wasn't strong enough to resist. I slumped against the ropes, drifting in and out of consciousness. Now, I only wanted the pain to stop, even if it meant death. My only hope was that I'd lasted long enough for help to arrive for Genaro and Brian.

"Leave him," Manuel growled. "Because he is a gringo, and because there may be more than he told us, we will try again later. After that—enough. Kill him. We cannot use this one for an object lesson to others. That role will be reserved for the traitorous peasant who led him here. His corpse will send the message. "Paco, tonight you leave with Moisés and Jose. Find this Genaro Chacon, this son of a rabid coyote, and cut off his hand. Stuff it in his mouth—before you kill him. Then hang him from the San Fermin Bridge."

"But Boss," Paco giggled, "I cannot fit a man's whole hand into his mouth."

"Make it fit, you depraved little devil! I have no doubt, you will find a way."

Chapter 38

CLARISSA

With trembling hands, I stroked my horse's neck and stared up at the great snaking limb above my head where the cougar had lain in wait. Monte snorted, every muscle in his body still communicating an uncontrollable fear of this place, yet he stood, and as the minutes passed, his head dropped and the corded muscle softened under my hand. I walked him away to let him relax before we faced the tree again. Each forward step became a victory, until in the end, he was quiet and responsive. It was a lesson in trust that might save me from an out-of-control, runaway horse at the next hint of cougar on the wind.

Later, we left the tree and followed the trail toward a high saddle between the peaks. I hummed a catchy Dave Forsberg tune, thrilled I'd made so much progress with Monte's fear. Far below, the mighty Fraser River carved an ever deeper channel into the great Chilcotin Canyon. Its deceptive current flowed placidly south like a chocolate serpent, depositing its cargo of nutrient-rich sediment into the fertile delta of the valley a hundred miles away.

The autumn-cured alpine grass clung to the slopes, shaded by the whispering pine and occasional mountain fir that hemmed in the rock-strewn trail. Often, I'd climbed to this quiet grotto between the peaks when my soul rebelled against the pain and bitterness in my life. Even my encounter with the cougar could never ruin this special place of healing.

When we broke out of the trees onto the grassy plateau, I tied Monte to a sapling, then skirted the towering rock face that led to the familiar wind-hollowed cavern. The ledge in front of me dropped away for a thousand feet, opening up a vista of rolling mountains and timber that reached to the distant coastal range. The words of the song played a backdrop to the miles of untouched wilderness at my feet. *"I stand amazed . . . I am strong in my weakness, I am brave when He throws my fear away."*

An elongated boulder formed a regal bench, and with my back nestled into the wall, I let my mind ramble through the morning. The thrill of my success with Monte still warmed me. How I wished I could have shared it, which made me wonder whether Lonnie had found Brian. Then I remembered the terrified response of the small-time drug dealer whose house had been incinerated. Silently, I sent up a prayer that God would bring both of them home safely.

That brought up the other question about my husband. Was it time for me to bury that part of my life? That sounded painful. Or could I forgive him and . . . and what? Darlene's words hammered against my defensive wall. *"Clarissa, you will need to forgive the woman who was involved with Lonnie.* Uh, yes, the other woman. Not going to happen—ever! Even though she lived far away, the bitter anger and hurt of that betrayal burned hot and corrosive.

Darlene had pointed to a verse one evening when we were discussing my shattered marriage. "Forgive, if you have anything against anyone; so that your Father who is in heaven may forgive you your transgressions." I wanted to bury those words. However, my sins were many, and there was no doubt in my mind that God had forgiven me. *But I'm not God,* I argued. *I can't forgive like He does.*

The words came in the stillness. "If you are willing to trust Me, I can fill your heart with enough love to forgive."

One step. Was that what He was asking? My eyes traveled down the sweeping mountainside and up into the brilliant blue pines on the majestic Pacific mountains. *Was it even possible for God to change this barren ugly desert of bitterness inside me into something of beauty? Could He replace hatred with forgiveness?*

I remembered asking Anna how she had become such a caring, compassionate person. Anna smiled, and gave me a hug. "Clarissa, you start with God—when you're very young." I knew then that when I was old, I wanted to be like that sweet, generous woman; not one consumed by long-held bitterness and pain. A tear slid down my cheek. I covered my face with both hands. "God, I forgive Lonnie. I want to show him the love that can only come from You. But I can never forgive that woman!"

His soft voice broke through my bitterness and anger. "Can you trust Me enough to forgive her just for today?"

The minutes passed. I couldn't say those words. I no longer felt amazed, strong, or brave. Regardless, the words ground from some inner, untapped chamber at the bottom of my soul. "We were best friends, and Rhonda Pearson betrayed me, but today, I forgive her for the horrible hurt and pain she has caused. Fill my heart with your love, because . . .

God, I don't have any of my own to give."

I don't know what I expected to happen, if anything. The wind still sighed through the fir and mountain pine. A Clark's Nutcracker gurgled its distinctive high o-ka-lay. I searched through my coat pockets for some tissue, and dried my bitter tears with hands red from the cold. Then, on that massive granite boulder, high on the west face of the mountain, a strange serenity flowed through me. Darlene had talked about this special kind of contentment. I thought it was all kind of a Christian cliché, but that morning I discovered the deep inner peace that comes with obedience to God. I hoped I wouldn't have to explain *that* to Lonnie.

Chapter 39

LONNIE

THE THIRST WAS UNBEARABLE. Somewhere past the broken ribs and the pain, my fevered mind drifted to the rippling water at the Messue Crossing. Brian and I had stopped in the middle of the river to let our horses drink. The stirrup-deep water gurgled around us, before skittering on to the placid lake. We'd been discussing a subject I usually avoided as a useless argument.

"Brian," I grinned slyly, "you've got a pretty good head—for a bull rider." He smiled, but like a wary trout, he refused to take the bait. I wasn't about to stop there. "So you believe that some mega-God in the sky just said some words, and up pops a house fly, and a squirrel, and over here a moose, and then a man?"

"He didn't even look at me. "Yep."

"That's absurd and unbelievable—an affront to any thinking man's intelligence."

Brian continued to ignore me while he studied some Canada geese that figured we were horning in on their territory. He watched them take off for quieter waters before turning to me.

"You're right. The whole idea is completely illogical."

This unexpected retreat made me wary. "You know," I said, enthusiastic over my headway, "there's some compelling new evidence that puts the deep-six to the old creation argument."

"I don't doubt it. It's a pretty far-fetched story," Brian replied lazily.

I sensed deep water, but I'd gone too far to stop. He leaned an elbow on his saddle horn, his face turned down river, but I could still see the half-turned-up corner of his mouth.

"No—seriously," he continued. "I agree. Creationism is completely implausible. So, I'm looking at the other options; evolution, big bang, everything out there, as well as believing in nothing, if that's possible. Some scientists now say the only part of evolution that is theoretical, is the mechanism that brought it about. That logic seems upside down to me, but that's not the real issue. My last day on earth, I'm going to stake my life on a theory, one on which I need to be one hundred percent certain. If I bet against the God who says he created the world, and I'm wrong, I've lost everything. So tell me, Lonnie, if eternity is at stake, what should I do? Should I gamble?"

Those far-away words washed over me like ocean waves while I drifted in and out of consciousness. Brian's words that day started a beginning uncertainty in me. To argue philosophy with nothing at stake is easy. Today I was going to die, and the concept of God was quite another matter. If Brian was right, was I good enough? Did it matter? Or would I be what I'd always staunchly believed; simply a lifeless block of rapidly decaying organic matter? Lying there on that hot Mexican dirt, bleeding, bruised, and hurt worse than I'd ever thought possible, I wasn't sure anymore. Then, what I'd thought was the cool water at the Messue faded, and the surging pain ground out the past.

They'd left me where I'd fallen, a couple hundred feet from the cave entrance. Manuel knew I wasn't going anywhere except farther down the canyon for a bullet in the back of the head. He'd probably let Brian out, hoping to avoid any confrontation over the flying routine. He couldn't afford to shoot Brian.

My head was propped up, and I could feel Brian again sponging the blood and dirt off my battered face. Not that there was any sense in that. They were going to kill me anyhow, but the cool cloth eased some of the pain, and I was grateful. My eyes were nearly swollen shut, but I focused enough to see Brian's face against the afternoon sun. Ramon stood off to the side; his pistol holstered while Brian tried to keep me from slipping back into oblivion.

My bloodshot eyes would barely focus. "They hurt me bad this time." I could only mumble through my shattered, bloody mouth.

"Yeah, I know. Just lay still, Lonnie." He swabbed my face and forehead with the wet cloth, but it wasn't doing any good. My head was pounding with the pain. Suddenly, I realized the banging wasn't inside my skull. Those were semi-automatic weapons. A muffled explosion followed the gunfire. Ramon tugged at the nine millimeter in his waistband, sprinted toward the cave, then froze. I managed to raise my head enough to see what had stopped him. Manuel barreled into sight, loping toward us, screaming curses. Brian, cat-quick as always, was instantly on his feet. My puffy eyes freeze-framed Manuel's hatless form. His tan shirt was open to the belly. Hate pulled his lips away from his white teeth. The angry barrel of a snubbed-off pistol in his left hand searched for me. Fifty feet away, he raised the pistol. Weary and resigned, I gazed at it, focusing on the minuscule black hole of death at the end of the barrel. My time had come.

A camo-clad figure burst from the cave entrance. The rifle in his hands snapped into position. Brian glanced down at me, and in that instant, I knew what he was going to do. For a moment, our eyes locked. Then, he turned and strode toward Manuel with his arms raised, blocking my still form. Manuel's gun steadied. Everything seemed so slow, and I tried to move . . . to help . . . but I could do nothing. At the last second, the staccato rap of the commando's automatic rifle drowned out the sharp crack of the pistol. Manuel stumbled, and swore. He was close enough his venomous eyes locked with mine. He tried to raise his arm as he struggled to force the muzzle of his pistol toward me. A trickle of blood dribbled into the black chest hair. He wobbled, then dropped to one knee. His right hand reached for his left, straining by force of will to fire the shot that would kill me. But when his hands came together, the gun was no longer there. It lay in the sand in front of him. Behind him, another burst of rifle fire drove his body into the dirt.

Ramon fired a wild shot toward the cave, then bolted down the mesquite-covered slope. He only made it a few steps before the metal-jacketed bullets found him. His body collapsed without a sound.

Relief washed through the fog of pain. Frederick's infantry had arrived. Other commandos filtered into sight from the cave. We were going to be okay.

I looked back at Brian. He turned, and stumbled toward

me with a puzzled, half-grin on his face. His hand slipped away from his chest, his fingers crimson. Blood soaked the front of his shirt. One of the commandos sprinted forward, grabbed him, and eased him to the ground beside me. He tore Brian's shirt open and yelled back toward the cave.

"Man down! First aid—on the double!"

Two others sprinted forward. Brian turned his head toward me, his face already a pasty white. "It's okay Lonnie. I'm ready to go." The blood welled up in his throat. His eyes locked onto mine, and though I tried desperately to roll over onto my knees beside him, I couldn't.

"Brian, don't die! You're going to make it!" He groaned and turned away, his eyes fixed on the fading afternoon sun. One of the medics worked over him while the other held his head up, so he could breathe.

"Lonnie!" Brian's voice was louder, and his hand fumbled for mine. "Lonnie! I'll wait for you at the crossing." What I've heard people call "the light," faded from his eyes. His head rolled back, and the big commando laid him gently on the ground.

I turned away. Cowboys aren't supposed to cry. I did. That shot had been meant for me. Manuel wanted revenge. Brian had placed himself squarely between me and that bullet.

The commando reached down, closed Brian's eyes, then stepped away. I had my moment alone, and I found enough strength to reach over and pull his still warm hand to my chest. He was gone, but I squeezed his hand anyway, and said good-bye. There wasn't time for anything else.

The two medics now swarmed around me, poking, prodding, and bandaging. It didn't take them long to decide I was in no condition to walk ten feet; never mind back to the staging area where they'd parked their vehicles.

Genaro appeared, and stood quietly in the background, watching the medics as they attempted to assess how badly I was hurt. All the conversation had been in English, which he didn't understand, but when they stepped aside to discuss their exit plans, he knelt beside me and took my hand.

"Thanks Genaro—for all you've done." I grated the words through the throbbing pain.

He nodded. "It was necessary. Our country has much sadness ahead unless we fight this great evil. However, I wish your friend had not died. I am sorry. Go with God, Lonnie." He touched my shoulder, stood, and turned away. One of the medics knelt down and emptied a syringe of morphine into my arm.

The danger was over for Genaro. No drug smugglers were left to identify him or deal out any retribution. He and his family would be safe back in El Vallecito. That was my last coherent thought before my drugged mind skidded into a tortured silence. Later, I remembered Genaro saying something about a better place for his children. He'd done his part, and if Mexico had enough people like him, they would win their battle against the drug cartels.

One of the commandos taxied Brian's plane out of the hangar and onto the runway. Four of them eased Brian's body into the stowage area, then poured me into the same passenger seat where I'd ridden white-knuckled through a hundred thousand miles. It didn't matter now. The morphine dulled the physical pain. No medicine would ever reach the other torment.

CHAPTER 40

LONNIE

I DO NOT RECALL the name of the El Paso hospital where they left me, but there was nothing wrong with the service. Perhaps the two capable-looking Stirling people outside my room gave the impression that I was somebody important. I wasn't, but the attention was nice for the time I was there.

A doctor prodded my misshapen, black and purple face, ordered a CT scan, and decided I would live long enough to get beat up at least once more.

A familiar, low voice outside the door jarred me from my reverie. Frederick Roseman padded into the room. He moved quietly for such a big man.

"Hello, Lonnie." He was guarded, watchful, perhaps expecting a cold reception from me because of how it had all turned out.

"Hi, Frederick." I mumbled.

"How are you feeling?"

I didn't figure that question deserved an answer.

Frederick muttered a simple apology. "We would have done anything possible to prevent Brian's death.

Unfortunately, accidents happen. I am sorry."

I nodded past the lump in my throat. As much as I wanted to, I couldn't blame him or the combat team. If I'd been more careful, I wouldn't have been captured. That could have changed everything. And what could they have done differently? It was a commando operation with a minimum of intelligence. They took out ten bad guys. We were supposed to be locked inside the cave. The second small cave where they had worked me over was behind a jutting shoulder of the canyon. Neither Genaro nor the commandos were aware of its presence, or that we were there. It seemed they'd done everything possible to get both Brian and I out of there. If there were recriminations, they could come later.

"Are they treating you well?" Frederick's eyes swept over my battered face.

"Yeah, but you can get me out of here any time."

"I talked to your doctor. He will release you whenever you wish. However, stay until you feel ready to leave."

"I'm ready." I tried to move and winced. I would have trouble walking because of the broken ribs, but they'd heal just as well elsewhere.

"Okay, there is a hotel suite reserved for you. It's yours as long as you need it."

"From two double beds to a suite?" My stock had skyrocketed.

Frederick shuffled from one foot to the other. He'd already apologized, but I guess he felt he had to do it again. Maybe later I understood that better, but I'm glad he cared enough to try. He stuffed his hands in his pockets and took a deep breath. "I've been in this business a long time. When we lose somebody, it still hurts. Please accept my deepest apology.

Words cannot convey how sorry I am about Brian."

"He and I were close." I clenched my teeth while I regained control of my emotions.

Frederick spent a few moments engrossed in the intricacies of one of the patient monitors by my bed, for which I was grateful. He crossed his arms and then immediately uncrossed them. "When you're ready, we can discuss the family details."

"I will contact his family," I replied. "They're a long way off the grid. Contacting them can be difficult."

"Yes, well . . . the company will pick up the cost of any transport, funeral, and burial expenses. That is something we can do. Because of the nature of the operation, I would ask that there be as little publicity as possible. Our people have prepared something I hope will be acceptable." Frederick handed me the *official* press release. I scanned the important parts of it. "A British Columbia man . . . killed in a hunting accident . . . Mexican State of Chihuahua . . . ongoing investigation."

I understood. The document meant nothing, nor would it change anything. I nodded, and flipped it back to him without comment.

Frederick tucked it in the inside pocket of his blazer. "Please convey our sympathy and support. I would appreciate it if you could inform me of the family's wishes. I will make every arrangement."

"Thanks. I will let you know as soon as I talk to them."

Frederick wrote a phone number on the back of his now familiar business card and laid it on the bedside table. He inquired about my injuries, and I told him about the various bruises and broken ribs, concussion and bruised liver, none of which would kill me. He made little comment, which was as I'd expected. Pain went with the territory. I didn't expect sympathy.

"I will see you this afternoon then. We'll need to go over a few details."

I raised an eyebrow, wanting more time, but he'd already turned and was at the door.

Later that morning, the doctor came in and discharged me into the capable hands of the two gentlemen who guarded my room. He gave me a proper warning to avoid any further head injuries. I thanked him. I wanted no more battles.

When I hobbled away from my bed, pain shot through every segment of my body. Nevertheless, with my two sport-jacketed lions on either side, we made it to the elevator and out to the waiting car. Both men looked familiar. I was sure I'd last seen them in combat fatigues wearing those floppy, military Boonie hats before morphine scrambled my senses. The quiet one on my right had a left-over Canadian accent, which fired an irresistible urge to go home.

We arrived at the Holiday Inn on Lincoln Street, and those folks were solicitous of my welfare. They supplied me with a toothbrush and the other necessities I'd left a lifetime ago back at that motel in Madera. Possibly, my beat-up mug wasn't good for business. They hustled me through their lobby and to a room, which was fine by me. More than anything, I just wanted to be alone.

The room was a real-live suite, a cut above ritzy for this beat-up cowboy. I reckoned I might as well make the most of it, so I called room service and ordered a bacon, lettuce, and tomato sandwich. That was a bad choice for my cut-up lips and battered mouth, but what I managed to eat still tasted better than Mexican tortillas and frijoles, or hospital Jello.

After worrying at the crusty bread with my swollen lips, I

shoved the half-eaten sandwich aside. The dreaded phone call couldn't be put off any longer. Clarissa needed to hear about Brian's death so we could start the process of reaching Bob and Anna. I dialed her number and glanced at my watch. She should be in the office, presuming her injured arm and shoulder were progressing the way they were supposed to. The cheery insurance girl opening came over the line.

"Hi," I mumbled.

"Lonnie?"

It was so wonderful to hear her voice. I tried to keep my voice strong. "Yeah, it's me. How are you?"

"I'm fine. But what about you? You're out of Mexico?"

"Yeah, I'm in El Paso."

"Lonnie, tell me everything."

"It . . . things didn't go well, Clarissa. Brian's gone. He . . . he was killed." My voice betrayed me, and I had to swallow my still fresh grief. She would have a tough enough time without me going into meltdown.

"Lonnie, Bob and Anna are here. They came yesterday, so they would be close if there was any news." She was in tears now.

"Do you want me to tell Bob?" I asked.

"It might be better."

"I understand."

Clarissa put Bob on the phone, and I had to give him the worst news any father can ever receive. His only son was dead, and I didn't tell it well. Again, I wanted to be the strong person, the one he could lean on through this heart-wrenching time, but I think that tough old rancher comforted me more than I did him.

After a brief sketch of what happened, we discussed all

those arrangements families have to work through when they are least equipped for it. They opted for cremation here in Texas. Brian's ashes would come home with me.

Bob and Anna were as near to family as either Clarissa or I could claim. I wanted desperately to be with them. We needed to grieve together. Tomorrow, I would make the long journey home to lend whatever support I could, to meld my grief with the heart-wrenching agony of parents who have lost a beloved son.

CHAPTER 41
LONNIE

I FUMBLED UNDER THE NIGHTSTAND for the phone book. "Lonnie Bowers, you're going home." I traced down the page with my index finger until I found a travel agent. Within minutes, she had reservations to Vancouver for the following afternoon.

The last item was to make sure Brian was ready to come with me. While I mulled over how to make that happen, Frederick called from the lobby and asked if he could come up for a few minutes. I told him that would be fine, then ordered coffee from room service. He arrived at the door, and we sat and discussed my health, or lack of it, until the coffee arrived. Frederick answered the door, and paid the bill. We sipped at the soothing hot liquid, neither of us ready to open the painful conversation.

Finally, Frederick straightened in his chair. "Have you been able to reach Brian's family?"

I set down my cup and nodded.

Frederick's eyebrows rose. "And?"

"They're okay with a cremation here. The problem is I

made reservations to fly to Vancouver tomorrow afternoon. I would like to take . . . what's left—his ashes, with me."

"I'll arrange it." Frederick reached for the phone on the desk beside him, called a number, and gave the necessary orders in his usual clipped, efficient voice.

"Everything will be ready by noon tomorrow. Will that be acceptable?"

"Yeah, that will work. My flight doesn't leave until two-fifteen. Don't you have to get some kind of clearance from a coroner or medical examiner?"

Frederick's smile was almost condescending. "Let us worry about that, Lonnie. The ashes will be delivered, packed and ready at the U.S. Airways customer counter. That was your airline, wasn't it?"

"Yeah, flight four-seventeen, through Phoenix," I answered.

Frederick walked to the window and stared out at the cityscape before turning and folding his arms. "Now, I need to know about Felix. What happened?"

I scrunched around in my chair, wishing I'd taken another painkiller. "Felix had been compromised. He ditched me on the steps of the motel, the day I arrived in Madera."

Frederick's teeth clenched. The muscles on the left side of his jaw worked back and forth. "What did you do?"

"Fortunately, I had a Plan B." There was no anger or resentment in my voice. Those emotions had drained away while I lay on that El Paso hospital bed. I told him about Genaro, and why I'd made the decision to go inside the cave. By the time I was finished answering all of Frederick's rapid-fire questions, my head was drumming for more Tylenol.

"You did well." Frederick shrugged. "But I knew you

would." This time, his backhanded compliment seemed more than a simple observation. He leaned forward, and the piercing blue eyes softened. "Also, I understand your grief. How I wish it had turned out differently." A momentary window opened in Frederick's eyes, and for a brief second illuminated a tragedy, somewhere in his distant past. Instantly, he rose to his feet, the curtain once more carefully drawn. He was again the Frederick I knew; clipped and efficient. "Your payroll checks will continue to be deposited until you are healed and able to resume your rodeo career, unless of course you decide to become a permanent employee of the company. I will contact you when and if that decision becomes necessary."

I nodded, grateful for this unexpected help while I got back on my feet. The employment offer needed no response. I'd made that perfectly clear before we started.

"Here." Frederick handed me a credit card. I reached for it, and glanced at the company name inscribed in the left bottom corner. Adelante Inc. Frederick noticed my interest. "It isn't necessary for you to know about the name. Pay for your airline ticket with it, as well as any other company business expenses you may incur. That includes any additional medical or dental work you may need. A car will be reserved for you in Vancouver. It will be a long-term rental. Don't worry about returning it. We'll let you know when that is necessary." The man stood, shook my hand, and without another word walked out the door. I wasn't one for premonitions, but there was a strong hunch in me that Frederick Roseman had not walked out of my life.

The next twelve hours were spent in a mostly prone position. My caved-in ribs and deformed face needed all of that time. By the next afternoon, with help from a handful of painkillers, I could manage a reasonable limp, but my face looked like it had been through a corn chopper. Frederick had assigned my tough-guy shadows to take me to the airport, for which I was grateful.

In Vancouver, I hobbled off the plane and had a shuffle race with somebody's grandmother for the second to last spot in the Canada customs lineup. The grandmother beat me by a nose, but she had the advantage of a cane, so it wasn't a fair race.

I gave all the right "yes, no" answers to the customs agent, and mumbled some nonsense about a Mexican bar in answer to his curiosity over my colorful face. He gave up, waved me through, and I hobbled off to the appropriate car rental counter.

Frederick had spent with lavish abandon. The keys to an expensive foreign hatchback lay beside the rental contract form, and I wondered if regret and sympathy warranted this extra expense or if there was something more involved. Actually, I wasn't at all interested in knowing the answer to that question, at least not now. Carefully, I maneuvered through the still frenetic Vancouver streets to Kitsilano Towers.

The apartment assaulted me with its familiar cold, musty smell, now synonymous with calling a real estate agent—which I still hadn't got around to doing. No food in the refrigerator, no messages, and no company were the usual welcome, and I wandered around trying to decide whether to walk down to the Brite Spot to eat. After glancing at my discolored mug in the mirror, I decided I'd rather order in real soft pizza. The swelling had subsided, but my face was still the color of a mud splattered rainbow.

Before food, there was something more important. I

eased onto the couch and dialed Clarissa's number. She answered on the first ring.

"Hello?" Her voice was muted, and sounded sad.

"Hi Love." Total silence. Somewhere under the yellow and purple, I could feel my face redden. I hadn't meant to use that old term. It just popped out—because of the pain and weariness, and maybe the way she'd answered. "How are Bob and Anna?" I hurried to carry on the conversation, trying to cover up the endearment, and my embarrassment. It had been a slip, and I scrambled for an appropriate response to the biting retort that would soon come.

"Hi Lon. I'm glad you called. They're not doing well. How could they? But they have a big, compassionate God, who has a purpose in everything. Their faith is all that makes this bearable."

She had just called me Lon! That way she said my name. . . . it was what she had always called me . . . during those intimate moments.

I jerked myself back into the conversation.

"I missed that," I said. "You said something about God?"

"Their faith is so strong, Lonnie. For them, there is no doubt that God is in control, and that this tragedy has some purpose. I know you don't agree with all that stuff, but . . ." A defensive note crept into her voice, which I'd become well used to whenever the "God" subject was broached.

"Clarissa, hold it. I've seen some strange things happen, events that are out of the ordinary, maybe miracles. I haven't told you all the details. I'm going to save that because Bob and Anna should be there to hear it."

"You will be here tomorrow?"

"Yes, and I have Brian's ashes with me."

"Alright. We're all waiting for you."

"I'll be there by lunchtime if the traffic isn't too heavy. See you then."

"Goodnight, Lonnie."

"Goodnight." Any more emotional endearments didn't seem wise, but I sat there and stared at the phone with a silly, lopsided grin on my bruised face, wanting the moment to last. We'd made it through a whole conversation without recriminations, which surely was a first.

Still elated, I reached across to the coffee table and pulled the latest edition of the *Rodeo Sports News* out from under the stack of bills. I turned the pages, sorted through the upcoming rodeo dates with all the entry details, then moved to the national standings. My name had not appeared in the top twenty since April. There would be no berth at the National Finals in Las Vegas for me, which should have been distressing. Today, it didn't seem important. I flipped through several articles, and then turned back to the national standings. Brian still held the number eight spot in the bull riding, which brought the too-familiar hard lump into my throat.

Chapter 42
LONNIE

Two tylenol and four hours of driving got me to Seton Lake and the long hill down into Lillooet. The glacier-fed water to my left lay quiet and regal, cradled like a rare gem between the darker green on the mountain slopes surrounding it, but I couldn't focus on the beauty. The people, and the grieving ahead kept my eyes glued to the road.

My ribs were beginning to heal, and my face was more of a normal shape, if not color. However, the pain pills I'd taken that morning were wearing off, so I was relieved to finally see the road that turned toward Farwell Canyon and Clarissa's house.

In the yard, I extricated my beat-up frame from behind the wheel of the low-slung hatchback. For a moment, I leaned on the open car door while I waited for my ribs to quit hurting.

Clarissa stepped off the porch and hurried to the car. The afternoon breeze ruffled a wisp of her long, sandy hair over her face. A thrill of tenderness brought a careful smile to my split lips as I followed her with my eyes. Nothing had changed.

She stopped, and her eyes widened as she took in my

battered face. "Oh, Lonnie!"

"I'm okay," I said. "I looked worse a couple of days ago. I have a few broken ribs and some bruises, which hurt a lot more than my face. They will heal. The other wounds—" My voice trailed away as my eyes unlocked from hers and followed the scars down her jaw. "How are you doing?" The red tracks stood out like jagged sentinels on the right side of her face.

Self-consciously, she turned away. "I'm healing. Maybe someday . . ."

Together, we gazed up to the blue-green peaks across the valley. The mountains towered above us, solid, immovable, bigger than our hurts.

"I guess we both have plenty of scars that need to heal."

"Lonnie, I'm so sorry." She turned and stepped toward me. I reached for her, and she slipped into my arms. It was a moment of desperate need for each other, an instant of sharing our deep hurts and common grief.

The embrace didn't last long, but it was enough for me to know there might be a small window of freedom to move forward, to maybe start rebuilding what we'd lost. We stepped apart and walked to the door. Bob and Anna were standing just inside. Bob grabbed my hand and squeezed my arm with his other hand, his jaw set against the grief. I turned, and hugged Anna. None of us spoke. There was only mutual sorrow. Words could come later.

Afterward, Bob turned to me. "You look to be beat up bad, Lonnie."

"Yeah, the cartel goons worked me over. They were efficient."

Clarissa made coffee, which wasn't any better than it used to be, but it mattered less than ever. We sat around the kitchen table talking about unimportant things: my flight, the trip from Vancouver, even the unseasonably warm fall weather. They were mundane subjects that meant little, but the words were a brief respite from the grief, a mustering of courage to face the subject uppermost in all our minds.

Later, Bob and I moved to the living room. "How long have you been here?" I asked.

"Let's see; eight days, I guess. We rode the bus down a week ago Wednesday. Seemed easier than driving that old Ford one-ton all the way."

"The service will be at the ranch?"

"No, it's easier if we have it in town. Tom and Brenda will fly in to Vancouver tonight. They'll be here in the morning. We'll ride up to Vanderhoof with them so we can take care of the final arrangements for the memorial service." He stared unseeingly at the floor, broken by grief.

I wished there was a way to lessen some of Bob's pain, but I knew there probably wasn't anything I could do. Besides, I was still coping with my own loss. How could I bid farewell to the partner with whom I'd shared so many hard, lonely miles? He was the best friend I ever had, and I couldn't let him go.

Bob walked over to Clarissa's big picture window, the one that looked down onto the meandering river below. For a time, he watched the brown swirling water, then turned, his big hands stuffed into the pockets of his jeans. "Tell me how it happened?" His shoulders were rounded, braced against the pain he knew the answer to his question would bring, but he needed to know; to make sense of his boy's death. I understood. Anna and Clarissa filed into the living room, waiting for my answer.

I'd tried to prepare, but now that the moment had arrived,

I wasn't any more ready than when I'd left the hospital in El Paso. I took a deep breath, and for a while, I was back in that brush-covered canyon in the wild, brush-choked Sierra Madre. Much of what I told came straight from what Derek, the commando leader had told me. Of course, the last part I'd seen, so I could give them my account of that.

"They let Brian stay with me. He was bent over me, trying to keep me conscious. We heard shots. Manuel ran down the slope toward us. He wanted to kill me, and probably take Brian as a hostage. But Brian walked straight toward him. He placed himself between Manuel's gun and me. He wouldn't let Manuel shoot me." My voice broke, and I had to stop and swallow the anguish that twisted my face. The scene was still so real. "Brian took a bullet right in the chest. He went quickly." That wasn't the way to break the news to his mom and dad, but I didn't know how else to do it.

Quiet weeping broke the silence. For me, the torture was back. *Why couldn't I have done something to keep Brian from dying? There were so many extraordinary events leading to that moment. Why couldn't there have been one more? If the bullet had been an inch to the right, Brian might have lived. Manuel didn't even intend to shoot Brian. That bullet was meant for me. Why couldn't the commando have shot Manuel just one second sooner?*

After a few minutes, I continued. "The medic was right there, but there was nothing he could have done." The grief was raw and fresh, the loss of Brian overwhelming every other emotion or need.

Later that afternoon, we talked more. I hoped it might help Bob and Anna if they knew some of what Brian had told me about his time there in the mountains of Mexico. Brian spent the last weeks of his life the same way he'd lived the rest, reaching out to others, meeting whatever need they had. It didn't matter that those around him were drug smugglers. Brian never doubted he was part of some great conduit of love and compassion for everybody who crossed his path.

At some point, we moved back to the kitchen. When the sun slid behind the western mountains, we were still at the table, the coffee cold in our cups, the tears slower to fall—for now. Hearing about those last weeks of Brian's life, and the effect he'd had on those around him perhaps made it easier for Anna. Bob was the one who worried me. He and Brian were uncommonly close, and he was carrying a grief that none of us could measure.

A car pulled into the yard. Clarissa stood, and peered out the kitchen window.

"It's Clint and Darlene."

When they walked in, Clint and I shook hands. He was still a preacher, and I had some long-held issues with any man of the cloth, but I figured one of their kind at this moment might not be a bad thing.

"It's good to see you again, Lonnie," Clint mauled my already bruised hand, but his words were gentle. "It appears you didn't escape unscathed. You look rough."

"I looked worse a couple days ago. I'm okay now."

"I'm so sorry about Brian, though I never had the pleasure of meeting him. He sounds like such an extraordinary man."

"He was." I could only nod and turn my head away, while that same hard lump softened.

Clint reached over and placed one of those big ham hands on my shoulder, though he had the good sense to say nothing more. He cared. That was enough, and I understood why Clarissa had warmed to these people.

I made more coffee, and everybody moved into the living room. By the warm look in Clarissa's eyes when she thanked me, I knew she was grateful I'd taken over my old chore.

"Clint, would you be willing to come and do the funeral service?" Bob asked.

"I would be honored. I'm sure I can make the necessary arrangements to be gone for a few days."

Going three hundred miles north for a funeral was a considerable sacrifice of time, and I resolved that Stirling Associates would pay a handsome retainer for Clint's willing services.

We spent the rest of the afternoon remembering, as well as planning for how we'd all get up-country to the memorial service. Bob and Anna had friends close to town. Their ranch by the sprawling Nechako River would be where we'd pay our last respects to Brian.

I left everything open with Clarissa, but I secretly hoped she might want to go with me. However, that was a lot of time together. I wasn't at all sure she would want to spend that much time in my company.

As if she'd read my thoughts, she turned to Clint. "I could ride up with Lonnie on Tuesday. I know you and Darlene want to take your own vehicle so you can get back right away, but maybe we could travel together." She turned to me. "That is . . . if that's all right with you, Lonnie."

After my heart started beating again, I stuttered out an answer. "Sure—of course. Going together makes the most sense." That sounded dumb, but I didn't know what else to say. I was going to spend at least seven hours with this woman who had been my wife. That was enough time for us to either resurrect the skeletal remains of our marriage, or it would . . . well, it would go the other way. Would she be willing to try?

Not likely. But when she had slipped into my arms, for a moment, it had been like—like old times. No. I scoffed at my juvenile hope. Whatever had been there was because of the sadness and loss. There was no reason to think anything between us had changed.

Clint and Darlene naturally wanted to know the details of what happened to Brian, so I related everything I'd told the others. However, I'd not shared anything about the cloud covering the moon only seconds before the *burros* had reached the indentation in the wall, and how they had walked by within an arm's length of our still forms.

"I have some issues with the God thing," I said. "But what happened that night on the canyon trail was too precise."

Clint nodded, as if he believed there was a God that would or could do something like that, and it wasn't a big deal, but he wisely never commented. Instead, he turned to Clarissa and said, "Hey, why don't I fire up your barbeque? We brought some venison ribs to go with the hamburgers. I'll start them cooking, if you want?"

I could offer little in the culinary department. Besides, another important job needed doing.

"Bob," I said, "I need to go for a walk. Would you care to come along?"

He raised his head. Much of the afternoon, he'd stared at the floor, too numb with grief to even speak, but he followed me, his usually square shoulders bowed from the knifing pain.

The evening air was sharp enough I drug my fleece-lined denim out of the back of the car. Bob put on his brown duck coat, and we faced into the chill October breeze blowing down from the rugged Coast Range. My ribs still threatened to grind with every step, but Bob matched his stride to my slow one as we silently wound our way up the mountain trail behind Clarissa's house. Every few hundred yards we stopped to rest. A thousand feet below us, the patchwork green alfalfa fields on the far side of the river clung to precarious fertile benches. Scattered boulders littered both sides of the trail. I'd gone as far as my ribs would allow. I eased down to sit on a fallen log. Bob did the same. Out of the corner of my eye, I glanced at his lined, weary face. Brian's last words made me uncomfortable on so many levels. I wasn't ready to share what he'd said with anyone, even Bob, but I blurted them out anyway.

"Bob, Brian said a few words to me before he died. He . . . I think he knew he was hit hard and wasn't going to make it. Both of us were hurt bad. He turned to me and said, 'Lonnie, I'm ready to go. You're not. I'll be waiting for you at the Crossing.'"

Bob only nodded, his head bowed.

Tortured by the memory, now, I couldn't stop. "I still don't understand, and Bob, I can't buy the Christianity package—at least not yet. But I can't get away from those words, and the way he died."

Bob picked up a dry twig, his fingers intent on pulverizing it while I talked. His gaze seemed fixed on something far in the distance, and I wondered if what I'd said even registered. Then, daubing at his eyes with a well-used handkerchief he spoke, his voice halting and strained. "Lonnie, there are a lot of beliefs a man can live by, at least reasonably well. We all believe in something. Maybe it isn't much, but we have to have some kind of guiding star through life. Where it all gets tangled is at the end. What has always seemed a workable philosophy to live by can suddenly become nothing but tawdry trappings in death."

I had never understood it that way, but then I'd never been as close to death as I'd been in the last week. I saw Brian's belief in God in his last moments. His faith was unshakable, solid enough to step into . . . whatever was out there. I didn't have that. In a way, it was our last argument—and I lost.

Bob reached over and put a hand on my shoulder. "Thanks for sharing that with me. I know it was hard, a very private thing between you and . . . and my boy, but . . . it means a lot." He took his arm away, but I knew things were okay between us, in a way that they hadn't been since Clarissa and I had split.

Bob took off his black felt hat and scrubbed at the brim with his thumb. "Leave me here for a bit?"

I glanced across at his grief-twisted face, struggled to my feet and limped down the mountain. Once, I glanced back to see Bob down on his knees, his face to the sky. His hat lay on the ground beside him. A sheen of tears wet his weather-beaten face. I turned quickly away. This was a private moment between Bob and his God.

CHAPTER 43

LONNIE

WHEN I ARRIVED at the house, Clarissa was outside in the twilight petting on that gray horse she liked so much. Maybe like Bob, she just needed time alone.

Concern clouded her face when she saw me in the yard. "Where's Bob?"

"He'll be back in a while."

Clarissa nodded. "No one can understand that kind of wrenching pain until you've been through it."

"Yeah, I'm concerned about him. How's Anna doing?"

"Better than Bob. For her, it will just take time. Every day will be a bit more bearable than the last. Someday, life will become more important than the grief."

We walked into the house. I tried to listen to the conversation around me, but my eyes kept straying to the kitchen window. At last, hunched against the cold, Bob trudged out of the darkness. When we filled our plates for supper, the set of his shoulders told me that someday in the future, healing might come.

We all picked at the food. Nobody was hungry, and after

I'd said my goodbyes, I slipped away. I would spend the night at the Concord Hotel.

When I pushed through the swinging doors, Ezra Parker's handlebar mustache was behind the desk. He grinned. "Hello, Lonnie. Good to have you back."

"Hi Ezra. How ya' doin'?" We shook hands, and he pushed a check-in form across the counter for me to fill out. "Same room all right?"

"Sure."

"You look a little worse than you did the last time." Ezra studied my beat-up face.

"Hope you gave the other guy at least half of what he gave you."

I continued filling out the form. "Nope, I lost this one. Wasn't quite a fair fight though."

"Oh?" Ezra was cautious, not knowing whether to believe me.

"You studying to do some more gold panning, or is this just a vacation?"

"What? Oh . . . of course." A quick glance revealed the twinkle in those washed-out eyes.

"Actually, this time I'm here to study sturgeon in the Fraser River. Real important, and top secret. You know—Indian work."

He guffawed. "Okay, you win. It's why I own a hotel. I'm a nosy old buzzard."

He handed me the key, and I struggled up the stairs with the pain and my clothes bag.

The hot shower eased some of the aches, and I stayed under the water until even my brown skin looked pink. The bottom corner of my clothes bag yielded a fresh shirt and underwear but no clean jeans. While I dressed, I mulled through the day. Maybe someday the pain would lessen. And Clarissa? There was no reason to be hopeful—but still . . . maybe.

Not ready to turn in, I made my way down the curved wooden staircase to the rose-tiled lobby. Maybe I'd take a stroll around the town, something to clear my mind from one more sad, depressing day.

Ezra was still behind the polished oak counter, giving his night clerk instructions.

"Hey, Lonnie. Where you headed?"

"I'm off to check on those big sturgeon fish," I answered.

He snorted. "Sure you are. Join me in the office for a nightcap when you come back."

"Thanks, I might." I walked out into the night, and made one loop around the block. My aching ribs and the cold made Ezra's office more appealing. Besides, I liked the old geezer.

Across the lobby, Ezra had left his office door open. I stopped at the antique, potbelly wood stove to warm my hands before announcing my presence.

"Come in." Ezra sat at his weathered roll-top desk, shuffling through invoices and bills; a two dollar pair of rimless reading glasses perched halfway down his nose. "Siddown!" He pointed to a burgundy captain's chair. "I'll deal with these later." He shoved the paper into a pile while I eased myself into the trouser-worn Naugahyde.

"What do you want to drink? You name it; I have it. I'm going to have a beer." Ezra rose from behind his battered old oak desk.

"Double it." Throughout my rodeo career, I was a near teetotaler. I'd grown up with far too much alcohol, and though I didn't subscribe to the crackpot theory that because I had some Indian blood, alcohol affected me more than folks with a lighter skin, I was still careful. I'd seen it make fools out of too many people—of all colors.

Ezra returned from the bar with two dew-spattered bottles and tipped back in his four-wheeled office chair.

"How long have you owned the hotel?" I asked.

"Thirty years next summer. I think I'm going to celebrate, maybe go on one of them cruises or something. I haven't taken a holiday in ten years, except for the time I went to my sister's funeral in Saskatchewan, and that doesn't really count."

"You married?" I figured I could meddle just as well as he could.

He noticed. The handlebar mustache rose a notch on the right end. "Nah, I was once. Went through a messy divorce, and then I came here and scraped up enough money to buy this place."

"Got any kids?"

"Yeah, haven't seen him in thirty years, but I've got a son. His mother got the kid and everything else when we split. I'd made plenty of mistakes, and it sure wasn't that I didn't deserve it, but I would have liked to have known that boy. I sent money—every month, all through the years he was growing up. I wanted him to have everything other kids had; I suppose trying to make up for him not having a dad. His mother was real bitter. She swore I'd never see the boy again." The old guy swallowed, and I politely looked away. "So far, she's been right." His voice was gruff. The distant, low hum of voices from the bar floated into the office, but they failed to mask the hurt.

"So." Ezra straightened his shoulders, and the handlebar mustache widened. "You got a woman here, or what?"

I ceased my contemplation of the floor pattern, glad the subject had brightened, but now needing to decide what of my business in Lillooet I would divulge. Ezra had seen a lot of pain in his life. It looked like I was headed in the same direction, minus the kid part. "Yeah, I guess I do. My wife is living here."

"Oh? What's her name? I know most everybody in this little burg."

"Clarissa—Bowers. You may not have met her. She's only lived here a few months. Works as an insurance adjuster for a big company in Vancouver," I added.

"Clarissa Bowers . . . no, I can't place her. So, let me guess. You're trying to put things back together?"

"Well, that would be nice, but I'm not sure she's interested. No, she got mauled by a cougar a while back, so I try to keep tabs on her. Then a friend of ours died, and—"

"Oh-h-h—now I know who she is. She was raised here. Her picture was in the paper a few weeks ago. That preacher fellow shot the cougar while it was standing over top of her. Yeah, that was quite a story. How's she doing?"

"Good—all considered. Lots of stitches. Her right arm's messed up. Maybe with enough physiotherapy she'll regain the use of it."

"So, are you going through some kind of counseling?"

"No, she's too bitter to be interested in anything but a lawyer."

"None of my business, but you had an affair, didn't you." It wasn't a question.

I glared. "What's it to you?" This old babbler had just gone too far.

He held up a hand. "No offense. It's just that I know the

symptoms. Been there, done that. The results aren't pretty."

He left to check in a customer at the front desk. By the time he returned, my belligerence had cooled.

"Lonnie, you know I'm a meddling old fool. I kind of told you my life story—at least the part that hurts the most. So, I'm going to just keep flappin' my jaws. It might save you some of the pain I've gone through. I reckon you can listen or leave."

I considered leaving. Upstairs, there was only more pain. I opted to stay.

"You've already broken the sacred trust, but you must still have some sort of relationship with your wife, or you wouldn't be here. Do whatever you have to do to rebuild it. I didn't, and she took everything from me—including my son."

"Didn't you ever think about marrying again?"

Ezra hesitated before he answered. "Yeah, once or twice. Every time I tried, I found myself looking for someone who was like her. That wouldn't have been fair to any woman."

Deep down, I knew I would do the same. Every woman would be measured against Clarissa. Suddenly, I could take no more. He was right, only it was too late. "Ezra, I gotta go." I grabbed my hat and struggled to stand, wincing at the spasmodic pain.

"Sure you don't want another beer?"

"No, thanks. One's my limit. It's been a pleasure—and thanks for the advice." I held out my hand.

"Sure, Lonnie. G'night."

"Goodnight." I crippled up the stairs, each step like a refrain. One's . . . my . . . limit. Well, it had been, except for a night in Fort Worth; which was why Clarissa and I no longer shared a table—or bed. I undressed, and eased my aching frame onto the lumpy mattress. Every minute detail of the afternoon paraded through my head. So much sadness. Was there any hope for Clarissa and me? Probably not. Sure, there was that moment of tenderness when we'd first met, but what did that mean? All day, I'd fooled myself into hoping for more, and now I felt cheated. *Cheated? Who cheated who?* That discouraging thought added to the melancholy of the day, and sleep eluded me until the early dawn.

***

THE SUN HAD LONG AGO RISEN when my eyes opened to the world. Standing hurt way less this morning, which meant my ribs and various other painful places were probably beginning to heal.

While I shaved and showered, I planned the day. First thing, I would go out to Clarissa's to help Bob and Anna load up when Brenda and Tom arrived. Not that I'd be much help. It was more just to be there. Then I would head back to Vancouver to spend a lonely weekend at the condo, wash some clothes, and just generally get ready to head north for Brian's memorial service.

After a quick breakfast at the hotel coffee shop, I drove up the now familiar road to Clarissa's. Brenda and her family had arrived and were already loading their van for the trip north. Everybody hugged, and shook hands. Clarissa assured Bob and Anna we'd arrive Tuesday night with Clint and Darlene. They drove out of the yard, Clarissa and I waved them on their way.

After they'd gone, I jammed my hands in my pockets, and she crossed her arms, both of us avoiding any eye contact.

Probably I should leave. Instead, we both drifted over to the pasture fence to visit with Monte, but the morning air had winter on its breath, and I hunched against the cold.

She noticed my coatless shivering. "There's some coffee left. Do you want a cup?"

"Sure. I've got time for one before I go."

We walked into the house. The kitchen still carried the sweet aroma of bacon and maple syrup. Clarissa found two cups, filled them from the pot, and sat across from me.

"Wednesday will be a hard day for them." She fidgeted, tracing the stenciled yellow lines on the tablecloth with the edge of her cup.

I sighed. "Yeah, no doubt about that. I called both Bobby Williams and Luke Tracey and gave them all the funeral details. They were going to spread the word at the Tucson rodeo. A lot of the guys will be at the Billings rodeo next week, but that's still a thirteen hundred-mile trip," I said. "I don't expect anybody will come to the service from that far away."

Clarissa nodded. "Bob and Anna will understand."

The conversation fizzled. Clarissa seemed edgy at my presence, and I couldn't think of anything else to talk about. This wasn't the time to overstay my welcome. We would be driving up-country together on Tuesday. If we were both this uncomfortable, that was going to be one long trip. I drained my cup, pushed my chair back, and started an awkward goodbye.

Chapter 44

CLARISSA

Ever since the day on the mountain, I'd waited to talk to Lonnie. There just hadn't been an opportunity, and though I didn't know how to start, I was determined he wasn't leaving until I said what I had to say. After that? It was up to God.

He reached for his cup and drained the last of his coffee.

"Well, I better go. I've got some things to do in Vancouver." He pushed the empty cup from one spot to another on the table, then stood, his eyes avoiding mine. "I'm going to sell the condo."

My eyes moved from the tablecloth to his face.

"Half of it is yours, so I wanted to make sure that's okay with you. I'll call a real estate agent this afternoon and see what we can list it for."

Whatever words I'd planned to say, fled like frightened rabbits. "Is that what you want?" My voice wavered.

"What do you mean? I know this maybe isn't the best time to talk about it, but we need to . . . well, deal with it." His eyes were now riveted to mine. "We bought that condo to make it easy for you to work out of the Vancouver office. And as much as I would like for things to be different . . ." His voice trailed off, and I had hope again.

I kept my hands in my lap so he wouldn't see them tremble. "Lon, why don't you . . . are you up to a walk on the mountain? Maybe we need to talk about it—just to be sure."

Something happened in the long silence between us. Maybe it was only a reprieve, a cease-fire, but his eyes held an unreserved warmness I'd not seen in a long time.

"Yeah, I think my ribs could handle a hike, as long as the pace is slow." His slow grin was the same one I remembered so well. "I've been putting off listing that condo for two months. Another few days won't make any difference."

Lonnie hobbled out and retrieved his mochila from the rental car while I threw together our usual trail lunch: bread, cheese and a little ham, water and store-bought cookies. I had only one item other than a bottle of water to put in my pack, but I hesitated. Did I have the courage to do this? Before I lost the little nerve I had, I hurried into the bedroom, and raised the lid on the heirloom cedar chest that had passed to me from my grandmother. Everything was as I had left it. I lifted the bit of intricate Victorian lace, folded it carefully, and placed it in my pack. We started up the mountain behind the house. Would it be too far for the condition he was in? I hoped not.

A hundred yards up the trail, Lonnie laughed, and reached over to touch my still useless arm. "Aren't we a pair?"

I smiled. Yes, we were a pair; two, bruised and scarred people with hurts that might never heal.

Slow and steady was the best pace either of us could manage as we climbed toward the backside of the high mountain plateau. An hour up the trail, a fallen fir log served for a lunch table. We munched on our sandwiches while I pointed out the tree where the cougar had attacked. Together, we tried to figure out where Clint had been hidden, up in the rocks. All the fear I'd carried had vanished, especially with Lonnie there.

Later, we slipped our packs on and climbed the last yards to the hidden plateau. Through a narrow gap in the wall, we stepped into the sudden and reverent silence. The trail, frequented by deer and the elusive mountain sheep led through a few scattered wagon-sized boulders to the sheltered overhang of an open cavern. The vista below us was a breathtaking drop into miles of timber and distant verdant meadows. The air, still as the rocky forest around us, allowed the feeble autumn sun to shed a promise of warmth. We sat together on the big rock, soaking in the peace of that wild solitude. I was well-aware the peace stopped at the edge of our rock. The gaping wound between us was only a cobbled together truce. Was it possible to ever have more? Somewhere inside, I breathed a prayer for help, a plea to God for our tattered, broken marriage.

I turned and lightly touched Lonnie's arm. "Excuse me for a minute." I picked up my backpack and resolutely walked behind another of the room-sized boulders on the north side of the grotto. Out of sight, I prayed for courage, and with fingers that wouldn't stop trembling, I pulled from my pack the treasured article I'd taken from the cedar chest. *What would Lonnie think? What if I had misread him, and he just wanted out of our marriage?* I pinned it in position, took a deep breath and stepped out from behind the rock. I clenched my hands to stop the trembling, and walked up to the man I'd once promised to love and cherish. When he saw the veil, he froze. Then he slipped off the boulder and stood in front of me. I looked into his still swollen face, and held his brown, serious eyes with mine.

"Lon, this has been a place of healing for me. I've spent

time with God here learning about forgiveness. This was where I decided I wanted to do whatever it took to save our marriage. And it's here where I want to ask you to forgive me for not being the wife I should have been." I had to bite my lower lip. I wouldn't cry.

"Lonnie Bowers, I wear this veil today, the one I wore when I gave myself to you on our wedding day. It is to remind you of my vows to you, to reaffirm my commitment to you, and you alone, as long as we both shall live."

My big, tough rodeo cowboy husband stood there like a statue, then crumpled. Through tears, he took both of my hands in his. "Clarissa, would you forgive me for what I've done to you and to our marriage?"

I nodded my head. "Yes. I do." Now a stream of tears washed down my cheeks.

"Clarissa Bowers, I love you more than life. Today, I commit to you alone, to love you, to care for you, to be true to you alone, as long as we both shall live."

Lonnie reached over, lifted the veil, and ran his fingers through my hair. "May I kiss the bride?"

"I'd love it if you would." His hands slipped to my shoulders. The embrace was desperate, passionate, beyond the physical need, a rejoining of two lost spirits. Time stopped—until the sudden rumbling of approaching thunder broke the spell.

Hand in hand, we hurried down the mountain as we tried to beat the rain. I pondered what I'd said on the mountain. For so long I had argued with God over those words I'd spoken. I kept telling Him it wasn't my fault. I wasn't to blame for my shattered marriage, but every time, He would gently remind me that He'd taken the blame for my sin. This wasn't about fault. This was about forgiveness, and healing, for both of us.

Epilogue

THE FAMILY slogged through three inches of still falling snow. On a south facing point, a few short steps east of the Messue Crossing, we stopped, and huddled together against the raw April wind. Winter ice still gripped most of the river, but it was thin, and rotten. A small patch of dark, open water swirled beneath us, and on the far side, a lone swan fed in another ice-free stretch.

Seven of us stood on the high bank. Brian's sister Brenda had come, and of course his mom and dad. Clint and Darlene were there, with Clarissa and me. This was a private time of sorrow. Bundled against the cold, we listened while Clint read words from a book in the Bible called Ecclesiastes. It said something about a time to be born . . . and a time to die.

I gazed out over that dark water, and reckoned Brian wasn't nearly old enough to die.

My mind wandered back to that last afternoon, high in the Sierra Madre . . . Brian jumping up and running toward Manuel . . . the sound of the pistol blending with the staccato report of a machine gun, and then Brian turning toward me and dying. That bullet had my name on it, and he'd taken it.

Clint finished the reading and said a prayer, committing Brian to the God he'd served, and thanking Him for the time we'd had him. The wind picked up, whipping the snow crystals around our legs. Everybody was shivering with cold before Clint reached the end of his prayer. My eyes settled on Bob Besser's profile. Every craggy line in his face was set hard against the grief as he shuffled to the edge of the bluff. His hunched figure seemed to wrap itself around the little jug, cradled like a blanket-wrapped baby in his right arm. Slowly, he took the urn in both hands and tipped it toward the dark water below. The ashes floated down to the silent Blackwater River. At the last moment, the west wind whisked them into a murky patch of open water. On the far side, the swan called for its mate, an aching cry of loneliness and loss.

I stumbled forward to the edge of the bluff. Beside me, a familiar small hand slipped into mine and I held her close, not ever wanting to let her go. We stood for a moment, gazing out over the river. My vision blurred. Brian, with his hat pulled low against the setting sun stood on the far side. I whispered into the wind. "Wait for me Brian. I'll be there."

Hand in hand, we turned and followed the others back through the snow to the wagon and the waiting team of horses.

The End

NOTE FROM THE AUTHOR

I'VE ALWAYS FELT authenticity mattered. With Lonnie, I've walked the trails in *Blackwater Crossing*, from the ancient ruins of the Paquime and Anasazi, to the remote Indian Grease Trail in the interior of British Columbia.

Thank you for reading *Blackwater Crossing*. I hope you enjoyed it, and if you feel so inclined, please consider posting a review on Amazon, or whatever other book site you enjoy.

OTHER TITLES IN THE SERIES